A Short Series
of Discrete Problems

A
SHORT SERIES
OF
DISCRETE PROBLEMS

Steven Jacobi

Secker & Warburg
London

Permission to quote from *Passion of Michel Foucault* by James Miller
kindly granted by HarperCollins *Publishers* Ltd.

First published in Great Britain in 1996
by Martin Secker & Warburg Limited
an imprint of Reed International Books Limited
Michelin House, 81 Fulham Road, London SW3 6RB
and Auckland, Melbourne, Singapore and Toronto

A CIP catalogue record for this book
is available from the British Library

ISBN 0 436 20235 2

www.secker.com

Typeset in 12 on 13 point Bembo
by Avon Dataset Ltd, Bidford on Avon, Warks
Printed and bound in Great Britain
by Clays Ltd, St Ives plc.

For my parents

Through what games of truth does man devote himself to thinking about his being when he perceives himself as mad, when he regards himself as sick, when he reflects on himself as a living, speaking, labouring being, when he judges himself and punishes himself as a criminal case?

Michel Foucault

I laugh at such things being done, but much more when no good comes of them, and when they are done to so ill purpose.

Robert Burton

— I —

Bathing

Everything was water.

That was Wislon Needy's first thought as his scraggy head slow-motioned out of the dirty grey water. He found himself blinking and looking around the bathroom. Bulbous pimples of soap slid down his bony face and plopped noiselessly into the opaque slush of used skin and wasted hair that surrounded him.

Despite this, Wislon had a feeling of hopeless optimism. He was perplexed by this. It seemed, frankly, unaccountable. But he thought, I'm going to be all right. Everything seems to be starting all over again.

For Wislon, everything *was* always starting all over again. It had to. 'Everything' would otherwise have been catastrophic, disastrous, hopeless – much worse even than the knowledge that the large-mooned toenail on his left foot was working its way loose again. It was the seventh time he had lost that nail. Or maybe the eighth. It didn't matter much. Nobody else was counting. Wislon dunked his head under the

I

water once more, vaguely aware that he was sitting on the plastic swivel top of the shampoo bottle. He felt its impress on the fleshier part of his right buttock. At least you know you're alive, he mused, and continued to massage his flaking scalp.

Before the bath, Wislon had made himself a cup of tea, something that he did not ordinarily do. Then, inexplicably, he had changed his mind. Immediately, he had a bath. Again, not something in his usual routine. No sooner had the warm liquid arranged itself around his irregular angles and bony crevices than a shudder had slid along and through his canted body. Not even a shudder, really. More of a tremor. Possibly a vibration. Still, he could not afford to be choosy. Not in his position. Tremor it was, then.

Wislon had stopped his hand, which had been vigorously soaping the spindly tangle of hairs on his legs, intent upon the strange thing that was happening inside him.

He had not thought of Armitage for six months – more? or was it less? – but now he couldn't get her out of his dirty little mind. He thought he might be about to cry when he realised with a tremor – no, this time it was a shudder – of relief that it was only some soap in his ping-pong orb of an eyeball.

Armitage was all of the things that Wislon was not. Her body was miraculously in proportion. There were no odd outcrops of bone or paunchy flaps of flesh. It all somehow fitted together. Shoulder-length black hair, bobbed, glossy, expensively coiffured,

2

curled Lolita-ishly under. A pout of a nose. Lips like fat worms. And, as far as Wislon could tell, long straight legs. In the general run of things, this wasn't anything special – not *that* special, anyway – but it was to him. Armitage was the first (and only) girl that Wislon had filed as 'Unavailable' who had so much as looked at him. Perhaps 'Unattainable' might be more honest, although if he was going the whole hog, how about 'Most Probably Absolutely Revolted by Me'?

They had met in Birmingham, at the Dog and Bitch. The bar ran near to the convalescing canal which pulled sluggishly on its dismal way to Evesham and Worcester. Wislon was between jobs. That was what he told Armitage, anyhow. It was only half a lie; he had never actually had a job. Twenty-five and never worked. It was a disgrace.

'I've been travelling,' Wislon said.

'For how long? Where to?' Armitage asked. She sucked noiselessly through a straw that lanced a crescent of orange before arrowing down into a thick reddish mixture.

'Months. Years. Australia. Malaysia. China. Bulgaria. Mexico . . . ' he lied wildly.

'And?'

'And? Well . . . there was Alaska. The States. Iceland. Greenland. Ireland. Scotland. Lapland. The Sudetenland. You know, the usual.'

'What were they like?'

'Which one?'

'Any one.'

'Oh – fine. You know. After a while, one place

3

looks much the same as the next. It's a global village now. That's why I came back. It sort of helped me to find a perspective.'

'What? On Birmingham?'

'Yes.'

'You had to do all that just to discover a point of view about Birmingham?'

'Yes. Kind of. About all of it. England, I mean.'

'Oh.'

It was about then that Wislon felt the initiative slipping away. He looked out of the window and thought he saw a dead cow floating past. Maybe it was a stolen car. He remembered an old exam question: 'Raoul gets £200 for stealing a BMW, £50 for stealing a Mini and £150 for a 4x4. If he has stolen two BMWs and three 4x4s, how many Minis will he have to steal to make £800?' He didn't know then and he didn't know now. He asked Armitage if she wanted another Dirty Red One. She did not, but they still arranged to meet a week later. She had even given Wislon her telephone number. He recognised it as being in a smart area on the other side of town.

A week later found him sweating it out in the bathroom, trying to get it right. The bathroom was the only place where he could somehow be made to work. It was a discreet, private area. Secret, Wislon thought, eyeing the stained, off-white porcelain of the lavatory. At times, the debris around its sloping bowl concerned him, but really (all things considered) it was a surprise that there wasn't more of the stuff.

He stripped and ran a bath, contemplating the night ahead of him.

He thought of a lot of things: how to be handsome, how to be witty, how to sweep Armitage off her feet. He even wondered if he could manage to be kind. Most of all, he wondered what she was doing with him. The last girl he had gone out with a long, virginal two years ago had studied biology in Leeds – the same place where he had been reading history. After a leaden couple of hours enduring something by Ibsen, the evening had nosedived whilst they ate a flaccid pizza in silence at The Flat and Floppy. Isabel had flickered her eyelids, smiled and said he reminded her of a pet annelid she had once kept. This rather pleased Wislon. Later that night, he had gone to the encyclopaedia and discovered that an annelid was a segmented worm or leech. Which was the worst, and which one had Isabel meant?

Talking of which, his eyes wandered reluctantly down his body. Then, quickly, with a grimace of disgust, up again. In the bath, he sometimes tucked it out of sight altogether, neatly folding it between his cantilevered legs. Could he be a man without it? In what ways did it define him? Could he be a woman *with* one? On the whole, he thought it was somehow neater not to have one at all. But not tonight.

He needed the devil in him to be active tonight. Wislon resisted the temptation to be scrupulous and lay back in the bath. White tiles with pencil-line cracks surrounded him. The ceiling was massively cratered in one corner and in another a wisp of grey web hung down in depleted strands. Wislon wondered where the spider was and whether it was watching him. Could spiders see? Maybe, but this one obviously couldn't be bothered. Wislon submerged his head. A pathetic but rebellious hank of hair flapped down his face, cutting his nose through the middle and dividing his face with absolute symmetry. Before massaging it back into place, Wislon stretched his tongue upwards and tasted the rogue shank. It tasted of nothing but the bitter remains of the shampoo.

Having done his best with what was available, Wislon navigated his body out of the bath and on to the cold but brilliantly white lino which covered the floor. If he was anything, he was at least clean. He inspected the obedient ranks of lotions, potions and assorted toiletries which were neatly collated along a small plastic shelf above the sink. He dried himself, rearranged his hair into something like hair, folded his towel carefully over the radiator and wandered into the bedroom.

A single bed sniggered at him from the corner, its duvet defiantly square and unruffled. Nothing had been happening inside that bed. Absolutely nothing. On the floor was a small tower of books: *Written in Blood*, *No Beast So Fierce*, *One Day in the Life of Ivan Denisovich*, *Soledad Brother*, something by Foucault (which was determinedly unread), *On the Yard* and *A Brief History of Western Cinema*.

Wislon considered what he ought to wear. Most of his trousers tended to hang loosely from a brace of inadequate hips. Jewellery? He didn't have any. And besides – jewellery?! Shoes? Not much choice there.

Black. Probably. Shirt? Brazen, restrained or sophistic-
ated urban libertine? All the sleeves were too long
and followed his arms down almost to the ends of his
fingers. He was bound to look obscurely handicapped. Hat? Socks? *Muffler?* Wislon did not really
know. Eventually, he settled for a pair of blue jeans,
hoisted and held by a large black belt. Up top, he
wore a white T-shirt with a small printed necklace of
caricaturishly naked men and women. Alternating
gender, they held hands around the neck of the wearer.
This, Wislon thought, was discreet but daring. He
folded all the rejected clothes back into their drawers
and strode off into the moist Birmingham air.

As he closed the door behind him, he was sprayed
with something like damp breath.

Whilst driving to the Triangle Cinema, where he
had arranged to meet Armitage, Wislon reflected on
some advice his best friend at school, Vivien Kind,
had once given him. 'Act flash. Act as though you
couldn't care less. Couldn't give a monkey's. *That's*
what they like. They'll be all over you.' The trouble
was, Wislon *could* care less. Not necessarily about
Armitage (although that might change), but about
the whole grubby business. And he was no good at
acting. What you saw was what you got – although
that was another problem. He remembered something he'd read about poor men only being able to
get lust. Love needed money, good luck, slick pack-
aging. He scanned the interior of his Metro and
caught an involuntary glimpse of himself in the rear-
view mirror. There were only a few small reasons to
be hopeful, and lust it was.

Wislon ploughed on through the networks of anonymous roads that eventually led to the collision of buildings at the city centre. He was constantly aware of how much he hated his body. Not just dislike, but loathing, abhorrence and (very possibly) estrangement. This was a marriage of inconvenience. He would divorce his physical self if he could. When he was particularly disillusioned with it, he would resort to violence. This often happened in the bathroom, when attempts to shape hair or hide blemishes or reshape bulges proved futile. He would, for example, take an offending knuckle of skin and slap it, squeeze it, garrotte it and rip it.

As he exhorted the Metro around the Bull Ring, however, Wislon felt pretty good. In general, taking everything into account, all things considered, *things* weren't too bad. No eruptions, hair (more or less) in place and his waist clamped tightly at thirty-two inches. He even found himself wanting to whistle. Something up-market, he thought, and spat out the first few bars of Elgar's Cello Concerto.

'Well of course. But I'm not sure that something – take music, for example – is really enough in itself – as the basis for a long-term relationship. Certainly any couple must have things in common, and – please don't get me wrong, shared interests are *so* important in maintaining a balance and a . . . what's the word? . . . a *sympathy* between people – but it's not the only thing . . .

'Far from it, in fact. There has to be something else

– a *frisson*, a tension, that provides something other for the partner to kick against, to help identify him – or her – self. It may work well for a short while, but believe me, Armitage, in the long term, we all need someone who is compatible yet different.'

Wislon felt in sparkling form. He and Armitage were back in the Dog and Bitch. Even so early on, he thought it unlucky to take her anywhere else. Maybe it was something to do with the lighting. Why else would she have looked at him? He even managed to find a table in the same dark corner where she had first noticed him. Or had she only returned the stare which Wislon later thought he must have given her? He couldn't remember. Anyway, here she was. Here *they* were.

Earlier, they had been to see *The Last Seduction*. Wislon had already seen it and rehearsed a catalogue of clever lines after tracking down some reviews. 'Grunge noir, I think,' he said, 'without the baroque overkill of *Basic Instinct*. This film really redeems the erotic thriller. Not so much in the explicitness of the sex scenes, more in the revamping of the classic noir theme of the woman who uses all her sexual powers – and any other psychological advantage [this was the moment for glasses; if only Wislon *had* a pair. His eyes were the only part of him that were holding up to the strain of 'getting through'] to bend weaker-willed men to her avaricious purpose . . .'

'Wislon . . . ?' Armitage asked.

'Yes?' Expectantly.

'What is that round your neck?'

'A motif.'

9

'Are those squiggles meant to be their genitals?'

Wislon cranked his chest out. 'Yes . . . quite interesting . . . isn't it . . .'

'If you say so. They're not in proportion.'

'What aren't?'

'Their bits.'

'I'm not sure they're meant to be.' Wislon was screwing his neck sideways. He couldn't tell from where he was. Too big or too small? He eased his head back into position. The muscles down one side of his face ached with the strain. His cheek, he felt sure, was glowing red with the exertion. He fixed Armitage with what he hoped was a mischievous stare. His memory had failed him, but he managed to add, 'It depends what you mean by "proportion".'

'If you say so. Sorry to interrupt. What were you saying? Something about avarice, I think . . .'

The conversation stumbled forward. Eventually, Wislon gulped down the last of his whisky with a single swilling movement. He didn't usually drink whisky. In fact, he didn't usually drink anything. The alcohol stabbed the back of his throat. Immediately, he regretted it. 'Shall we go?'

It was while he was twirling the Metro's steering wheel and turning into Paradise Circus that Wislon knew he wouldn't make a pass at Armitage. His belt was pressing too tightly against his abdomen. He could feel the doughy overhang of his stomach straining the top of his jeans. The unusually sudden neck movement in the Dog and Bitch was causing him pain. The whisky had set his chest on fire and a curious form of indigestion was on the cards. His head was liquid. He was fast becoming incapable.

And besides, he didn't think Armitage would let him.

'Drop you off at your flat?'

'Fine,' she said, and glanced thankfully across.

'No problem,' showing her his teeth.

She smiled back.

This is easy, thought Wislon. Just be chivalrous. Don't overdo it. He wondered whether he ought to add something complimentary about what she was wearing, or flatter selected parts of her body. He looked round again, quickly appraising her whilst feigning a cautious and exaggeratedly sensible check for turning traffic. The legs look nice. Maybe the arms. Something smaller, perhaps? Eyes? Too obvious. Ears? Surely not. Hands? Nose? Mouth? Teeth? Wislon couldn't do it.

'Nice earrings,' he eventually said.

'Thanks. They were a present . . .'

An image of glistening Chippendale pulsed through Wislon's mind.

'. . . from my father.'

'Lovely,' he said, the words sounding strangely high-pitched.

The rest of the journey to Armitage's flat was filled with what Wislon thought was a highly promising variety of topics: salads, football hooligans, earrings, films, fashion magazines, the importance of weaving in South America, and libraries. He thought that Armitage must find something in that lot to interest her. However, she continued to look straight ahead, hardly bothering to blink.

Her flat was at the end of a small cul-de-sac. The road was undoubtedly genteel. There were trees, street lights that worked, walls without graffiti and a sprinkling of BMWs. Wislon didn't want to spoil the impression he thought he was making. He mumbled something pleasant and promised to call again next week. She said, 'Yes, that would be . . . fine.'

Driving back to his own shabby flat, Wislon reflected on what another friend of his had once told him: 'They don't want to be *impressed* – just be yourself. If it happens, good – if not, it doesn't matter because it wouldn't have worked anyway.' There seemed to be wisdom in this, even if its essence was elusive. Still, Armitage was a girl and he knew that he liked her. *Liked* her? Be honest, he teased himself, you'd like to reinvent the good bits of the *Kama Sutra* with her, wouldn't you. *Wouldn't* you?

Next week seemed a decade away.

Wislon drove sharply home. It was raining. The sky did not look angry, but it had decided to rain anyway. The weather was turning. It was turning bad just for the sake of it. Zipping past a row of houses, Wislon noted dark shapes with halos of light from the street lamps softening their obscurity and illuminating the shards of rain. He was balmily comfortable in the Metro. He could see how much rain was falling and at what angle, but its mean, needling nature was lost on him. Here was rain which just didn't care, going about its business with a faceless, bureaucratic efficiency. It rained because it did. The porous houses that lined the road stoically soaked up their punishment. So much, he thought, for all that stuff about droughts and greenhouse effects. Where was the rain when you wanted it? Here – and a ton of it. Going out in it made the getting back all the better. Sheets of news-paper on the hall carpet, shaking an old umbrella out on the porch before finally retracting its spokes, ready for the next time. Bent people stooping into corner shops to get the milk they had forgotten to buy earlier in the day. The floors invariably dotted with greying pools of muddy water. Small islands of scratched, indistinct lino bubbled up between them. Wislon was looking forward to a hot bath. He used to enjoy the rain. He used to spend long hours out-side getting drunk on it. Not now.

He watched as someone swept an assortment of drenched fruit, soppingly limp paper and mutilated vegetables from the pavement outside a shop. They cascaded over the lip and swirled on along the gutter to join a torrent of gathering detritus. The man had a cat perched on one shoulder. Wislon stared blankly ahead and wondered about Armitage.

He wiped the soap from his reddening pot-bellied eye and ducked beneath the water again. In the instant of time during which Armitage filled his thoughts, Wislon's bath water had inexplicably turned lukewarm. Lazily, he pushed his better toe towards the hot tap and gently swivelled it in an anti-clockwise direction. Somewhere, the boiler juddered into life and a few squirts of scalding water shot out before settling into a steady dribble.

Wislon thought about it. The ooze of water ran

13

from the tap to the bath without stopping. Its beginning and middle and end only existed in people's minds. Experience, life – they couldn't be neatly split up either. Trying to divide his life into past-present-future seemed senseless to Wislon. But he still tried. He knew he shouldn't; but he did. After all, the past had been pretty bad, so he had to have *something* to be going on with.

He gave the tap another flick. Hot water flooded into the bath. That's better, he thought.

Wislon contemplated that drive back to his flat after he had dropped Armitage off. Now, he could remember only the weather. Assessing his body, he remembered only too well why he had stopped cavorting around in the rain. He could even remember how old he had been: eleven. Nearly twelve. It was from that age that his scrappy, colourless, unpigmented pale imitation of a body had been covered with spots. Body butter. Marks, welts, flaws, defects, disfigurements, scars, blots, physical graffiti, blotches, pimples, poison pancakes, plonks, zits, blackheads, whiteheads, greyheads, carbuncles. You name them, Wislon knew that he had them. He had had them right up to his neck and then some more.

The only way to remain anonymous had been to burn them off in the sun. Now, he recalled the agonies of his adolescence. If he could get a good dose of sun in June, then things might be satisfactory for a month or two, especially if he managed a top-up later on. 'Ultraviolet light breaks down the DNA in overexposed skins,' his father had told him. Thus he had been condemned to lonely summers in search of the sun. He was never able to afford the one scorching holiday which, Wislon felt, would have made all the difference. Instead, he pinched and scraped and stole and grabbed odd hours behind a lumpy knoll in the local park. He avoided swimming unless he had managed to take advantage of a particularly hot day immediately beforehand. His body continually complained and grumbled. From May to October, Wislon's life had been structured around giving his skin a dose of sun. Sometimes it didn't work, but the routine was ruthlessly maintained. Sand dunes, long grass, lonely mountains, deserted parks. These were Wislon's real friends for several years. Even if there was no improvement, he thought, think what things would be like if I *hadn't* gone. Christ . . .

Eventually, he had abandoned himself to fate. Still, it didn't make things any better. But at least he could suffer alone now and eat what he wanted, away from the psychopathic, brute world of childhood.

He knew that in the school up the road, boys up to the age of thirteen had to swim naked once a week. Even the P.E. teacher took his kit off. Mr Brando was middle-aged and overweight; he looked more like a butcher than an athlete. Still, he had led from the front, as it were, and the stories about his purplish backside disappearing beneath the water had stayed with Wislon for the past twenty years. Going naked was bad enough, but with his affliction, even plain costumed swimming became murder. Toni Childs asked if he had leprosy; Sasha Screwbie thought it might be syphilis. Many others refused to swim in his segment of the pool, afraid of catching some unspecified disease.

Wislon wished to be alone with the sun, the air, the muted sounds of people at a reassuring distance. At the age of twelve, he had decided that he wished to be alone with his hideous lumps, to allow himself and Nature to work it out between them. He had become prematurely existential.

Before long, his father had decided to smear a gamy, offensively sulphuric lotion all over Wislon's body. This had taken the skin off in slices of shrivelled peel. Its fetid odour also made him hum with corruption. 'You'll thank me for this one day,' Mr Needy had said.

Wislon's mother did not think this was right. Mind you, Wislon reflected, after years of ill-treatment she was bound to disagree with any opinion her husband offered. It had been a bad marriage. Wislon thought that he disliked both of them, but he hated his father, who was now dead. 'I would like to be buried at sea,' Mr Needy had once announced over a bubble-and-squeak supper. 'I'm going to burn you,' his wife replied. 'More peas?'

Wislon's parents were getting married when everyone else wasn't. In the mid-1960s, they had dropped in when all around them were dropping out. Wislon despised them for it. He seemed to recall that they argued about everything, even his name. His father had wanted to call him 'Wilson' after the Prime Minister. His mother had gone for 'Lonnie', a skiffle singer she had obsessed over as a teenager. He sang 'My Old Man's a Dustman'.

16

Wislon was the skewed compromise.

A chair; a transistor radio; cutlery; an entire Chinese meal; a hammer; an ink bottle; a Boy Scout's knife; a battered copy of *War and Peace*; a candle; a cricket stump; cushions; a bra; a tabby cat; a copy of *Exile on Main Street*; a small tree; a bird table; four pounds of cashew nuts; an oxygen mask; an empty dustbin; five light bulbs; dog excrement; a shampoo bottle; shoes; a vase; a set of egg cups.

These were only some of the things that Wislon could remember his parents throwing at each other towards the end. There were others, but none that he could recall. Nor did he know what had happened after he had left home to go to university in Leeds. His father had died suddenly about two years after that. Maybe his mother had burned him. Or was it a heart attack? Or cancer? He couldn't exactly remember. He did recall his mother saying, 'I've only got one regret. It's simply that I was unable to look down on his open coffin and spit in his eye.' She had done something, though. Although the coffin was sealed and lying in its grave, Wislon seemed to remember that she had dropped a handkerchief wrapped around a medium-sized stone on to its lid. The pattern on the handkerchief showed a squadron of pink pigs floating on a vivid mauve background. It hit with a dull, sterile thud. Only Mr Needy's sister, Aunty Jack, said anything: 'He didn't even like pork.'

Wislon had kept up a meticulously calculated list of things he hated his father for. After the funeral, it was finally compressed into a catalogue of eight items:

1 Always having the last word
2 Always having the first word
3 Miserliness
4 Never allowing money for trips to the barber (and using Fairy Liquid to wash hair)
5 Premature baldness
6 Inability to swim
7 Dirtiness (e.g. rarely flushing lavatory)
8 Bullying

As a child, Wislon had loved to swim. His father had always frowned on it. He suggested anything from health to morality as reasons. The real reason, Wislon quickly guessed, was that he could not swim himself. To confound and anger his father he became a keen swimmer. More than that, he studied the sport. In the nineteenth century, the English were the best swimmers in the world. In London, there were six permanent pools. In the summer, floating baths were moored at Waterloo and Westminster Bridges. The fastest swimmer in the world was English – E.T. Jones of Leeds. It was partly because of him that Wislon went there to study history. Beckwith, Jones himself, Jarvis, Mather, Johnson, Aspinall and Poulton; Wislon was in awe of them.

The honeyed memories he had of childhood swimming were consecrated in his mind. They were violated by the carbuncles that sprang up in adolescence. In those early years, swimming had been a romantic protest against the bitter experience of family life. Wislon himself was a figure from pagan mythology. Then life had got its own back, and how.

Since his father died, Wislon has frequently had the same dream. He has gone back to a swimming pool he used to enjoy. Now, it is empty: the sides are streaked with a green sludge and dead leaves hurry around the sloping edges. The young children who swam with him are still there, but they are grotesquely changed. Middle-aged men with bloated stomachs and puffy legs sit around the pool side. Their hair is growing in tufts, colonising the most unlikely parts of their bodies. Varicose women loll and smile, buttocks swaying like full udders at milking time, legs streaky and blue. Slowly, they all close in on Wislon, trying to force him into the empty, scruffy pool. Always the dream ends as he strikes out at the nearest man. The man is invariably Wislon's father, who gives out a cold, cancerous stare.

Wislon also knew all the other stuff about swimming. That it suggested a hidden desire for a return to the security and freedom of the womb and its amniotic waters. Someone once said that civilisation ends at the waterline. Wislon could not agree. The water line was only the start of it. Once past that, you were into water's own dark mass, its unfathomable mess, an infinite, moving and disordered place. There was an uncertainty about water, a sense that every immersing and embarkation could be your last. Away from the reason of solid land, solid towns, solid streets, solid houses, was where you found out about yourself after being cast adrift. And the bath he was in constituted a meagre parody of the real thing.

With these thoughts clouding his mind, Wislon

19

hauled himself out of the bath. Immediately, he was startled by what he saw. In the mirror he beheld what looked like the smallest penis in Birmingham and, on his neck, the largest pimple this side of Watford Gap. His twiggy body was more or less hairless, except for the great clumps of fuzz that frothed underneath his arms and between his legs. In these places, he was positively fleecy. Wislon sat down again, lay back and, once more, flicked the hot tap. He closed his eyes.

How hideous am I?

Wislon was standing in front of the mirror in the Gents at the Dog and Bitch. It had been a week since he last saw Armitage. She was now sitting in the main bar, noiselessly sipping some kind of liqueur. Looking at his hair, Wislon remembered one of the reasons for hating his father. Being bald as a billiard ball, he had told Wislon that it was because of the helmet he had worn during his time in the fire service. His father had never been in the fire service. Wislon couldn't decide whether it was a lie or a joke. He had been perplexed by the occasion. His mangy hair reminded him and brought on a sensation of repressed nausea. Something was happening in his stomach. Something was trying to get out.

In general, Wislon avoided mirrors. It depended on the light. Sombre, filmic bars and twilight restaurants with red candles were usually the best bets. Lights in their cloakrooms tended to be grey, gorgeously bleary and comfortingly anonymous. Public lavatories and McDonald's were the worst. Their searing lasers of shame were neither kind nor hospitable. They *ordered* people not to loiter. Still, the Dog and Bitch was better than most. Wislon supposed that was why he liked it. Here, he looked good. Or rather, he did not look as bad as he really was. The place had also become a talisman for his meetings with Armitage. Three times, and still the possibility of a fourth had not been denied.

'So why do you like it here?' she asked.

'Oh, you know. Good beer, ambience of the canal, no music. It's been a good place to me. Over the years. A lot of rough times. People have been kind to me.' Wislon raised his glass to the barman. Along his arms, the man had tattoos of snakes and what looked like dragons. A scar ran up and down his hooked nose. The nose was savagely indented and came to an end about an inch to the right of its bridge. The man had a persistent scowl set into his face. He gave Wislon a look of intense fury. Wislon smiled back, then quickly peered down into his beer. At this moment, a tear would be useful, he thought. He looked up and smiled. Armitage's lips curled in response.

That evening, things had gone pretty well. They had been to see another film at the Triangle. It was called *Love and Human Remains*. The film itself had not been a great success. It included serial murders, drug addiction, theft, AIDS, betrayal and a character called Candy. At least there was plenty to talk about afterwards.

Wislon felt his research into drug abuse had been a sound investment.

'I've never taken drugs,' Armitage was saying, 'unless you count coffee and cigarettes. The loss of control frightens me.' Her voice was a high falsetto.

'Absolutely.'

'Have you ever taken any?'

'A few experimental ones.' Wislon shrugged, rather convincingly he thought. 'But nothing now. Khat, magic mushrooms, benzo, diazepins, cannabis, toads, amyl nitrate, some downers . . .'

'Like what?' She eyed him suspiciously.

'The usual. Barbs, Seconal, Amytal, Tuinal, Nembutal, quinalbarbitone, amylbarbitone, butobarbitone . . .'

'You're an addict,' Armitage mock-giggled.

'No. They're all legal. Well, virtually. Certainly no Class A stuff.' He leaned back and took a carefree swig of Colombian beer.

'How did you take them?'

'Pills, capsules, elixir, injections,' came the robotic reply. He knew that he was taking a gamble here. Armitage's father was a surgeon. She was clearly from a comfortable family, and accordingly he had pitched his trangressiveness fairly well down the scale. He hoped she would see him as respectable but adventurous; a flawed boy needing protection. Who knows, he might even graduate to 'Man Who's Seen Life'.

He scanned her mostly blank features. Eyes wide open and looking at him. Lips slightly parted. What did it all amount to? Nothing that he recognised as approval, but possibly interest. Yes, *definitely* interest. Wislon took the opportunity to cast a wistful, sensitive glance at the canal, as if recalling some painful memory. A pensioner from Washwood Heath had drowned there ten days ago. He was a regular on the bank side; an angler who sat there for hours in most weathers, even though he knew there were no fish to be caught.

Wislon was concentrating hard on the preparations he had made before leaving for the Triangle. Now, he remembered standing in the doorway and scrutinising his flat. It was not well appointed, well furnished or well decorated. However it was scrubbed, clean and suffocatingly tidy. He had breathed deeply, and set about creating organised chaos. Books were strewn, cushions scattered, his bed unmade, drawers opened, clothes chucked, socks uncoupled and bottles toppled. Finally, a number of plates were taken from their cupboards, plunged into the greasy remains of the waste bin and then piled haphazardly into a bowl of scummily cold water. That should do it. What does this flat say, Wislon thought. I'll tell you what it says. Help. Succour. Be kind. Pour oil on troubled waters. Go on. *Mother* me.

The business of actually getting Armitage back to his flat wasn't as tricky as Wislon had anticipated. Maybe she really did want a coffee or a liqueur or wine or whatever it was he offered. When they got there, Wislon took a long time finding a bottle of wine. He and Armitage then arranged themselves on the sofa.

'Excuse the mess,' Wislon said hopefully.

'Not at all. It's fine. At least it's clean.'

'Is it?'

'A quick tidy. That's all it needs. No problem.'

23

'Oh. No. I mean, I suppose not,' Wislon croaked.

He put on a tape; a soundtrack by Michael Nyman. 'Have you seen *The Piano*?'

'Oh no,' Armitage said, 'where is it? Do you play?'

Wislon gave her a pained look.

'Don't worry,' she continued, 'I'm only flirting.'

'Ah,' said Wislon.

She settled back and closed her eyes for a few moments. Then she picked up one of the carefully pitched books and searched through it. It was called, *A Local History: Mysterious Birmingham*. The pages that Armitage found told the story of Mary Ashford who had lived in Erdington in 1817. She had been found dead in a pond near her home. A patch of blood and some blood spots had led a labourer to notice her on his way to work. The obvious suspect was a man called Abraham Thornton. He admitted to 'possessing' Mary, although a jury acquitted him of murder. The case seemed to hinge on whether the blood was menstrual. The court reasoned that a girl who is starting to menstruate would not feel like yielding her virginity.

Armitage closed the book. Wislon noticed that she had drawn her legs underneath her body, revealing the full flow of ankle, calf and thigh. The sequence ended at the junction of maroon skirt and the darker band at the top of her shadowy, opaque tights.

Wislon bided his time.

There was an awkward, fetid silence. If this was a film, Wislon thought, spirals of smoke from expensive cigarettes would be climbing towards a slowly rotating fan high in a vaulted, stark white ceiling. As it was, a chill sharp breeze cut in through the thinly protected window. The tree immediately outside shifted uncomfortably in the wind. The whole garden creaked.

Wislon got up and walked around. The music churned on. Armitage looked up and he aimed a smile. He leaned forward, not quite knowing what the next bit was. His face was angled towards hers. If he kept going, some kind of collision was definitely on the cards. He kept going. Eyes shut. Lips on standby. At the last moment, Armitage's face pulled away and ducked underneath Wislon's arms which were reaching mechanically forward for some kind of purchase on the sides of the sofa. He was bent almost double before he realised that no one was there. Armitage was busy playing with the cassette deck on the other side of the room.

'I'm not sure I like this,' she said. 'Do you have anything less monotonous? Some words, maybe?'

Wislon gathered himself together, his face a riot of disgrace. He tugged his hair back into some kind of shape and ambled over, though not all the way.

'Elvis Costello?'

'Mmmm,' she almost replied. 'And I'll give you a hand with the washing-up. Then I really must be going.'

Wislon thought that after the first kiss you can usually do one of two things. Either liberate your lips and simultaneously manage a cooing smile, or simply get on with it. What do you do after no kisses, though? None whatsoever.

What he did was the washing-up.

'Where's the Fairy?' Armitage asked.

'In the . . . oh, I don't know. Have a rummage. Somewhere . . .' Wislon recovered. He found some rubber gloves and briefly considered placing one of the gloves over his head and blowing it into an inflated cockscomb. Instead, as was his habit, he blew loudly into them. The fingers came up like sausages. Armitage raised an eyebrow and then turned back to the curious marks she had found on the dinner plate in her hands.

It wasn't all bad. She was in the kitchen. She hadn't slapped him. She hadn't said she wouldn't see him again.

He thought about his bed and the fact that he would have to remake it before clambering in. A number thirty-seven rumbled past. Someone was singing about passion going out of fashion.

No. It wasn't all bad.

The slow-burning memories of Armitage receded from Wislon's mind. A few seconds on and he began to question their validity. Was that what really happened? Life was made of uncertainty, travesty and twists of the truth. At least, that's the way it seemed. Wislon reflected that some people seemed to be certain of themselves. But no one could be that certain. No one could even be *that* certain. The most certain men and women you know – they don't really believe it. No one does. They're bluffing. They're insecure. They just don't know.

Take dreams, for example. Lately, Wislon could not

remember them. Yet he knew they were important. Surely he should take heed, write them down, speak them into a tape recorder? Something. It was what Agnes had told him to do. Or rather, he imagined, it was the sort of thing Agnes ought to be telling him to do, which amounted to about the same thing. Apart from the one about his father the only dreams he could bring to mind were about Armitage. That was because they were all the same, with a slight variation. His dream was that he found Armitage in bed with a succession of film directors: Scorsese, Altman, De Palma, Capra, Powell, Mackendrick, Leone, Cimino, Allen, Coppola and Spielberg. One by one, she had them all. At one time, she'd been through the French New Wave and – and this *hurt* – Hitchcock. He didn't even like women! There had been only one deviation in the sequence. Once, Wislon had come into the room to find her under Sir Peter Hall. What had he done to deserve her, Wislon wondered. This lone aberration disturbed him. He could manage the symmetry and predictable patterning of the others; it seemed like a game. But Sir Peter was trespassing. He somehow made the whole thing *real*.

Thrown into disorder, he pulled himself out of the bath. The water dripped off him on to the towel that had been carefully placed where his feet would fall. Wislon stared at his legs and then moved slowly forwards. Avoiding the mirror, he moved into the hallway and turned into the lounge. He ignited the television. Nostalgia. A repeat of an early episode of *Steptoe and Son*. A comedy without jokes. Harold had

27

been jilted at the altar and the relatives had arrived to reclaim their presents.

There was a sour taste at the back of Wislon's throat. He must have swallowed some soap. His mind was infinite and empty, like a stillborn sky. He filled it with a mental catalogue of what he needed to do before going to work the next day. Then he went to write it down, meticulously numbering each item. He remembered his mother's lists which had been left all around the house. Once, he had found himself lying on one after climbing into bed. He had turned on the bedside lamp and read the crumpled paper. It said, 'Don't forget to turn the light off.'

He settled in the sofa. It was nine-nineteen p.m. He watched the digital display on the video player as it recorded the fact. There were no other lights on in the room. A faint red glow faltered in the darkness around Wislon.

— 2 —

Working

The radio-alarm kicked in at seven a.m. Precisely. The same as all the other mornings. Radio Four. Slowly, Wislon became more or less conscious. Or rather, less unconscious. Generally speaking, he had to admit, the mornings were not a problem. He liked mornings, which arrived before anything could happen. Plenty of zip and optimism there. It all went wrong after that, when he had to deal with the rest of the stuff around him. Then, life belly-flopped. Try as he might, there was no escaping it.

Wislon felt uneasy whilst listening to the less significant items on the news. He had got out of the habit of bothering with them. News of dismal little lives sent him scuttling quickly to the bathroom. This morning it was peace in Northern Ireland and then something about an actor who had gone missing. Then, farming or schools or pensioners. Or something. Ordinary things terrified Wislon. But the big business was out of reach, abstract, even soothing in its sense of process combined with an inability to touch him.

Wislon sprang out of bed with the taste of metal gripping the inside of his mouth. He wrenched open the curtains and glanced at the day that was waiting for him outside. He watched it like television, scanning the image for anything of interest, then squeezed his eyes tight again. The day needed more channels. Then, bath, shave (if his skin was up to it), a quick clean and tidy, breakfast (coffee, orange juice, cereal), gunk down the lavatory, get dressed and empty the rubbish.

Wislon pulled at the thin loops of polythene, pressured the pedal at the bottom of the bin and lifted the bag of garbage through its open jaw. Even though he was used to it, the stink hit him with some force. Wislon could hardly believe that he had somehow created this stench. Did it really belong to him? The bag was only half full, its contents moving around in an almost organic manner. He thought he could make out a used toilet roll holder, two battered milk cartons, maybe some newspaper, several knots of hair, the crumpled remains of an old toothpaste tube, several ear swabs, a broken biro, an odd sock and a foil tray which must once have contained something edible. It now seemed to be the source of a brown, oily stain which was threatening to gather itself into a pool at the bottom of the bag. In the middle, between these items, Wislon was aware of a mass of unidentified objects which had compressed into an indistinct sculpture. He wondered whether the bag was a clue to his existence, whether it was active with his own habits, patterns and inclinations. If so, he wanted to find a more exotic collection of rubbish rather than the rubbish in his rubbish – maybe a condom leaking chicken soup or even underwear of some kind. Most people's rubbish is private, but Wislon's was simply forgettable and almost invisible. Wearily, he tied the sagging loops together, more to plug the smell than anything else. He dropped the bag back into the bin, releasing the pedal with a sudden theatrical flip so that the lid clanged shut. The last hurdle to negotiate before setting off to work was the post. This morning, there were only bills. Well, one bill. Even the bastard services were giving up on him. Where were the piles of gaudy junk-mail that everyone at the office was always complaining about? Free gifts, prize opportunities, holidays, cash, special-edition pottery, time-shares; he wanted a piece of the action as well. But who did you *talk* to about these things?

He was waiting for a letter from Armitage. Although he had not heard from her for months, he was expecting a communication any day now. No, really; he was. After all, Wislon reasoned, she couldn't just let things go, could she? Not the way things were when it all finished. *Could she?* He could not remember exactly how it had all ended. The precise, tangible details still eluded him. He knew it had been pretty bloody, though. The circumstances demanded a spirited, womanly riposte. He knew that the letter – when it came – would be drenched in bile, threatening, hurtful. Possibly even truthful. She knew how to give him a hard time. There was no reason why she should *not* do it. For heaven's sake, if people *can* do something, they always do.

31

Wislon slipped the electricity bill into his leather-ette briefcase and slipped out through the peeling front door. There were two other flats on his level. He knew the occupants were lurking behind their doors, listening and watching. They might be in-discernible, discreet, but they were there. Raymond Doughty: war veteran, good at coughing, two cats, prize ear hair. He was there. So were Zasu Pitts and Tempe Pigott, the mummified pair who lived directly opposite. Their story was that they had been actresses and even worked in Hollywood. They wore enough make-up, even now. Their faces were caked and cracked, dusty fossilised contours mapping fogeyish landscapes of obsolete looks.

He hurried past their doors, down three flights of stairs. Each landing was lit by a single naked light bulb. Each one of these was suspended by a brownish plaited cord and gave off a sullen, reluctant glow. Even during the day, even in the summer, each bulb's glowing trickle of light never faltered. There seemed to be no switches. When a bulb failed, it was invisibly replaced within a matter of hours. Wislon could not remember seeing anyone perform the act.

The time was eight a.m. The temperature was forty-seven degrees Fahrenheit. Wislon encouraged the Metro up the road. The engine eventually fired with a grudging regularity. The road was lined with houses that looked more or less identical. They had been extended, converted, modified, improved, trans-formed, knocked through, modernised and partially knocked down. Essentially, though, they were the undifferent.

Wislon usually took the same route to work each day, arrowing the Metro towards the city centre. He headed up Tailbush Road and then on to the Soho Road. Today he had decided on The Alternative Route. It made little difference in actual miles travelled but the alternative was slightly less civilised. It was, in fact, entirely uncivilised.

The road he took had become a kind of makeshift high street. All the shopkeepers were selling derelict merchandise. Handmade signs on sheets and cardboard moved reluctantly in the meagre breeze. One man had boxes of calendars from 1991 and a wooden tray with last year's top-selling cassettes. He was slumped on the pavement and eyed everyone who walked past with a defiant and guilt-seeking stare. Wislon wondered if *he* had been there since 1991.

He drove at a sharp speed through the flashing streets, handling the car with a kind of casual, absent-minded violence. He grappled and pulled the wheel, stammered aggressively on the clutch, and routinely stampeded the brakes. Bits of canal, trees that once boasted leaves, avenues that used to be avenues – and then a wide ribbon of tarmac, buzzing with cars and slicing between stacked rows of squalid housing. He manoeuvred the Metro into the choking stream and set about working towards its mouth.

This was a suburbia that had lost its virginity. It had been gang-banged by formless executive cul-de-sacs, ravished by smooth chromium business parks and abused by glossy edge-of-town superstores. It was an empty, graceless world devoid even of sin. Scavenging clumps of adolescent boys hung about the more dilapidated buildings that had survived the unravages of reconstruction. A strip club, The Metropolis, stood out only because of its flickering neon. It was flashing despite not being open until lunchtime. Then, office workers would pull themselves into the dank bar to watch the acts. When he drove home in the evening, Wislon could often hear the nightshift at work. 'Get It On' by T. Rex would clatter tinnily from a half open door at the side of the club. On the inside, a sign read, 'NO ENTRY. PISS OF'.

Wislon wondered what would happen if a stripper simply walked on stage already wearing no clothes. Strip a woman naked and she is instantly desexualised, *un*sexy. She can't help it, but she is. Wanting, need and fantasy – all mugged at once. The same woman must do the same things, probably in front of the same people. Women past their prime, haggard, stretched, grey-white mottled skin, cellulite dancing on the thighs, lying on their backs, opening their legs and giving it their all. Whenever they glanced down, they would see the same rows of hopeless, emetic faces.

Why did Wislon allow himself such thoughts? It was not just because thoughts had a life of their own. They weren't merely psychic hooligans. Not really. Or so he hoped.

In front of the Metro was an off-yellow bus with an advertisement rudely plastered on to its backside. A shiny brat of a car glinted from the rippled paper. 'The back of a bus doesn't need to be ugly', the slogan asserted. It does, Wislon thought. You don't know the half of it. It does.

Wislon did not like arriving at work. He did not like working. The days needed filling. The job became what he did. Lots of people do one, thought Wislon, so it couldn't be that bad.

He had not worked since leaving university. Somehow, he had shambled through the year after his father had died. His mother had moved to a small village somewhere between Worcester and Stratford. He thought his job would provide an identity, maybe the routine would settle him. (Fat chance.) However, he did learn something about money. It bought him a Metro – white, C reg., 85,235 miles – but good enough for him. He rented a flat. He found a chair, a bed, a sofa, a television, some cutlery and a table. He had a lowly foothold and he clung on.

He worked for a small insurance company. Still, he did not really know what he was doing. Or, come to that, what he was *supposed* to be doing. Sometimes he wanted to ask, just to make sure. But then no one else seemed certain either. Wislon knew that he sold what Fat Mike and the others told him to sell. Policies mainly, mostly by telephone. They'd told him to follow the manual and he couldn't go wrong. So far, they'd been right. He bluffed his way through each day, shirking responsibility and dodging decisions. The others knew and they didn't let him forget it. Virgil Young, Fat Mike, Simon Monks, Matt Jackson, Faith Dawkins, Tony Tuesby, who was known as 'The Truth', Napoleon Jones and Phoebe Steel. All apart from Amy Facer. They were all up there waiting for him.

An office job, he thought, gave the illusion of

having things under control when, of course, there is actually nothing *to* control. Insurance seemed, at best, a superficial business. Wislon thought that this was probably because it *was* a superficial business. That wasn't too bad because it meant that he thought he was quite suited to it. Wislon was not imperfectly suited to the superficial business of insurance. Or rather, it suited his present state of mind not imperfectly. Or something like that.

The company had lodged itself in a three-storey Victorian warehouse at the centre of the Jewellery Quarter. The decline of the jewellery business – real jewellery, he had been told, not the machine-miser trinkets which the area now pumped out – had led to the establishment of other uses for many of the buildings. Wislon could not help thinking in terms of the current mediocrity in contrast with the rich workmanship of bygone ages. He thought of the building he worked in as parasitical, greedily squatting where it should not be. It reminded him of something his father used to say to him: 'You're nothing but a big fat cuckoo.' He used to pronounce the word as 'koo-koo'. He had never fully understood what his father meant. Now, looking up at the building in front of him, he still felt the complexity of his father's unfriendly distaste.

As he walked in, he felt strangely at home. Phoebe Steel was just ahead of him. They were heading down a neatly lain floor of frozen silk. The old red brickwork had been left exposed along the walls. Ancient timbers criss-crossed the roof and long poles of tubing threw out a sharp but unsatisfying light.

Wislon could smell the sharp tang of Phoebe's perfume. As her heels clacked along the corridor, he watched the mechanical stabbing actions that her legs made upon the floor. Her hair had been piled into a bun which revealed a virtually transparent slope of pale skin running from the nape of her neck to the top of a dark blue suit. Wislon felt ungainly, loping along behind her, carrying the burden of his body with him.

Phoebe stopped at the end of the corridor and flexed her forehead. She was frowning, uncertain, as if she had lost something. In a single industrious movement, she turned back down the passage and swept past Wislon.

'Morning, Wislon,' she said. Her mouth didn't open, but words still came out.

'Low.' Wislon knew how little he understood about women. He thought he understood them less than other men, and that wasn't saying a great deal. In fact, it wasn't saying anything. During his life, when faced by women, he had been tongue-tied, verbose, sweaty, dry, nervous, compulsively arrogant, rude and blandly polite. Sometimes, in frenzied orgies of emotional confusion, he was all these things at once. There was something wrong with him. He knew he couldn't cope. His father had once told him that 'the right one will come along eventually. You won't be able to miss whoever it is – blind, one-legged and covered in warts.' Now he was dead, but that didn't make things much better. Being near to Phoebe had brought him out in a drizzly sweat. He didn't even like her. Besides, she was probably Virgil's girlfriend, whatever that was supposed to mean. Anyway, she wasn't with Wislon. There was something about the partial logic of women that paralysed Wislon. He felt scrutinised and perused by them. Except by Armitage, of course. The celestial mystery that surrounded her didn't fool him for a moment.

Fat Mike could do anything he liked. So far, he hadn't bothered, but one day he might. He had a murky office to himself. He thought he had Phoebe Steel too, but she was working on it. Two months ago, he tried it on once too often and she pissed in his coffee – but not so that he would notice.

Otherwise, there were five others in Wislon's section, or rather, the section in which Wislon worked. Simon Monks was neither fat nor wrinkled, even though everyone referred to him as 'Jumbo'. His head was always buried in the middle of papers. His white skin and his cropped, thinning white hair gave an impression of anaemic shyness. He found it difficult to talk about anything other than his work or himself. What's more, he seemed to be even worse at his job than Wislon. Virgil Young was young and smart and repulsive. He was being 'groomed' by the company which meant he was always smug. Matt Jackson went on about football. He was slow-thinking and always seemed to have an infection in his eye. Twenty years ago, Tony Tuesby was going to be a troubleshooter. Amongst other things, he sniffed out false claims. His reputation was based on the exposing of a jewellery fraud in Hockley. It had involved false claims being submitted about several hundred diamond solitaires that had never actually been stolen. All the paperwork seemed to be in order, but The Truth was having none of it. His was a life built around suspicion and meanness and he had become defined by it. His hair was greying and his nose was bent and crooked as if specially adapated for his job. Form and function were one.

Napoleon Jones was younger and more junior than Wislon. No doubt he would prove to be an inspiration to those around him. He would demon-strate ambition and determination by going to college, reading the right books, even taking a degree in something or other. After all, anybody could do it these days. He would probably even marry the course darling and eventually rejoin the company as a supervisor or team leader or whatever. At the moment, Wislon was still grateful that he made the tea and carried messages. However, he could feel Napoleon catching up. Fast.

The only one who didn't seem out to get him was Amy. Or rather, she was the one who Wislon didn't think was out to get him, and he thought that it probably amounted to much the same thing. He found it possible to think of her as a virginal school-friend. She often sat with her arms folded under her breasts and stared directly in front of her. Her expression was one of eternal trust. Wislon wondered whether she had experienced a single bad or un-happy thing during her life.

What was Wislon's standing amongst this lot? He arrived to find a memo propped on his desk. It said,

'Fuck off, pimple features.' It was unsigned. Wislon put it in the bin.

Napoleon took orders for mid-morning refreshments at eleven. He asked everybody except Wislon. Phoebe never communicated with him in anything other than shrill squeals as she tap-tapped around the office. The Truth treated him with silent disdain. Simon Monks hated Wislon for being less bad than him. To be humbled by Wislon was unforgivable. He blamed Wislon, and muttered incoherent, dark obscenities at him during the day: 'Bertie tosser' or 'Bastard creepy code'.

However, Virgil Young was the worst. His teeth were rotten and he smelled of stubbed cigarettes and menthol. His intelligence was apparently geared to doing one of two things, although he quite often did them together:

(i) Getting on

(ii) Fucking up Wislon.

'Don't you understand, scabby,' he was saying in a voice specially designed to ricochet around the office, 'the expected claim rate times the expected claim size equals the prime premium. So what don't we do . . . *Never*?' He pushed his face close to Wislon, whose senses reeled from the breathy odour of rotting bark.

'Sell a standard policy to someone who wants to move his piano to South Africa?' ventured Wislon.

'Exactly. And why not?'

Wislon pushed his hair back and tried to ignore the fountains of sweat underneath his shirt. He thought that he knew the answer. He would have to give it. 'Because the smaller the group, the more accurate the premium . . .'

Virgil interrupted. 'Therefore, we have to work out a policy from cold. *Not* issue the standard one. Clear?'

Wislon despised himself for letting this happen. This was Wislon being pushed around. This was Wislon being fucked up. Virgil continued, 'And watch the one behind your ear. Christ, Needy – I've never seen one *there* before.'

The rest just listened. They knew that Fat Mike liked Virgil Young. Jumbo kept his head down, his bleached skin glowing red with self-consciousness. Phoebe did her little dance around the office. She still had a worried frown on her face. Napoleon sniggered. Amy Facer sat in the corner like she always did. She didn't look up or down. She was invisible.

So that was Wislon's standing in the office. He did not so much stand as subside.

Lunchtimes were different. Usually Wislon sat by himself in the Ruptured Bachelor sipping gassy lager and eating grease while everyone else went to the Fleece and Go-Between. Sometimes he went to see his doctor. Sometimes he went to the other doctor, the one he talked to. He knew he had difficulties. Nothing he couldn't handle, you understand. So why not share it with someone who did understand? Besides, Armitage wasn't around any longer. Now he couldn't talk *to* her he talked mainly about her. Since she had left, it was the least he could do.

Once or twice in the past, he had even met

Armitage for lunch. The mouldy stench of the Ruptured Bachelor wasn't for her. On one occasion she had insisted on a stroll around the art gallery followed by soup and a Constable Salad in the Edwardian Tea Room. It was some time in April. One of those days when the sun shines luridly for a few mocking moments before the clouds dash in front of it. Then the rain, stinging and cold, before the sun messes you up again with its faint suggestion of hope.

Armitage met Wislon on the marble steps. They went inside and two men dressed like traffic wardens took her hat and umbrella, swapping them for a numbered plastic disc. Wislon did not have anything to hand in and was dank pretty much all over. He wrinkled his nose as the smell of old carpet slunk up and into his nostrils. In the four (or was it five? or six?) months that he had known Armitage, he had never known her to go to the hairdresser's. Yet her hair always looked exactly the same – same length, same style, same gloss, same smell, same shine. She was a marvel of engineering. She wore . . . what did she wear? Short black skirt, vivid mauve blouse (probably silk) and plenty of gold jewellery. As usual, her manner was one of off-handed interest, almost as if she had turned up despite herself. She acted as if she was unaware of Wislon, alternately coming close to and then retreating from him. He found it difficult to decide which Armitage he was actually seeing. Consequently, he was uncertain about her feelings for him. Still, she always showed up – she was never not there. In that department, at least, everything was fine. He had her down as someone who took her punishment and came back for more. If only there was a definite, final version, Wislon would have been a happier man. As it was, he waited with nervousness for her ultimate identity to show itself. Would she allow him a glimpse? A tiny peek? His blood raced, his heart jumped wildly and his skin came out in damp rashes. He was impatient and waiting for her decisively naked self.

Now she led Wislon through the gallery's hard cavities. They reverberated with the slop and jostle of footsteps, and the low drone of occasional conversation. He was thrilled to be there and to be with her. Every so often, her hand touched his or took hold of his arm for a few seconds. He could not begin to describe the intoxicating strangeness of such moments. As she led him, Wislon shuffled behind her. He watched the way she moved, bored holes in her clothes, observed the flashes of skin and enjoyed the small detonations of pleasure that were set off inside his own body.

What of the paintings? Armitage seemed to know it all. Wislon was not up to listening in much detail but he caught the general drift. Besides, he preferred it when pictures were moving. This lot, they just hung there and returned your stare. Wislon saw himself in each painting's glass covering, reflected against a variety of landscaped backgrounds. He thought that people and lives didn't resemble paintings. *They* changed, accelerated forward, moved sideways, were dynamic. This art ignored time, and you couldn't do that. No. Not in Wislon's experience, anyway.

They wandered through the various rooms.

Bundles of yawning schoolchildren littered the floor eating sandwiches. An elderly couple crawled past, inching after their walking sticks. Two women in their thirties, their arms bound around each other like seaweed, confronted a gawky Indian attendant. They wanted to know where Judith and Holofernes were.

Armitage had a bruise of lipstick at the corner of her mouth and decamped to the Ladies for a few minutes. Wislon put his hands in his pockets. Like an obedient son, he stood and waited. In front of him Valentine was rescuing Sylvia from Proteus. Good for Valentine, Wislon thought. He leaned forward and peered at the printed words discreetly mounted on grey card. 'W. Holman Hunt, 1851. Kent. Oil on canvas, 38¾ x 52½ (98.5 x 133.3). First Exh. R.A. 1851.' A further explanation followed: Valentine was disillusioned with Proteus, whom he had considered to be a good friend. He had just foiled Proteus' attempted rape of Sylvia, who was Valentine's fiancée. The two men were making up. Proteus was kneeling. His hand rested on the back of his neck as if he had just swatted a fly. Valentine was holding his other hand and looking all magnanimous. Wislon wasn't sure that Proteus wouldn't do it again, given half a chance. Given *any* kind of chance, probably. His face betrayed no remorse. In fact, he looked rather pleased with himself. Sylvia just looked nonplussed and embarrassed in the kind of way that some people say women are meant to look after somebody has tried to rape them. 'Couldn't have been that bad then, could it?' Someone else was leaning against a tree, although Wislon didn't know who it was. It was all happening in a wood. The ground was a riot of symbolic leaves. Behind Wislon, an old lady chewing toffees wandered past and commented to no one in particular, 'Nice mushrooms.'

Wislon wondered how he would act if someone tried to rape Armitage. He didn't really have friends, never mind best friends, so he could not be specific. A convoy of malicious but compulsive spite rumbled through his mind. Forgive and forget? You must be joking. What kind of a man is this Valentine?

Armitage came close. She took his arm. 'Thoughtful?' she cooed.

'Nothing,' Wislon instinctively lied. He did not, on the whole, think it was a good idea to know what people were thinking. Nor did he think that people often bothered with the truth. He also suspected that his mind never contained anything worth listening to. He therefore thought it best to make something up that was more entertaining than the truth. And, of course, might even show him in a better light. And really, anything was better than just saying the truth, which was usually that he *was* thinking about nothing. 'I was just wondering what the soup was today. I'm hungry.'

She pulled him gently away. Wislon's mind was dithering. He went where she directed.

This lunchtime, Wislon ate a battered sausage and potato salad, washing it all down with a pint of bilious Mexican lager. He went back to the office, made some calls, day-dreamed about sex, not having

45

sex and why he didn't get sex, and endured Virgil's verbal abuse. Who said that being alone set you loose for carefree womanising and a life of extended sexual pleasure? Being alone meant only being *alone* in Wislon's experience. Napoleon spilt coffee over his trousers. Jumbo smouldered in the corner glowering at Wislon every time he picked up the phone. Fat Mike said something about the company's policy on the policies they had about selling policies. Phoebe rattled nervously around the office keeping one step ahead of Fat Mike's opportunistic breathy pursuits. At this rate, Wislon thought, his dodgy feet would start playing up again. They all had to endure a technology update from Faith Dawkins on the new computers that were to be installed. She also had some words of advice about telephones, saying that they were the company's nervous system whilst computers were its virtual epidermis. Matt Jackson dozed heavily and Amy Facer looked on politely. She unfolded her arms and smiled carefully. Wislon watched as her heavy breasts sprang free and lurched forward at the same time as she looked down and concentrated on her work once more.

By five p.m. they were all gone.

Wislon looked at his desk. Telephone. Pens. Calendar with antique car, a parody of its type. A calculator, which was glued tenaciously to the desk's surface. Two trays brimming with buckled paper. The contents of his desk were what brought him there every day. These were the materials which rendered him anonymous.

Wislon thought about it on the drive home. The

Metro dawdled in the infectious limb of traffic. He observed the thickening clump of men, boys, sick urbanites and ragged outcasts who had somehow transformed themselves into a single ugly group outside The Metropolis. Wislon wondered whether the same vile homogeneity would apply to a group of women. The buildings around the club formed an inlay of stubby, rotten teeth amongst gleaming, symmetrical porcelain. They wobbled all right, but they just wouldn't come out. On one wall Wislon noticed, 'FUCK OF THE POLICE'. A large fox sat in the alley between a newsagent's and a tawdry video shop. In its mouth was a bulky sanitary towel, the streak of red running along its middle now faded to a dusky pink. The ends of the towel drooped down. The fox looked as if it were sporting a cartoonish moustache.

Wislon took the stairs three at a time and burst through his front door. He wanted to avoid the weird sisters and the old man. He knew they would have been in position behind their peep-holes as soon as the entry door clunked open. Back in the privacy of his flat, he had a long bath and brought his body to heel. Then he went to see *The Discreet Charm of the Bourgeoisie* at the Arts Centre, working out an impressive thesis he could save for . . . what? Well, he'd save it anyway. The film was the last in a Buñuel season. A knot of oily Spaniards in the row behind him talked throughout the showing. Wislon huddled forward in solitary, suppressed rage.

When he got back there was a message on the answer machine. It was short and the tone was even, polite and measured. It said simply, 'I know, Wislon.

What are you going to do about it?'

He considered, then calculated. He was not afraid. The message must be from Armitage. It was what he had been anticipating. She always turned up in the end. But why was it delivered by a man? Was she trying to tell him something? After all this time? He thought that she would be more of a letter writer. No. Perhaps not.

He went to bed, his head heaving with the dreams which he would never have and certainly never remember.

So who is this Armitage anyway? What was a single woman doing in the Dog and Bitch on the night that Wislon had met her? Did she have a job? Exactly what kind of relationship did she have with Wislon? Let's be honest; did they *do* it? In order. She had told Wislon that she was at the pub to meet a girlfriend and that she had been let down at the last minute. A message left at the bar, no way of knowing beforehand. (Nothing wrong with that, is there?) He thought she did have a job. Maybe she had told him once. A consultant somewhere, something in the arts. Not very demanding. Beauty and brains. She had everything, but did she want Wislon? Difficult to say. She teased and incited him without actually meaning to do either. Perhaps that was the trick. Anyway, Wislon was puzzled, so it was definitely working.

Wislon summoned the courage again about two chaste months after his first fumbled attempts. In the meantime, he had seen her on only a handful of occasions.

This time had been better, though you couldn't call it in any way satisfactory. No way. This time, at least, contact had been made. Wislon had taken a few swigs from the liqueur bottle in the kitchen. Armitage didn't drink much – he felt that he would have to do it for both of them.

He had backed her into the corner of the sofa during a monologue about the political significance of Spanish films post-Franco. He thought he had better get the kissing out of the way. After all, it was only meant to be a prelude, an anticipation of better things to come. So. He tried everywhere: neck, ears, nose, hands, hair, chin – all the while keeping an eye on her lips. Every now and then (more then than now, in fact) Wislon would gently land one on Armitage's mouth. He was gauging the response, estimating what would happen if he dared to stray there for longer than a few micro seconds. This went on for a couple of minutes. Wislon thought he ought to up the stakes and be more ambitious. So. His hands began to move in what he assumed was an erotic manner. He stroked the back of Armitage's hands. With the other hand he traced the little ravine of flesh at the back of her neck. To do this he also had gently to lift the glossy wall of perfect hair it was hidden beneath.

So far, so good. He was getting *away* with it.

Moving on, he rubbed her thighs – inside and out – and then made some circular, swirling movements roughly around the contours of her breasts. All the

49

time, his head was bobbing and weaving around, his lips offering little kisses over the bits of her upper body he could reach without contorting himself.

Striking a natural balance between the measured movements of his hands and the more general opportunism of his mouth was tricky. Wislon thought he was getting the hang of it when two thoughts stopped him cold. First, if things really got going, how would Armitage react to his body? Could men keep their shirts on? Probably not. There was no point in wearing one unless you could take it off. He might just as well be carrying a placard: 'Danger. Stop now unless you really enjoy pus.' He couldn't even keep it on in the spirit of sexual abandonment; it wasn't going badly, but bloody hell, she might at least wriggle or sigh or *something*. That's what women were meant to do, wasn't it? And that brought Wislon to his second thought. This was more alarming and prevailed over the first thought at almost exactly the same time as he was having it.

Actually, it was more of an observation than a thought.

It wasn't that Armitage was objecting to Wislon's crabbed assault or his biological doggerel. Quite the opposite, in fact. Armitage was absolutely unmoved by it all. Not just unmoved, but exhaustively unmoved. Unmoved to the point of not moving at all. She seemed quite relaxed but it was as if all the blood had suddenly and inexplicably drained from her. She was staring impassively, unthinkingly ahead of her. And if she was thinking, what could have been going through her mind? The colour of her skin had paled to reveal a filigree of blue veins that mapped her face and the backs of her hands.

Wislon responded by changing his tactics. He arranged his body around hers. One knee impressed itself against Armitage's right thigh. The other leg was swung imperiously over and between her leaden, prosthetic shanks. She didn't budge. Her legs stayed exactly as they were, two stubborn branches on an unyielding trunk. Wislon had expected them to leap apart, if only out of shock. Still. On he went. He rubbed every bit of her more vigorously than before. Daringly, he went for the stomach. Mischievously, one hand strayed beneath it for a few seconds. He was bolder with the kissing, too. At one point, he found his mouth lumped with hers for a good five seconds or so. The next time he was in the vicinity, he made it ten. He was counting, and he knew. Then fifteen. He established a rhythm. Rub–caress–kiss; touch–kiss–fondle; then back to rubbing . . . and so on. Apart from the kissing, of course, which was always in the same place. Being a natural romantic, he was (for the time being) exclusively a lips man.

He had worked and tracked most of Armitage's body when, after exactly twenty-two minutes of silent and personable molestation, she grabbed hold of Wislon's hand.

'Pardon?' he blustered. 'What?'

Armitage squeezed. Only a bit. But definitely a squeeze.

'Wislon.'

He had his head buried somewhere underneath her armpit. 'Yefffspp?'

Now he would get his tongue ready. Perhaps this was it. He looked up and she even flickered an eye. His mouth had almost dried up and he salivated madly. His hand moved back to her stomach, by far the least unresponsive area so far. He even considered using both hands at the same time and rotating them in opposite directions in a kind of sensual symphony.

'I think I've got something in my eye.'

'Oh.'

'Do you mind if I use the bathroom?'

'No. I mean no, of course not. Go ahead.' Wislon had forgotten to dirty the bathroom. Still, she would have to confront the reality of his cleanliness at some point.

'And Wislon?'

'Yes?'

'Your trousers are dreadfully creased.'

'Yes.'

A pause.

'Do you mind moving your leg?'

'Yes. I mean no.'

Wislon blinked like a small boy as she raised her still fully clothed body languidly on to the floor. It seemed to flow into an upright position as if ignorant of its individually complex components. He watched as she made her way noiselessly across the room.

From start to finish – sofa to bathroom – exactly twenty-eight minutes. Well, it was a start. And he got to keep his shirt on.

Before going to bed, Wislon drew up a list of things

to do the next day. It was much the same as most other days, except that tomorrow he was also going to the doctor's. Next door, the weird sisters were having a sing-song. Nothing from the old man. Something thumped upstairs. Proabably the Greek-looking saxophonist. Mid-thirties, barely five foot. She often ran a bath at two or three in the morning. Wislon glanced at the morning newspaper which he'd taken from Virgil Young's desk. It was by now redundant. More on Ireland. A woman had drowned her three sons in the local lake, invented a kidnapper, and then confessed. A man had beaten his wife to death with a wrench in front of their children.

What is love? He supposed it was the kind of question people living by themselves often asked.

Wislon could not answer it with any certainty. He didn't think he could even think about it very constructively. He wasn't the type people loved. No one had ever bothered him with it. Armitage implied something like it a few times. His mother. Maybe.

Wislon wanted someone to love. He didn't even mind particularly whether or not he was loved back. Presumably the one followed on from the other.

He was once in love with a girl at school. Her name was Jane and she was good at geography. Wislon would get up early to do his hair. This was a time when doing things with it was still feasible. His father would hammer on the bathroom door. 'What in God's name do you think you're doing in there? What is it that takes more than a minute?' Then, a few minutes later, 'I wouldn't bother if I were you. It's hopeless. You know that, don't you. Hopeless.'

53

Then he would go to the boiler in the airing cupboard and turn off the hot water. Wislon was convinced that he would have removed the sink and bath if it wasn't so inconvenient. After a short while his mother would tuck notes beneath the door. They said things like, 'Come out before your father loses his temper' and 'Quickly. Breakfast is getting cold.' Wislon knew she was acting under instruction. Even the dog had been trained to join in and growled whenever Wislon went near the bathroom, her tongue lolling elastically over labial jowls.

Jane never noticed Wislon's hair. Of course not. He must have been stupid to even think she might. Sometimes he did her history homework for her. He was a trier if nothing else. Once she kissed him chastely on the cheek. They had seen an Indiana Jones film together. Then she met somebody else who seemed to kiss her all the time. Wislon's heart shrivelled. He stopped caring about his hair. He got over Jane all right. The trouble was, he never got over himself.

Next morning. Radio Four. Anna Ford? Or was it John Humphries? They all sounded the same after a while. Anyway, Ireland. Again. Wislon was tiring of it. He was not feeling himself that morning. But then, he thought, who is? Nothing but sodding Ireland for five days now. After all, news was meant to be *news*. Into the bathroom: hair, ears, teeth, face. The usual breakfast. Wislon paused in the hallway, knowing there was something he ought to remember. He thought of Armitage. She had made some kind of contact; there could be more. You never knew with women. He needed to know where he stood.

Out through the front door, and the old man is standing there. Coughing.

'Good morning, Mr Needy.'

'Yes – hello. Look, I'm in a bit of a rush. Work. Early morning meeting. Important. You know.'

'Yes. I've got something for you.' He handed Wislon an envelope.

He tried to take it in as the transfer was made. It didn't look like a bill. But then, bills these days, they never did. Armitage? His mother? But it wasn't his birthday.

'*Reader's Digest*. Prize draw. You've been entered. Well *done*,' said Mr Doughty with a contemptuous snort. He produced a handkerchief and wiped something barely liquid from his mouth. He handed the envelope over, turned and mooched back into his flat. Wislon perused the wadded rectangle in his hand. I'm on the map, he thought, and sprang down the steps into the Metro, suddenly remembering what hope felt like.

Work was . . . work. It was only the middle of the week. The others in the office were tetchy and sullen. Wislon wasn't the stooge that morning. Midweek and noses were to the grindstone, heads were down, people were *getting on with it* and making the most of a bad lot. They were waiting for Friday. Fat Mike was on a war footing. Someone upstairs had had hard words with him *and* Phoebe was moving far too quickly for him today. In fact, she'd been moving round the room at speed all week. He couldn't get near her and his feet were beginning to play up. At about midday, Matt Jackson received twelve dead roses from Interflora. Wislon noticed that he had a perfect arc of scratched skin across his cheek.

'So that's finished,' said Virgil with admirably sardonic polish. Nobody else said anything for a while.

'Claim here from a bloke who got bitten by a snake,' said Virgil, eventually.

'Where?' Phoebe asked.

'Australia.'

'Where on the body?'

'Leg.'

'Nasty?'

'Yes.'

'Serious?'

'No. Not really. Sounds like it was his own bloody fault, anyway.'

'How do snakes eat? I mean, it couldn't have thought it could eat a whole man. Could it.'

'Search me.'

'Peristalsis,' said Napoleon, 'and then they lie still for hours, days at a time, digesting whatever they've eaten.'

'Oh,' said Virgil, 'did you know that, Matt? Needy?'

'Isn't snake meat a delicacy,' asked Phoebe.

'Does it have meat, as such?'

'I thought it was alligator that was a delicacy,' suggested Napoleon, 'maybe it was alligator you were thinking of.'

'Maybe.'

56

'Isn't that suitcases and handbags and shoes and such like?'

'You mean not meat.'

Then there was silence again.

At lunchtime, Wislon went to the doctor's to get a skin prescription. Skin? He didn't think there was much of the stuff left. He went to get a prescription for whatever it was that was now holding his blood and bones together. Whatever it was, it was now beginning to play its middle-of-winter tricks. Not only would he have to wash his bed sheets when he got home, he'd proably have to vacuum them first.

The afternoon came and went. Wislon picked up the telephone a few times and blethered to people in Bath, Croydon and Derby. At the end of the day, he tidied his desk and checked off the list he had made the previous evening.

Wislon stayed behind for half an hour after the others had deserted the office. He found a strange well-being in the solitary ordinariness of the room. It was defiantly anti-heroic, being neither ethereal, lofty or impressive. There was no ninety-second floor view, no mahogany panelling, no corporate-grey carpeting, no glacial lengths of brass railing, and no squadrons of desks banked with burnished communications systems and shimmering computer monitors. The only clock showed the time in Birmingham: six-fourteen p.m. It wasn't even digital. There was nothing to indicate what the state of play was in the offices the company didn't possess in Tokyo, New York, the Middle East or Sydney. There was no sinuous forty-foot-long ticker tape urging stock quotes into the office. There wasn't even a coffee machine. Not one that worked, anyway. There was no point in connecting the room's occupants to a television screen that would relay important instructions from their superiors. After all, Fat Mike had a desk just inside the door. Even when his feet had a bad day, he could get information to them pretty quickly.

Neither had an addiction to the buzzing colour and perpetual mania of urban life taken its intoxicating grip. If the economy chattered for twenty-four hours every day, this office was hard of hearing for much of it. Nobody was addicted to drink or pills or even coffee. Especially not the coffee. Napoleon was still refusing to offer the molten contents of the refreshment trolley to Wislon. The chemical peace of charlie, jellies, tems, skunk, white and khat were not needed. They weren't even heard of. Fat Mike drizzling over Phoebe Steel did not constitute a sex scandal. There were no sharp suits.

Wislon sat at his desk swathed in normality and drinking in the mundane. This was the earnest nineties, after all. For Wall Street read Bull Ring. When you looked, it wasn't clouds with gashes of silver linings that floated puffily past the window. It wasn't anything, really.

Still. *Still.* Wislon found it all rather comforting.

He looked around the room. Seven desks. Seven cracked and finger-greased computers. Wislon knew why he was there. When people couldn't do something for love they did it for money. Not much money, but some. In all kinds of ways, insurance kept life in its place. 'The expected claim rate times the expected claim size equals the pure premium.' What could be simpler? Life could be estimated and gauged in clean no-nonsense ways. Arms, legs, heads, eyes, digits; all had a calculable value. Shoes, condoms, toiletries, dolls, jewellery, paintings, wigs, whips, wallpaper . . . everything could be computed. Efficient, swift and discreet machines did the job. An individual's entire life, even his internal organs (*especially* his internal organs) could be reassuringly tabulated in an endless sequence of figures. The machines remembered. Even time is money. It's what makes men different from animals. No animal can count. Men can and they do. That's what makes them have money. It's not the quantity any more, it's its fact. Wislon respected its determining, absolute nature; you could always get an answer with money if you put your mind to it.

A man of twenty-five should cram his thoughts with women. However, Wislon could no longer cope with the discrepancy between *his* thoughts and the rest of life. Money could restore order and put things right. He knew that even a little of it could make an inventory of his psyche and docket his damaged mind.

Suddenly fortified by these apparently bold thoughts, he pulled himself across the shadowy office, sat brazenly at Virgil Young's desk and lifted the receiver off its set. Perhaps now was the time to call Armitage. No. Almost immediately, he replaced it.

Not now.

Maybe never.

What would he say? What *could* he say?

Driving back to his flat, Wislon noticed some new graffiti. The bricks beneath the whitewashed walls of the building were haemorrhaging through its flaking skin: 'SUPERBEE SPIX COLA 139 KOOL GUY CRAZY CROSS 136.' It was like a scream and meant nothing.

He pounded up the stairs. The weird sisters were at the top looking like autistically iced wedding cakes and smelling faintly of mints.

'Ah. Mr Needy.'

'We've been waiting for you.'

'Your phone.'

'It's been ringing all day.'

'A terrible nuisance. And what a noise.'

'Hardly hear ourselves think, could we, Zasu?'

'Couldn't you possibly do something?'

'All day you say?' Wislon said. 'Important calls. Probably from abroad.'

How long had they been waiting? Didn't the old fudge-brains have anything better to do?

Wislon went in and cursed. He was sure that he had remembered the answer phone that morning but now it was turned off. Shit and fuck and arse.

He didn't go to the cinema that night. For some unfathomable reason the Arts Centre was holding an Arnold Schwarzenegger season. Tonight was a double bill: *Conan the Barbarian* and then *Total Recall*. Wislon had seen them both. He had a bath, listened for the phone, ate a liquid Linda McCartney pie for dinner and watched the news. Ireland was no longer the top

60

story; it had been knocked off by money. 'About time,' Wislon thought, 'the natural order. Money always gets its way in the end.'

Some barrel-jowled young trader had lost billions gambling on the market. His picture flashed out on the screen. It showed a frightened hamster face that was already middle-aged. A threadbare carpet of hair perched on top of his head. The head was half-way through outswelling the wispy threads that were left. Second up, a boxer was in hospital, put there by another similarly muscular rhomboid. No doubt he had been insured and everything was accounted for. Something about his image on the screen suggested big insurance coverage. His family would find out when they flew in from the States. There they were now, distraught and filling the television. Wislon closed his eyes, lay back and tried to dream.

Not being able to dream, Wislon tried to remember the time he felt that he'd first made an impact on Armitage. He had decided to break the usual routine and suggest something other than a film. He decided on ballet. He couldn't remember what it was (his memory was appalling these days), but he knew that Armitage had been impressed. She even squeezed his hand; a proper squeeze this time, not a please-get-off-me one.

Wislon hadn't really noticed at the time. His mind had been miserably fixed elsewhere, namely on the oversized priapic bundle that each of the male dancers had affixed to the front of his tights. Tights?! They were virtually another membrane, sliding between all the cracks and crevices they could find, proclaiming a new, redefined and scientifically manufactured version of manhood.

Wislon thought that the ballet was taking its time, deliberately time-wasting. Whenever one of the dancers executed a pirouette or twirled with elasticated abandon, she (or more probably he; *especially* he, in fact) would twinkle to the front of the stage, smirk at the hypnotised rows of bodice bandits, foot fetishists, knicker peepers and breast imaginers, before heading back to the others.

'Bastards,' Wislon murmured.

Armitage moved close. 'Many of the dancers refuse liquid for twelve hours before a performance,' she said, 'so that they don't sweat so much.'

'Ah,' said Wislon.

On stage, there was a hairdresser who loved the daughter of a fat barman. They were running away from a couple of flash but obviously unlovable libertines. An old man with a knotty beard was following them around. Wislon wondered what the hell he was doing. At one point, he seemed to be attacking a windmill. Eventually, all the dancers came on for a climactic sequence of manic rotations. If Wislon had been the girl, he wouldn't have married any of them. The hairdresser got her, which had been the obvious conclusion right from the start. Surely, though, once a hairdresser always a hairdresser. Love really must be blind, Wislon thought, and shuffled awkwardly in his seat.

Armitage was *still* holding his hand.

Wislon had been wrestling with himself the whole evening. In the interval, he went to the Gents.

Afterwards, he sweltered in the spoiled heat of the theatre. The radiator grilles blew a constant stream of warm, cabbagy air at the audience. Armitage wrinkled her nose. Wislon felt his anxious body inciting some prickly, tumescent swellings.

Then it was all over. Wislon wiped his one free hand down the side of his jacket and placed it on top of the hand that Armitage had on top of his other hand. The awkwardness of the moment was sustained for about twenty seconds before Armitage took Wislon's hand in her two and gently pressed it to her face. 'Thank you, Wislon,' she said, 'that was wonderful.'

He could barely hold the steering wheel on the way home. For one thing, he could smell Armitage – the oil and even the colour of her hair, its secrets. He felt shamed by the smoothness of her thighs where the skin appeared to shine and was stretched silky tight. She talked about the ballet during the journey. The girl was called Kitri and the old buffer was Don Quixote. Wislon nodded and pretended to be concentrating on the driving. His flat was horribly and undisguisedly organised. This time, he would take the initiative and be spontaneous. He didn't even offer a drink at the Dog and Bitch.

Now. No drink and straight on to the sofa. Wislon flattened Armitage beneath him and skimmed his lips everywhere he could manage. As before, she appeared to be completely inert. He moved his legs, intruded his knees and massaged her body. Nothing. He grabbed a hip and traced the inside of her left thigh until his hand could go no further. She remained firmly unsociable. Her body had closed down again. Wislon renewed his frenzied assault and rubbed Armitage's stomach. He rubbed all the other bits he could lay a palm on, too. At the same time, his knee was drunkenly cranking itself. The sofa was making a series of muted but regular eeee-ing noises. He stopped for a second and looked down. Armitage's eyes were tightly sealed and her mouth had distorted itself into a childish grimace as if she were expecting physical pain of some kind. After counting her teeth he decided that enough was enough. This should have been exhilarating and it wasn't. It was hard work. Wislon's hair had simultaneously combusted and flopped. A pearl of sweat clung to the end of his nose. He was panting. He doubted whether even he would have sex with himself. He gave up, but eyeing Armitage's small puckered forehead he felt compelled to plant a single chaste kiss on it.

That was when her eyes opened. She craned forward and cupped her hand around the back of Wislon's neck and – *all of her own accord* – she pulled him down and offered a moist kiss.

Well . . . that was it. She left soon afterwards. Wislon was astounded by the sudden movement. Perhaps she had a taste for the deformed. Anyway, that one kiss, her lips slackening and slithering, was enough for Wislon. Its effect lasted for several days. For weeks. Probably for ever. Sometimes, Wislon wondered if it had happened at all. He replayed the moment thousands of times in his mind, having set up dozens of cameras to capture it from different angles. Here it was from reverse angle, now behind the sofa, now from a specially adapted camera hidden inside one of the cushions. He invited a team of experts in to discuss the trajectory, intent and instant of impact. Should a kiss feel like this, Wislon thought, and was it really all his?

Steady. On the other hand, everyone was at it. In the street, in cars, in hotels, in aeroplanes, even in the Channel Tunnel. Sometimes even in bedrooms. So what? Armitage had probably done it many times herself − full-lipped, open-mouthed . . . whatever. She had done it to him so she must have done it to others. Wislon could not believe for a moment that it had meant as much to her as it did to him. She had probably forgotten all about it. She had probably only done it to stop Wislon trying to get one in the first place. She had paid him off.

For a week after the kiss, Wislon could not bring himself to see Armitage. Just in case. But, he reasoned, I like her. I *really* like her. After she had left that evening, he repuffed the cushions, resisted the temptation of a bath and instead opened a bottle of rum left from the previous Christmas. He really felt that he had made an impact. For a few seconds, he had mattered.

Whenever he had these thoughts, Wislon would wake up the next morning revitalised. He would tear through the bathroom, sometimes even skipping breakfast. This morning, he remembered the answer machine before bounding down the stairs and almost yanking the Metro's door off its hinges. The traffic was easy and he arrived even more on time than usual. The others percolated in over the next half an hour or so.

Fat Mike was the first. His foot problems were getting worse. He now wore an alarmingly jazzy pair of Reeboks. Wislon thought that if his feet revolved any further he would be waddling one way whilst facing the other. He abseiled past Wislon with a large chocolate doughnut wedged in his mouth. 'Wekfirst,' he said by way of explanation, pointing a stubby finger at it. The other hand, the one that wasn't backing it down his throat, gripped a copy of the *Sun*.

Matt Jackson was still brooding for lost love in a melancholy, self-indulgent way. This morning he was wearing sunglasses. The Truth did not speak all morning. His kinked nose was stuck in a pile of papers that sprouted from his desk. Wislon gathered that he was sniffing out a fraudulent claim from a credit-card company. Virgil simply told Wislon that he was a cunt and more or less left it at that.

In the afternoon, Faith Dawkins gave a short introduction to the new technology that was about to be unleashed on them. 'Machines don't need to be frightening,' she pleaded, 'and anyway, even we are no longer *natural*. We are stuffed full of anti-bodies, our teeth do not stay in of their own accord, our hair is artificially coloured . . .' Wislon took her in. As far as he could remember (which wasn't very far), this was the first time he had ever seen her being still for longer than a couple of seconds. She had her own office at the other end of the building, and only came in for specific purposes. Her skin was a spurious, brightly simulated orange. The tan was so obviously fake that it had to be real. Her hair was a metallic blonde. Each day it was sculpted and clamped into new and impossibly threatening shapes. Now it resembled something like an anvil. Her clothes were nothing more than stretches of material buttressed by styled wads of foam. Today, her shoulders were so wide that it seemed as if two smallish UFOs had been balanced on either side of them. Her legs sloped down to a sharp point just above her shoes. Wislon did not think she had any feet but she must have been held upright by some ingenious hydraulic system. She spoke with a chiming but mechanical sing-song. She was saying something about the democracy of machines and was keen to point out the move from an information society to an experience society. She concluded: 'Modern computer technology has generated an explosion in our ability to describe, investigate and control our world. It is nothing less than a new stage in human evolution. We have an opportunity to change what we are . . .'

Wislon doubted it. She didn't know. How could people change what they are? He looked around the room. The others were leaning forward, intent and watchful. When he got back to his desk after the talk, Wislon looked at his computer screen. The word WEIRDO shone neatly out at him. His skin boiled, but he kept his head down and called Cirencester.

No. Some things never changed.

The drive home. More graffiti had been added to the

expiring cluster of red-bricked buildings. 'DUKE SPIRIT SUPERCOOL KOOLKILLER' and 'THE VEZ SUCKS COCKS'. When did this stuff get written? A knuckle of about thirty men were bunching around. That was what men did. They were all sizes, colours, shapes and textures, but men didn't usually discriminate about things like that when they were bunching. There was some inhuman, high-pitched yelping, a frightening squawk that rose above the general medley of shouts and banter. Slowing as he drove past, Wislon saw two large dogs break the circle. The one in front looked like a monster poodle; its bottom jaw was flapping loose, snapped by a bite inside its mouth. It hung straight down, hinged only by a few feeble shreds of skin and a stubborn knot of matted hair. It was tracked by something that resembled all known species of dog. It had the head of a chihuahua, the jaws of a rottweiler, the body of an alsatian and the stumpy legs of a dachshund. As the two dogs darted down a thin alley, Wislon saw several of the men gazing at him with undisguised suspicion. Without hesitating, he stood on the accelerator and sped home.

Up the stairs, breathlessly picking up his mail. Something from the Folio Society. *The Folio Society!* What did they want? 'Dear Mr Needy, As an intelligent and literate person you must have considered the possibility of expanding your library. If you do not already possess one . . .' He sensed Doughty lurking behind his door and rammed the letter through its brass flap.

The red light on the answer machine was winking.

He pressed the 'Replay' button. A woman offered him a free double-glazing estimate. Then something from his bank. Then, *that* man again. 'I still know, Wislon. We will have to meet at some point. And you know that. We all know, don't we?'

Strange girl, thought Wislon. Who is this man delivering *her* messages?

He stayed in that night and made the most of some weeping pasta he had bought the previous week. There was a documentary on television about women who tried to uncover their partners' infidelities by having them set up with other women. Looking at the decoys, Wislon thought that he would have paid to have himself investigated. Come to think of it, he would have paid to have a partner who would allow him to pay to have himself investigated.

After the programme, he ate an organic yoghurt, did something with his hair, made some lists and went to bed. He probably dreamed about Armitage, but it didn't really matter.

You don't think you're doing this right. Not altogether at least. There's some explaining to do. Quite a lot, actually. There's much that can be averted but not forgotten. You know you'll get there in the end. Memory, after all, is an act of will and you'll have nothing to do with this botched business of involuntary memory. Or, indeed, with anything involuntary. You must be lucid and courageous. Where's the old inner knowledge, the stuff that haunts even the happiest occasions of its avoidance? Come on; out with it.

You've been through worse. Much worse. You think of

your father reading to you at bedtime. You remember him reading the same story to you over and over again. You simply can't forget Alice's adventures – in Wonderland, through the looking-glass, wherever. Once he discovered you liked it, he couldn't stop reading it to you. He was like a cook serving a favourite dish until it no longer tastes as it originally did. You don't know whether this is because it has changed or because you have become insensitive to its individual flavouring. Whatever, you know that it is not the same and that is all you care about.

For you, the fact of the story itself is no longer enough.

You recall your father leaning over you. He fixes you with his eye and reads in a brisk, jarring monotone: '. . . and tied around the neck of the bottle was a paper label, with the words "DRINK ME" beautifully printed on it in large letters.' You are forced to respond and look back into his eyes and smile. 'DRINK ME,' he repeats. You continue to smile though inside you are aching and even a little afraid. Sometimes when you are having your tea, he says, 'EAT IT'. During homework he tells you to, 'READ IT' or 'WRITE IT'. All the time, you must look. He doesn't tell you to do this, but somehow you know that it must be done.

You remember him saying, 'It's a very fine day for croquet.' Out into the small garden you go. You think you can remember a large rose-tree near the entrance of the garden; but now you are not sure. Each time you play, your father explains the rules to you, even though you know them off by heart. You quickly begin to understand that your father is a good one for rules. Although the garden is tiny, he has devised an intricate route for the hoops. You don't know whether he is playing games with you.

Or rather, making games out of emotional issues. Soon, you understand that you must just follow the rules, keep smiling and hope for the best. Soon, it becomes hard to imagine a life without games and without rules.

At night, your father reads to you about the caterpillar:
' *"What size do you want to be?" it asked.*

' *"Oh, I'm not particular as to size," Alice hastily replied; "only one doesn't like changing so often, you know." '*

You look at your father's face and watch his lips and try hard not to not smile. You wonder where your mother is. You wonder if the same thing is going on in all the houses in all the streets. You look at your father's eyes and wonder if you are afraid. But surely, you think, this can't be fear. After all, he is your father.

He seems to be saying, 'LISTEN TO ME.'

No. You've been through worse.

Come on.

Come on.

Surviving

Wislon was doing something which not many people get the chance to do. Everybody must have thought about it, though. Some were probably desperate for it.

As usual, he had arrived precisely two minutes late (fear? embarrassment? sheer panic?) and ventured down the pinched alley to the right of the house. Be fair, Wislon thought, you couldn't very well go in through the front door now, could you? The neighbours would talk if they found out what was going on. Before long, the whole street would be in the know. He reasoned that such a discreet entrance not only protected him but it also helped 'her'. Wislon knew he wasn't much to look at, and to be glimpsed visiting the house more or less every week for the last three years couldn't be much fun for the visitee, either.

He walked down the cracked path which split the wall of the house from the soldierly wooden fence between it and next door. Then he squeezed past the dustbins and turned sharp right and up a couple of steps into a cosy, hollow porch. The door was pale blue and the buzzer was set into the wall about six feet up from the polished stone steps. Wislon thought the same thing each time he reached up to press its white circular nipple set into a black rectangular case: absolutely no dwarves allowed here. It didn't seem logical or even reasonable. After all, wasn't she meant to be indiscriminating? Who cared what size or shape or height you were? What happened, Wislon supposed, was much the same no matter *who* you were. And Wislon was sure that she wouldn't mind – not that much, anyway. And after all, she put up with him for fifty-eight minutes every week (excluding two weeks in the summer and one at Christmas).

The buzzer's low drone sounded somewhere inside. Its muted ululation was followed by a forbidding 'clunk' as the door mechanically sprang its latch and fell a few inches into the house. Once in the cramped hallway, with its oatmeal carpet and moonlight illumination, there was only one more door to negotiate. Wislon turned as it swung open. It was at this point that his blood turned to something like porridge and simply stopped moving around his body. His feet would have stopped as well if momentum were not already taking him in the right direction. His throat contracted as he felt his spine trying to escape through his mouth.

Agnes Tunnelle stood in the doorway. Her arms extended down the front of a billowing but strangely desexualised cotton skirt. Her hands were clasped in front of the whole arrangement as if she were

74

just about to swing an imaginary golf club. Her smile was one of intimate formality, a knowing, welcoming but businesslike crescent of virtually invisible lipstick. Modestly, she looked downwards. Her face was slightly flushed as if she had just completed some vigorous but silent and ultimately secret exercise.

Wislon shambled inside. Despite his habitual foreboding, he thought that everyone needed someone like Agnes Tunnelle. (He never actually called her by her first name, of course. That was a wickedness he reserved for the rugged privacy of his own mind.)

She could sort you out, or at least try to sort you out, which amounted to much the same thing. Wislon took off his jacket, folded it bureaucratically on to the floor and automatically made his way to the couch in the far corner of the room. Over the years, he and Agnes had tried several different positions and contexts for their activities. The chair seemed altogether too courteous for what they had in mind. The floor seemed to trivialise the whole process and made Wislon feel rather too Californian. That left either standing nonchalantly around or settling roguishly on the ample desk situated in front of the bay window. Wislon had reservations about the couch, but it still seemed the best bet.

And that was what Wislon was doing now – lying on the couch, eyes softly closed, arms splinted to his sides; waiting. In fact, he had been waiting for over twenty-five minutes and nothing had happened. It never did, of course. Not unless he initiated it.

Finally, he said, 'I saw two dogs fighting the other day. One of them was badly hurt . . .'

He looked up to see if Mrs Tunnelle was showing any signs of interest. She was statuesque in her chair, merely looking intent and looking intently through or at Wislon.

'Anyway, that's not really the point of the story.' He was sure that, in the presence of one such as she, he was stating the obvious. He blundered on regardless. 'The dog that had committed the injuries, the chasing one, was made of all kinds of other dogs. You could see its lineage in its shapes, its furs and skins.'

There was a slight but definite raspberry as Mrs Tunnelle adjusted her position in the leather chair.

'Well, I was wondering what it would be like if people could achieve the same kind of obvious dissimilarity as dogs. Could they adapt themselves to life more . . .'

Wislon was also thinking how suitable it was that he should think of himself as a dog. Among other things, it was a common form of abuse; not for nothing was 'dog' the same as coward, bully, traitor, bastard, meddler, head-case – and more besides. The only good thing about being a dog was that you eliminated the possibility of choice; you were a *dog*, and that was it.

The silence between Wislon and Mrs Tunnelle curdled, but it was still silence. Eventually, she said, 'I find it interesting that you do not consider people as being various.'

'It depends what you mean by various.'

'I wonder.'

'What *do* you mean by various?'

'What do *you* mean by various?'

'Ah.'

Mrs Tunnelle's chair was now making moist, satisfied sighs. Once again, she was perched and vigilant. Wislon observed the box of tissues sitting on the desk about eight feet away. She never placed it within his grasp. What would happen if he suddenly broke down and sobbed? It could happen, you know. In all his visits he had not yet mananged a tear – but who knows? A stabbing childhood memory; a long-buried but undead incident suddenly resurrecting its traumatic self, coming back from its mental grave. And where would he be then? He was only Wislon, but even he had feelings. So what if they were on the chronic side? It wouldn't take much. And, Wislon reminded himself, he had worked hard at being inconsolable. It wasn't his fault that his feelings weren't doing what he wanted them to. In his time, Wislon could remember crying on numerous occasions: crying as a child (broken toys), blubbing as a teenager (broken heart), wailing as an adult (just broken). He could manage it all right – but never *here*. If the box was in the right place it would at least offer him some form of encouragement. If the box was in the right place who could predict what would happen? Then Mrs Tunnelle might see Wislon hollering and giving it his all: live.

Another period of non-talking commenced. Wislon could sense Mrs Tunnelle's unconcerned, neutral curiosity wearing down his reluctance.

It was always like this. The talk was intermittent and on occasions Wislon would say something, anything, simply to break the quiet. *Quiet.* It was never really *silent.* He could say what he wanted. He could lie and cheat and change the story of his life, manipulating it into any shape he preferred. Mrs Tunnelle would meet each narrative diversion with the same considered seriousness, sometimes offering a few words in response, most often not. Wislon's words simply ricocheted back at him, as unmediated and pure as the moment they left his mouth. You couldn't deceive Mrs Tunnelle because she listened to *everything* and did not discriminate between false- hood and truth. She didn't have to. It was all the same to her. He often thought that was why he found it easy to tell untruths outside her room; he couldn't get away with it while he was there, with her, face to face. Everyone else was easy. They were queuing up for misinformation. Most of them had already decided what they wanted to believe before they even heard it.

'I was thinking of Armitage a few days ago . . .' Wislon started. Not absolutely true, he thought – you think of her *all* the time. Mrs Tunnelle hunkered forward again, her eyes unblinking. 'I was exhilarated when she started to see me, when she allowed me to meet her, to take her places. But after a while I worked out that girls, women, have usually decided who they are going to go out with before they actually go out with them. It has nothing to do with men. They don't feature. It has nothing to do with me. It had nothing to do with me. I had nothing to do with it.'

Mrs Tunnelle waited for Wislon's sentence to fade into the still air. Then she gave a brief and grave and husky reply: 'And why do you think that?'

Now it was Wislon's turn to pause. It always came round to him again in the end. He screwed his face up until it became a landscape of uneven, irregularly nervous ridges. He picked at the bottom of a tingling ear lobe. 'I think because nothing else seems to make sense. I mean, men always assume that because a woman chooses a man it must be because there is something different about him. It confirms to each man what he wishes to know about himself. But men also know that this isn't *absolutely* so. Men know that they are liars and rapists and serial-killers. It's only men who do these things. Even the ones who don't . . . there's something in them. They might. They *could*. Women know this. But they can't just hang around checking all the men, assessing, categorising them. So they take whatever's on offer, more or less, whenever they feel like it. Quite often they don't feel like it. But when they do . . .'

'Yes?'

'. . . when they do, it doesn't really mean anything, does it? They're just helping out.'

'I think you must ask yourself what your motives were.'

'With Armitage?'

'I think so.'

'Yes.'

'And whether she was looking for a penis.'

'Sorry?'

'Whether she was looking for happiness.'

'Oh.'

'Yes?'

'I'm not sure what she was looking for. We just met. I didn't know why she chose me. I still don't really understand.'

'Did she make you feel different? Special?'

Wislon thought for a few moments and heard his body ticking. He couldn't answer her questions. He had felt 'privileged' – but was that the same thing? On occasions, Armitage's presence had the opposite effect. He had been compelled to scrutinise himself, trying to put himself in her shoes. What did she see? What was in it for her? Did this absence of seedy self-congratulation make him different from other men? He decided not to say anything. It could be used against him. He had silence in a clinch and he hung on to it, taking deep, exhausted gulps of air.

Outside he could hear the rain starting to foul things up. Good. It beat a gusty, fitful tattoo against the window and strafed the parked cars.

'I think we have to stop there,' Mrs Tunnelle said after a few more minutes of churning quiet.

Wislon hauled himself off the couch and picked up his jacket. By the time he had slipped his arm inside its sleeve and wrestled it on to his back, Mrs Tunnelle was standing by the door. She had assumed exactly the same mannequinish posture as when he'd arrived.

'Same time next week?' he offered.

'Goodbye,' she replied, in an even, predetermined tone. She's not human, Wislon thought. Can't be. Good for her. Nothing gets in, nothing gets out. But as he stepped out into the little alley again and made his way back to the Metro, he repeated to himself that everybody needed a dose of Agnes Tunnelle. Damage limitation was her game and we all need it. We're all wrecked and damaged in one way or another. Usually one way *and* another, he thought. Something told Wislon that he would be having a lot more to do with Agnes Tunnelle before he was through. Survival wasn't enough, but it was all he could manage for the moment. Wislon was hanging on. Just.

He walked over to the Metro, climbed in and turned the engine over. At the third attempt, something happened and the car lurched unevenly forwards.

You know that this is all very well, but you wonder about the truth. You wonder about the kind of truth that matters. You know, true truth. You hope that you are going to be all right. It seems inconceivable that you managed to get yourself into this jam. Then again, you know that you've only got yourself to blame. Still, in your own way, you suppose that you are trying to do something about it. It's not much, but it's something.

Incidentally, you decide to have a look at 'truth' in the dictionary. It's worth the visit. It gives you quite a degree of latitude. Better still, you try the thesaurus. (Rules. Again?) Truth, fact, fact of life, undeniable fact, positive fact, stubborn fact, matter of fact . . . Truth is important, you decide. You should value it. But — here's the trick — you find that several truths can co-exist. They don't necessarily have to cancel each other out. You think about that. You decide that — after all — you're not an amnesiac. You decide that — after all — you've got nothing to lose. Absolutely nothing.

So. Now you can remember your father playing chess with you, and the patient but tense manner in which he explained the rules.

'Do you understand?'

'Yes,' you said, and nodded vigorously.

'Do you think I could mate you in three moves?'

'I don't know. Probably.' You smiled.

In the kitchen, you could hear your mother sluicing the dishes after Sunday lunch. It was the same routine every Sunday. You wondered why it was so hard to imagine life without these games and their rules.

'Your move,' said your father. He had advanced a pawn two squares forward leaving a gap immediately in front of his king. You stared at it, aware of your father's expectations heaving down upon you. You sensed his psychic weight and it felt as if your own physical stature was about to be determined by what you did next.

Last night, your father had read to you about several little children who had got burned all because they would not remember the simple rules their friends had taught them. You understood all about rules and bodies. There were other stories, too; the one about the boy who bit his nails and then had his fingers cut off by the Scissor Man. Then the girl who would not eat and wasted away to become as thin as a pencil before dying. And then you were always asked whether you were able 'to sit quite still at the table'.

You looked at your father and worried about yourself.

82

Sometimes, when you dropped a plate or forgot a chore, your father would appear in the doorway with a meat cleaver raised comically above his head. 'Off with your head,' he would shout. 'Off with your head.'

'Don't be daft,' your mother would say nervously, 'we've got people coming for supper.'

Then your father would forgive you with all kinds of elaborate smiles and caresses, trying (you supposed) to make you feel better.

Better? Somehow, it only made you feel worse. His patting and touching and cooing didn't seem right. Even your mother disapproved – though she never actually said anything. It was the point at which she turned away and inflated the washing-up gloves with a blast of perfumed breath or started to do something with the dog's bowl.

Meanwhile, your father was in the process of forgiving you. It was really only a ritual that re-emphasised his authority.

As you grew up, you understood what was happening but you were unable to do anything about it. Growing up was a poor substitute for knowing how to play. It was as though you were aware of your bodily changes instead of true wisdom or knowledge. The one was a kind of compensation for the lack of the other – but you wanted both.

You looked down at your father's pawn again. It hadn't moved.

You wanted to cry, but when you cried your father told you that you would drown in your own tears if you weren't careful. Mother just gave you a handkerchief and told you to blow hard. It didn't matter, because she was doing a wash tomorrow morning anyway.

83

Wislon drove back to the office. He had arranged it so that he saw Agnes Tunnelle during lunch rather than after work. That way, he didn't have to spend too much time with himself straight afterwards. He could spread himself around.

He tried to make himself invisible as he sneaked darkly back to his desk.

'You're late. Freak,' Virgil Young said casually, a soft hand temporarily cupped over the mouthpiece he was speaking into.

Wislon sat down heavily. He looked at his desk top and was gratified to see that everything was neatly in its place. He took a paper-clip and straightened it out before using it to scoop out some lingering dirt from underneath his thumbnail. It was only quite recently (since he last saw Armitage, in fact) that he had grown any nails to have dirt under. Up until then, he had chewed and gouged the tops of his fingers and thumbs, leaving them as ruined, spongy stumps. With the onset of nails, he worried that his fingers might be too feminine. In the end, he had decided that he couldn't win either way and had gone with aesthetics. Still, the dirt *was* a problem.

A few minutes later it had been prised out and a crumbling snake of soil substitute lay on his desk. He flicked it into the bin and surveyed the scrupulously stacked piles around him. He looked at the list attached to the antique car calendar, put a tick next to 'Mrs Tunnelle @ 1.02 p.m.' and considered the rest. Wislon was priming himself, getting sorted. He started the first of the calls he had to make – a florist in Kidderminster. He pressed the phone tightly to his ear and dialled.

Fat Mike was away at the chiropodist's that day. His feet had finally given in and refused to carry him any further. Maybe all the potions and pills and pedal manipulations weren't enough; maybe feet also needed to talk.

Without Fat Mike as an audience, there was nothing to stop Virgil Young being Virgil Young except Virgil Young, and he wasn't enough.

'You like her?' he suddenly started.

Matt Jackson was taking in last night's football reports at the back end of the *Daily Mail*. He was picking his nose with expert concentration. There was a picture of Princess Di on the front of the newspaper. She was wearing a pair of new boots. The headline read, 'Di shows she is the bee's knees'. One of the dead roses still lay on his desk top. 'What?'

'The one who sent you the roses. Tanya? Marina? Laetitia? Did you like her?'

'Not much,' he replied.

'But you must have seen something in her. I mean, for heaven's sake, you'd been seeing her for four years.'

'Three. Not that it's any of your business.'

'No. Of course not. But Matt. Still. It must. You know. Hurt.'

'Sod off.'

'Right. And – oh – send us a postcard when you get to the top.'

'What?'

'Your nose, Matt. Your nose.'

'Piss off.'

'Right.'

But Matt Jackson's eye was playing games now. It was weeping and bubbling and squints of salty water were already irrigating one side of his face.

Virgil glanced at Phoebe who was taking her time with everything today. After all, Fat Mike's absence was a rare pleasure for her. She swapped a complicit smile with Virgil. This was *his* office for the day. He was aspiring, territorial and expectant.

Wislon had his head down (the rogue shank doing all kinds of interesting things) but was listening hard. He remembered what Virgil had once said to Fat Mike about establishing a 'wonderful thing with insurance. You organised it and made it your own, Mike,' he went on, 'and now nobody can take it away from you. It's all yours. This is the centre, the source, of everything important that goes on in this com—pany. We all know that, Mike. This is Mike's Office. It must be very satisfying for you.'

Wislon shuddered at the memory. It helped to make his senses more or less alert and he looked over at the vertically slanted textured fabric louvres that covered the windows. He saw that they were linked together by teardrops of steel beads. Somewhere amongst the silence, a couple of swivel chairs were gently eeking. Everybody else was used to Virgil's abuse and was busy not noticing it. However, Wislon found that he was both appalled and enthralled by it. A memory of something else came up for air in the soup of his mind. Amongst other things – quite a lot of other things – it made him nostalgic.

Around him, in the office's fuggy atmosphere, he listened as the small acclaimless lives gathered into something like meaning, or at least something like the lack of non-meaning. Still, it was better than he could manage. For the moment, all he could do was to tidy his desk. Every paper-clip was rounded up into a plastic container and highlighting pens were triumphantly sheathed in their transparent wallets.

Wislon took in Tony Tuesby on the far side of the office. It was a close run thing between his father, The Truth and the beggarly drunk who had made his home in the abandoned skip across the street. On the whole, he thought Tuesby shaded it as the best reason he had come across for packing it all in before he reached middle-age. Was that all there was to come? Was that *it*? Bloody hell. Now was only bearable because it looked better than then. But what happened when you reached then? Or didn't you know when you got there? Was that the deal?

The Truth was on the phone and speaking to a woman in Wales. His head was bowed and weary. His steamy Amazonian eyebrows had spread upwards towards his frazzled, greying hairline forming a pair of furry stick-on miniature rugs that were clearly part of some creative game for children. He was scratching the spannered crook of his nose. His desk was covered with charts and maps, one of which showed 'The Flood Defences of the West Coast of England and Wales. Map based on the Report of the Departmental Committee on Coastal Flooding.' Another showed the potential effects of climate change in the UK. Great chunks of Norfolk, Wales and other coastal areas had been shaded in and the shape of a new, future Great Britain outlined in red.

The portfolios of catastrophe were being conscripted to prevent a woman in Wales claiming for a new gas cooker.

This is what The Truth was saying: 'Yes . . . I know it was insured . . . but look at the exclusion clauses . . . That's it. I'm very sorry. Twelve (b). That's the one. Have you got it? Good, good. It makes everything quite clear . . .' His eyes were almost black. Neither did they move. The Truth was getting his way. Wislon could tell from his manner that he thought there was something heroic about this pinching and fussing and bickering. There was a palpable pleasure in his daily fault-finding, his warping of human activity to fit the impoverished facts laid out before him. It's only a fucking oven, Tuesby. Give it up. The woman is probably a single parent with seven children, most of them handicapped. She's probably lost her house and her car has floated off into the Atlantic. *Come on*, Tuesby.

He was finishing off. 'So sorry. I do hope you find your cat. And to you. Goodbye.'

The Truth put his phone down with a celebratory shimmy. Wislon didn't know that a phone could be made to pop in such an exuberant manner, but The Truth had the knack. Only stopping to ink a few numbers on to a form, he made his next call and ground himself forward.

Wislon considered: The Truth's career was a miracle

of ordered decline. He had started off with a jewellery fraud; then financial fraud. So far, so good. Things began to go wrong when he was assigned to fraudulent property dealings. It wasn't that he was ungifted in this area, but rather the opposite. He was so thorough in his investigations that he gradually lost sight of the larger issues. From there, he deprogressed from warehouse fires and home disasters to individual domestic items which were of increasingly diminishing significance. Now he was dealing with a cooker in Wales.

Phoebe Steel and Virgil were arranging a meal for that night. The arranging was very loud.

'This isn't the lunch I'd planned for myself,' said Phoebe. She gestured at a small apple, a packet of nuts and a couple of compressed cheese sandwiches. 'I was seriously thinking about chicken and pasta.' She pouted sulkily and continued, 'The bloody shop sold out of anything decent.'

'You always say that,' said Virgil, 'but you keep buying that sort of stuff.' Now it was his turn to gesture.

'But I never eat it,' she said, sweeping the contents of her desk into the bin. 'There. Now you'll have to take me out to dinner.'

'Where would you like to go?'

Soon they were running through a prescribed litany of celebrity restaurants, bars and grills. Maybe they didn't *mean* to be loud, Wislon thought.

'How about the Chamberlain Grill?'

'Na. Let's try the Moody Blues Bistro.'

'The Trevor Francis Cellar?'

Wislon knew what was coming next. The Brian Lara Calypso Club. They couldn't very well miss that one, could they? Wislon grimaced to himself and ground his teeth together. Phoebe's voice rose and fell like some kind of artificial lung. An obscure machine on the other side of the office made a small peeping noise.

'The Brian Lara Calypso Club?'

A pause. 'Oh – is that new?'

'Opened last week. Expensive.'

'I don't mind the money,' said Phoebe. 'Let's do it.'

'At seven then,' Virgil announced.

Wislon didn't think that Phoebe was stupid. It was just that women tended to act that way when men were involved, generally because they did what men wanted. For men it was different. Mostly, they were stupid to begin with so they couldn't help it. (And it was easy after that.) But women could. So why did they join in and gee the lads up?

Anyway, it was all cant. In Wislon's view, everyone was afraid that other people would discover their secrets, even if their secret was that they had no secrets. He looked around the office. He knew that Matt Jackson was afraid of Virgil prying even further into the demise of Ur-Laetitia. He knew that Simon was fearful that Phoebe and Virgil had athleticised sex and *enjoyed* themselves. His own plodding marriage, mediocre occupation and dismal existence were thrown into disconcerting relief by anything that deviated from the monotonous. Wislon knew that The Truth was panicked by the thought that his life had already run its course, that what he was doing now was nothing more than a convulsion. He feared everybody in the office and everybody else he came into contact with, everyone who might benefit from life.

If only they all knew the sad facts about adult life – that is, that you can actually see your fears coming towards you. You hang around and spend time worrying about them, taking precautions and putting things in place. You try to fashion change in your life and yank it to some safe haven. Only you can't. Not really. Because it's usually too late. No. It's *always* too late. Wislon's mother always said that if they could only get through 'this year', then 'next year' would be better. He had never really understood what she was talking about, but now he knew.

People cheer the future on convinced that things will get better. By anticipating fears, the sad fact of adult life is that it is effectively over before people really know about it. They are so worried about life that it has slipped past before they *know* it. A theatre audience will spend so much time anticipating a gunshot that the rest of the play will pass them by. When the crack finally arrives, it's too late. Who knows what its significance is?

Fat Mike was worried about himself from the feet up (but especially the feet). And that was only the start of it. Phoebe was worried about getting old – i.e. within stretching distance of twenty-nine, when her body would begin to develop a mind of its own. And Wislon? For one thing, he was worried about the past, particularly as so much of it just didn't seem to be there. He wondered where all the forgotten moments had disappeared to. Were they gone for good or were they recoverable? Only the fact that he was still in there, surviving, convinced him that he was *meant* to find it all again. Otherwise, what was the point of being around? Another thing. He was afraid of the future. There were the phone messages, for example. But more importantly (or so he thought), the solemn voices in his head were on to the job, connecting what had happened with what *will* happen.

Wislon wasn't sure how it all fitted together, how things were related, but he had a nasty feeling. He was thinking about it and that thinking made him afraid.

About two months after they had first met, Armitage's parents invited Wislon for dinner. He and Armitage had decided to meet beforehand at the Dog and Bitch. Safety in numbers, Wislon thought, although as he walked into the bar he was also worried about the jacket he was wearing. Armitage took a single attentive look at the contrast between the tight drainpipe sleeves and the sheer capacity of the rest of its billowing bulk.

'The colour is fine,' she said, 'but the shape needs work.'

'What? Me or the jacket?'

Armitage inspected the whole ensemble by walking slowly around Wislon as if he was a used car. She pulled and yanked and smoothed wherever she could, then stood back and said something about it being fine so long as he took it off as soon as they arrived.

Dr and Mrs Small lived in Moseley, only a mile or so from Armitage's own flat. She directed Wislon past the county cricket ground, along the perimeter of Cannon Hill Park and, eventually, into a particularly flawless avenue. The houses were large mock-Tudor galleons which stood imposingly behind a variety of shrubs, bushes, saplings, small trees, fastidiously barren flower beds and tidy fences. The lawns were symmetrical slabs of weedless green. He remembered his own childhood garden and recalled the creosoted gate, the spindly hedge and fence, the lacklustre grass and the tiny green space which always seemed to be full of croquet hoops.

Wislon had told Armitage that his mother always wanted him to be a doctor.

'Mothers do,' she replied.

'And what sort of medicine is your father in?' asked Wislon, it sounding the right sort of thing to say.

'He's a pathologist.'

'Yes.'

'Diseases and so on. All rather morbid. But he doesn't talk about it that much.'

'No. I don't suppose he would.'

When they rang the doorbell, there was a brief delay before Mrs Small answered. She was a large, comfortable woman who still mananged to look undernourished and strangely trivial. The same kind of paradox also characterised her manner. Although constantly smiling and talking, she gave the impression of being nervous and darkly anxious, as if expecting a physical blow or jagging verbal abuse at any moment. The skin on her face was remarkably soft but etched with lines. Wislon was having fun working out where Armitage came from when there was a flurry of movement as a small boy of about five or six years old sped down the stairs, across the room and into another room. Not, however, before he had a chance to say, 'You're ugly. Is this the ugly one?'

'That's my brother,' said Armitage.

'Can I take your jacket?' said her mother.

'Yes. Please,' said Armitage.

Wislon dredged himself out of the jacket, eventually ridding himself of the sleeves with a final spluttering tug. His mind was frankly elsewhere. Come to think of it, he thought, Mrs Small is no beauty. Although long hair, an oxymoronic face and colourful clothes had given him one impression, the close-up, considered reality was quite different. Moles were strategically positioned around her nose (actually sharp and rather severe) and there was a large lozenge of flesh hanging loosely from her forehead.

On they went, turning left down the hallway until they came to a door. Mrs Small knocked discreetly and the barked response indicated that they might enter. Dr Small was a substantial man with black (no – *really* black, Wislon thought) hair which seemed to sprout from all available parts of his body. Although he had clearly shaved that morning (that afternoon? that evening?!) the hair ducts on his face looked about ready to release the next rounds of stubble. A faint chemical smell hung in the room.

Introductions were made and Wislon got the definite impression that the Smalls were not really so bothered whether he was there or not.

When the food arrived, he saw that it was a tureen of thick, unfathomable stew. Irregularly shaped wedges of meat poked through the top of a brackish, glistening soup. Armitage's brother, who Wislon could now see was a full-grown dwarf, threw things off the table and on to the floor throughout the meal. Mrs Small attended to him with a cowering, quiescent patience, not to mention the odd fretful blink at her husband.

Dr Small himself seemed oblivious to almost everything else around him. However, he made some kind of effort for the first few minutes.

'And which university did you go to?'

'Leeds . . .'

'That's in the north, isn't it?' said Mrs Small, juggling a bit of pork elbow with a giant sprout on the end of her fork.

'Leeds. Yes. Good medicine. Good pathology department.'

'That's not to say we don't like it here,' interrupted Mrs Small. 'I'm not complaining. I like it here. A smallish town. But big enough for someone like Dr Small to make an impact. He's established a wonderful pathology department here.'

'I did history,' said Wislon.

'You did history.' Dr Small made it sound like one of the less exotic diseases he dealt with.

'Yes.'

'Why?'

'Well, because I enjoyed it at school.' Wislon sensed that only Armitage was listening but when he looked across the table at her she widened her eyes and silently urged him on. Just before he continued a half-eaten carrot flew from the other side of the table and, after hitting Mrs Small's side plate, rolled into his lap. 'And because I'm interested in the different ways that facts can be interpreted, retold, be ascribed different versions of themselves . . .'

'But you never got a job out of it?' interrupted Dr Small. 'Eh?'

'No, he hasn't. Not yet,' Armitage offered.

'Thought not.'

'Dr Small secured a post as soon as he left the university,' Mrs Small said. 'And now, nobody in the whole country can really say the word "pathology" without a nod in his direction. The hospital is internationally renowned, you know. It has an identity.'

In contradiction of Armitage's words, the rest of the meal was spent listening to her father talking about the cadavers with which he had recently dealt. Wislon heard all about skin discoloration, the appearance of a network of bluish veins just below the surface of the skin, the shedding of skin, the formation of a grey, fatty substance (known as adipocere), the presence of maggots, the liquefying of eyeballs and skin blisters. 'Even when people are dead,' Dr Small ended, 'they never do what you want. There are just so many unpredictable factors.'

Like death, Wislon thought. Like dying. He imagined Armitage's father in the post-mortem room. He was wearing a black rubber apron and his impressively hairy forearms were plunged deep into somebody's diseased lung. He found it uncomfortable sitting next to someone who was probably wondering what colour his urine was.

Wislon managed about two and a half hours of it. Armitage's brother asked Wislon to tell a story and a joke. Then he asked him about his 'most embarrassing moment in life' before telling his own joke which concerned a motorway accident.

'Goodbye Dr Small, Mrs Small. Say goodbye to Toby for me. I'm sure he didn't mean it. None taken. And thank you for the delicious supper. It was very nice meeting *you*. And, of course, I hope I see you again, too. Soon.' He turned through the front door, not wanting to be in the way when the Smalls said their goodnights to Armitage. However, she was quickly beside him, so that couldn't have taken very long.

Wislon wondered what they should do next. No, that wasn't strictly accurate. He *knew* what would happen next. He would drive Armitage home. Then he would be given a modest kiss on the cheek and a sensible arrangement would be made for another week. No progress had been made in that department. On the other hand, a part of Wislon was rather taken with this doing-it-properly type of thing. He reasoned that it was noble, chivalrous, adult and admirably restrained. Anyway, she wouldn't let him even if he wanted to. It was quite clear who was calling the shots and she wasn't having any. It was

(Wislon was afraid) as simple as that.

Still. She did look good tonight. Dark blue trousers and matching jacket (with a cream trim) and one of those fabulously expensive Italian scarves that probably cost more than Wislon's jacket. No. It *had* to cost more than Wislon's jacket. But then, everything cost more than Wislon's jacket, he reminded himself. Her hair was so very black that it was almost blue-black. As he watched, Armitage reached up and delicately pushed a stray hair from her face.

How could that family have produced her?

Armitage was a moving mirror for Wislon. He saw himself in her two-fold. He did not want absolute truth (on no account. He couldn't afford that kind of truth, even if it existed, which he doubted). Just a bit of truth that admitted the concept of flexibility. First, Wislon perceived himself as being a part of her simple, handsome beauty. Second – and he had rather less control over this one – he felt shamed by her simple, handsome features. The one was good, the other not quite so. Somewhere in-between these nuggets of reality lay the real Wislon. As he dropped her off, his eyes followed her to the door with a look of infinite sadness before he turned the Metro round and drove north.

Things had started looking up over the past couple of weeks. First, there had been no more phone messages. Initially, Wislon was not sure whether or not this was a mixed blessing. He wanted to keep in contact with Armitage (no matter how indirectly) and yet the male voice disconcerted him. He reasoned that 'she' was bound to try again. Maybe she had even initiated a nuisance rethink, if that's what it was.

Second, his skin was drying out nicely. The cold, dehydrated weather was doing its stuff and keeping things in check. Third, he had spoken to Amy Facer. He still found this difficult to understand. He had never spoken to Amy Facer. Usually, Amy Facer didn't speak to anyone. As far as Wislon was aware, Amy Facer didn't speak. Amy Facer was not desirable or rich. She was an enigma, a voiceless presence somewhere else in the office, no more or less apparent than a chair, a desk or a paper-clip.

It happened during one of the evenings that Wislon stayed behind. The others had already abandoned the ordinariness of the office. Amy was late to leave, although he hadn't noticed her until she spoke.

'Life seems rather crowded at the moment, suddenly, tonight, don't you think?'

Wislon looked round, suspicious that what was being said didn't actually mean what was being said. He took in Amy's face, her virginal eyes and the bulky upper torso which was stacked neatly behind her desk. Nothing too threatening there, he thought.

'Yes. I suppose so.' Wislon juggled a clipful of papers and pushed a couple of greenish folders across his desk in an attempt to simulate purposeful activity, even a crowded life, whatever that might be.

In fact, life in the office was anything but crowded. That afternoon, Wislon had spent at least half an hour staring at the off-grey carpet tiling which oozed across the office floors. It had been advertised as being 'indestructible'. It was called something like 'TuffTile'. He had been fascinated by its almost total lack of discernible weave. It was just a gristled chaos of fibre, a collection of skinhead pelts. How did it all hold together?

That was his crowded day.

'There's just so much to do.' Amy rolled her eyes and took in the neat piles that surrounded her. Then she folded her arms, a familiar gesture which seemed to re-inflate her breasts. 'Well, I'm tired. Fancy a coffee?'

Wislon started and said anything. 'Where?'

'There's a new place. Henry's.' She spoke with a comic Brummie accent. For a moment, after recovering from the shock of hearing Amy talk, he assumed that what she said and the way she was saying it were meant as some kind of feverish parody. 'I'll only be a minute. I'll just get my coat.'

'Yes . . . er . . . fine,' Wislon replied.

He knew that Amy was overweight, but as they walked to Henry's he saw that in actual fact she was quite enormous. Not that it particularly mattered, he thought, as the aggregate of her hilly curves and rolling flesh was a pulpy but succulent voluptuousness. There was also a kind of inherent honesty in such bulkiness. For some reason, people trusted a certain amount of bulk in others, especially women. Yellow hair poured down her back in thick luminous handfuls. She wore a tight-fitting purple dress of crushed velvet which fizzed and popped about her body.

Wislon generally preferred girls like Armitage, their boyish glamour admitting a sense of lewd possibility. The trouble with women like Amy was that the mind had no room for manoeuvre; there was just too much of her. She was so completely and absolutely herself. And that was it. For Wislon, and (he presumed) for most men, that was no good.

Still, all this made it easier to talk. When men and women got together, sex was usually hanging around, loitering intently. Her face was plump but pretty with a vital, packed sheen not given to those women who bypassed skin and only had room for complex bone arrangements. Although Amy was oddly attractive, Wislon did not feel attracted to her. He wondered momentarily about the rational conjunction of these thoughts. He felt sure that she felt the same about him, perhaps without the bit about him being oddly attractive.

What was the catch? Before he knew where he was or what he was doing, Wislon had told Amy about his parents, about Armitage, about the phone calls and about Agnes Tunnelle. And that was only the start of it.

Maybe he was tired.

Possibly, Amy had caught him with his guard down.

Conceivably, he really did need someone to talk to.

And perhaps he even had something to say.

Whatever, he was saying it. Loud and clear. He didn't mean to, but once he had opened his mouth, he couldn't stop.

She had a way of closing her eyes when she was listening to Wislon with a tiny fluttering of the lids. He found this both frightening and appealing.

Wislon even told her of the time when Armitage had taken him shopping and how he had waited near the changing rooms in Rackham's while she tried on some skirts. Occasionally, he would peer round the corner and observe the rows of cubicles. He could see her feet and calves framed by the gap between the door of her cubicle and the thickly carpeted floor. They made twisting movements as they moved in and out of various skirts. He imagined the bare legs above them. When Armitage eventually emerged from the cubicle she was carrying the crumpled garments in her arms. Wislon smiled but what he really thought was whether he should kiss her. His face heated up. Armitage read the look and said, 'Don't make things difficult.' Then she chose one of the skirts and went to the cashier to pay for it. Wislon's heart throbbed in its injured place. Afterwards, they went for a coffee and Armitage crossed her hands in her lap and brought her knees together as if protecting them. She said, 'You're too honest, Wislon. Or rather, you want to be absolutely honest. It makes you easy to read. You should tolerate something a little less truthful. Nobody can manage it even half the time.' Wislon replied that in his opinion nobody should be intentionally mysterious to another person. He tried to sound coolly philosophical but inside his body was giving him away. It felt vulnerable to all sorts of forces and currents. He wanted to go over and embrace Armitage, but woudn't that be an intrusion? Would it be right just because he felt like it? He thought that his feelings were too obvious and he looked away. As his head turned, his hands came off the table they had been gripping. He felt the whiteness of his knuckles and wondered if Armitage knew how he was beginning to feel about her. That is, *really* knew? Wislon feared that, after all, maybe he was only what his body allowed him to be. And suddenly his heart felt ugly and he was sick of himself. It wasn't even as if he was good or sincere or affectionate. He didn't even feel nobility in his failure. Inside, of course, Wislon didn't *want* to be like this. He wanted to please people even if it kept coming out wrong. But it seemed as if nobody was able to show themselves without a sense of exposure and disgrace. And while this was going on, you had to somehow appear stronger and better than you really were so that people wouldn't ignore you. Yet in doing that you weren't able to be truly yourself and with all this happening nobody was able to work out what was real. Nothing seemed to be genuine and Wislon wondered whether this was simply what is was like to be human. Whatever the game was, he not only wasn't very good at playing it, he wasn't even certain what the rules were. He stood by and watched the cheats get on. And all he wanted to say to Armitage was that he liked the way her throat would suddenly grow full and did she see how he was beginning to feel about her? And how degenerate was that?

When Wislon had told Amy all these things, and about how he blamed himself for the gap that had opened up between his desire and all its clumsy expressions, of the whens and wheres, he began to hate himself even more. After it was finished he felt worn out because it was like living through it again. He also felt threatened because he never let anyone close. Normally he felt it was a sign of weakness. The rude essentials of his life were yielded to Amy in less than half an hour. She had achieved more pure information than Mrs Tunnelle had managed in two years. That was what frightened Wislon. In the face of such winsome credulousness, it all came gushing out. He wasn't even telling that many lies, just enough to retain the kind of dignity which he calculated was still important to him. Nor did he say anything about his father or his childhood. He had already made himself feeble and poor and he had to retain some standing.

'But what happened with Armitage? Why did you do it, Wislon?' Amy was sipping an espresso. The cup looked like a doll's-house beaker in her sappy hands.

'It was the voices.' Wislon did a stare out of the window to give the answer gravity. The trouble was, he thought, I *mean* all this.

'Which voices?'

'The ones I told you about. The ones that mess up what I want to be and what comes out.'

'But they don't instruct you?'

'Not really. They're just there. All the time. In the end you have to do something just to keep them quiet. They seem to require action of some kind.'

'Maybe you ought to see a doctor.'

'I do.'

'Do you ever tell the voices to be quiet?'

'Yes.'

'And?'

'They take no notice. They're like that. Independent. You've got to admire them in that respect.'

'They don't listen?'

'Oh, they do. But they take pleasure in ignoring me.'

'Tell them again.'

'It won't do any good.'

'It might.'

Wislon glanced around Henry's, anxious that others might be listening. All the waiters sported goatee beards in various and mostly adolescent stages of growth. The waitresses wore short skirts and toyed with biros in their mouths while taking orders. Everywhere was finished in brass or chipboard made up as wood and the bar area was landscaped with tubs containing small palm trees and lolling cheese plants. One of the waitresses was carelessly dousing the foliage with water.

'I could do with one of those squirters,' said a woman behind Wislon.

'But I bet they don't wipe the leaves like they ought,' her companion replied. 'You just watch.'

The gentle hum of conversation grew and resonated in Wislon's ears. A waiter brought him another coffee.

There seemed to be a predetermined, agreed equilibrium holding all the people together in this place. He looked back at Amy Facer and recalled the events of the last thirty minutes. He distrusted himself and despised his own vulnerability. Amy was smiling, her cheeks puffed, red and firm. She talked about herself so easily and told him about the group of volunteers she belonged to who read to the blind. Once a week she read to an old man named Brunt who lived on the edge of town.

Life just wouldn't leave Wislon alone.

If Wislon had had a partner then Amy could well have become his non-sexual mistress. As he did not have one, he wasn't quite sure what she was. Despite his misgivings, he found himself discoursing guiltily to her about cinema, about swimming – about almost anything that came into his head. They never spoke at work, but once or twice a week (and it was regularly becoming twice) they met at Henry's or The Gibbet or the Languid Greyhound for a coffee. Wislon had never really experienced talking *qua* talking before. Now he could recommend it. It was actually quite good once you got into the swing of it. No, really. It was.

Wislon decided that Amy must be the difference. She made no demands on him and accepted all that he said with cheerful, impersonal good sense. With Mrs Tunnelle and even Armitage – no, especially with Armitage – there had always been an agenda. It took him a while, but eventually he had calculated that the agenda was himself. It always had been. And if he thought about it, he had always known that it always had been. The lies he told Armitage and the carefully selected information that passed between him and

Mrs Tunnelle were determined by the aggregate sense of himself. It was now strange to find himself nudged aside in a discussion about (say) education, or elbowed out of it while there was a mutual fuss made about slaughtering animals for meat. Not that Wislon particularly cared – what else are animals for, he thought – but at least he did not constantly find his own identity radically enrolled in the world's problems.

Amy was a local girl made mediocre, and happy with it. She was happy with her job, content with her life and generally satisfied with just about everything. 'And how many of us can say that?' thought Wislon, consciously echoing a favourite phrase of his mother's.

She had no education to speak of: left school at sixteen, no prospects, no qualifications, no beauty to tout and no brain to scheme. At an early age she had come to terms with her limitations. Nor was it merely her volume which kept her honest. Her laugh (ready, willing and loud), her clothes (resolutely post-hippie), her wide-open rheumy blue eyes (so trusting) and her wide-open roomy character (so unchallenging) were all asking for it. The fact is, when you *ask* for it so completely, you don't usually get it. Not completely. Wislon wondered whether that said something rather good about the world. On the other hand, he had never asked for it, spent most of his life trying to avoid it, and yet he was always getting it. Virgil Young gave it to him; even Napoleon Jones gave it to him. Since his father, everyone had taken their turn in giving it to him. But Amy? What was the point in giving it to someone when they didn't care? Where was the fun in that? Leave her alone. Don't touch. There's just no point.

The other thing about Amy Facer was that she was a full-souled, dense woman. Not any woman, mind you, but a proper, justifiable woman. Simply walking through the streets of Birmingham at any time of day or night, Wislon could see hundreds, thousands of defective, incomplete women. Many had decided to become more like men and some had redefined womanhood in idiosyncratic and post-feminist ways. But Amy was uncompromisingly herself. The soft gut and yielding skin were all part of it. She knew all about men and emotions and evasions. Despite herself, she knew and she didn't let on. She listened and she answered, frowning and hushing at what Wislon instinctively recognised as the right moments.

When Wislon became desperate, Amy acknowledged the fact of his melancholy but never asked, 'What's wrong?' He would never have to tell her that *nothing* was wrong. Nor would he have to bother about all the other stratagems, the wearily constructed responses that would keep truth and the unanswerable at a distance. No. It was never that simple and Amy Facer simply understood.

About three weeks after their first coffee and after their ninth meeting, Wislon noticed something strange about the stuff that was going on around him. In short, he started to notice it.

He even began to pay attention to where he lived.

This was a painful experience as so much of his time up till then had been spent deliberately not paying attention to where he lived. Given its location, this was not surprising.

His flat was in Winson Green, which hadn't even made a name for itself as a ghetto, despite being a ghetto. The riots in the early 1980s in Lozells, about two miles away, had disallowed such notoriety. Lozells had been replanned, rebuilt and renewed. People in Winson Green cursed their luck. They should have done some damage of their own, but now it was too late. Driving past the prison in the evenings, Wislon noted the ways in which the perimeter wall was made both forbidding and strangely inviting. You knew that you would rather be on the outside – but the inside? It didn't look so bad from where Wislon was sitting. He thought about his own divisible life; the known and the secret.

He heard the irregular arrangement of sounds in Tailbush Road, where he lived – and listened to its music. He looked hard at the Indians, the Pakistanis, the Bangladeshis, the West Indians and the Africans who teemed through the territory. Wislon saw that they drove, shopped, cried, murdered, shambled and contemplated like anyone else. It had come to his attention that the small Indian who ran the post office kept an iron bar under the counter and gave packets of sweets to local under-agers. He was alert to the blind Irishman who sat on the bench at the end of the street, the husband who beat his pregnant wife because he wanted her to stop smoking and the tatty, unravelled whore who every day at eight tried her luck in Tailbush Road before heading north to the Soho Road.

He could say with certainty that he and Amy didn't dislike each other. Sometimes, they talked without substance about work. And sometimes – occasionally – they tried something more ambitious.

'Do you know what the hardest part of our job is, Wislon?'

'No.'

'It's that people expect us to make things better. To make them all right.'

'Yes.'

'When they call us – rather than us calling them . . .'

'Which is altogether different.'

'Altogether. When they call us, they want to be compensated. They want to be made to feel better. They want somehow to be better people.'

'I suppose so.'

'It's not just money. Not just. They want comfort. Succour.'

'Right.'

'They *expect* things to be better. But it's impossible. We can make things worse or we can not make things worse.'

'How do you mean?'

'Sometimes things seem worse simply by not being better. If you're *expecting* better and you don't get it, I mean. If you know what I mean.'

'I do know what you mean.'

And sometimes, Wislon's conversations with Amy went like this:

'How are the voices, Wislon?'

'Receding.'

'Quieter?'

'I don't listen to them so much now.'

'That's good.'

'Yes. I was quite attached to them.'

'Yes.'

Sometimes the conversation went like this:

'Did you see Fat Mike today?'

'Yes . . .'

'Funny the things you get used to.'

'Us or her?'

'Phoebe?'

'Both. Probably.'

'He was so . . . hopeless with her.'

'I think she enjoys it.'

'Fat Mike's sweat?'

'And Virgil. He adores having something that Fat Mike can't have.'

'Still. Those hands. That look. All day . . .'

'You're not a woman.'

'No.'

'It could be worse.'

'Ah.'

Amy never asked what was wrong. She never asked Wislon what he was thinking, even when he *was* thinking. She didn't need to know and he never had to say 'Nothing' or 'Pardon'. Amy's prodigality could absorb anything, even Wislon's morose silences.

It would be stretching the point to say that Wislon

was beginning to find humanity more humane, but things were moving in that direction. On Sunday afternoon, and he still wasn't quite sure how it had happened, he found himself drinking tea with Tempe Pigott and Zasu Pitts. Or was it the other way round? Anyway – the weird sisters. In their flat. They had caught Wislon on the dusty landing as he was taking the black swag-bag of rubbish down to the bins. As far as putting the trash out was concerned, Wislon was predictably regular, as he was with most things. The two old women could have guessed that at some point during the day he would be there with his sack of scraps, litter and good riddance. They had never bearded him before, however. Maybe, Wislon mused, my specifications have altered. I've been recategorised, earned a second opinion. He wondered about Amy's part in all this. After dumping the rubbish he made his way into their flat. They had even left the door on the latch for him. He walked straight in.

The first thing that struck Wislon was that the flat was not at all as he had expected. He had anticipated the odd puddle of urine, a battery of two-bar electric fires, a medley of purring cats, an anti-macassar mountain. The prosaic reality did not fit the imagined scene.

Although the flat still contrasted boldly with the ordered, hard-lined severity of his own, it was by no means bad. Perhaps a little ornate here and there, but everything more or less as it should be. Even though the sofa had a spidery palm frond printed on to its covers, you could still sit on it. The room was uniformly heated by an apparently efficient heating system which whirred and gurgled contentedly somewhere in the kitchen. There was, in other words, no squashed conference around a solitary heat source. It was forty-two degrees outside (Wislon had checked) yet the room was undeniably and disappointingly comfortable. The pale curtains (which showed a pair of giant flamingos looking sharply at each other) were scrolled tightly back, allowing a grey but luminous light to range freely in the room. No; this was a living room that people lived in. He remembered his own childhood when his father had routinely 'closed' rooms for the winter months in order to save on heating. One of them was always the living room, which became for almost half the year the un-living room.

They asked Wislon what he did and whether or not he had gone to university. One of them seemed surprised that there was a university in Leeds and the other asked him why he had 'taken' history. Wislon did not have the patience for the full, heartfelt version and simply said that he enjoyed the subject.

'Though not any more?'

'Pardon?'

'Though not any more. You've stopped doing it.'

'Yes. I had to. Once you've finished – that's it, you have to get a job. Earn money.'

'Of course he does,' said the other one rather sharply, throwing a protective glance at Wislon.

The three of them talked and drank tea for about forty-five minutes. The old women claimed that they had both been in silent films, had known von

Stroheim, and that the talkies had undone them. Neither Zasu Pitts nor Tempe Pigott appeared to have any family other than each other. When Wislon told them he was 'in insurance' Tempe Pigott told a story about a boyfriend who had lost his thumb in a machine at an eel pie factory. 'It came clean away,' she said, 'right down to the webbing. Of course, in those days – no insurance . . . just a few pounds' compensation. Pity. Nice man.'

Wislon stared at her freakish features while she was talking. Even underneath the mascara, the powdery foundation, the shadows and painted lines, he could now see that Tempe Pigott had been a beauty, a dazzler. Probably about sixty years ago, but there were still signs. As with most hopelessly attractive women, there was a single feature which stood out from the others. By itself, it would seem insincerely abnormal but somehow it worked well enough inside its facial ensemble. Tempe Pigott's feature was her lips. To date, they hadn't caved in, cracked or diminished (like so many do) to become mere rubbery bulwarks for a row of dodgy teeth. Her lips were still *lips*. Wislon thought of Armitage and wondered whether she would make it to eighty – no; nearer to ninety – and whether her looks would continue to defy the passing years. Only once did the conversation falter. Zasu Pitts was slightly deaf in one ear and, although she coped intelligently with the disability, sometimes there was no disguising it. They were discussing old man Doughty and complaining at the way he was always complaining.

'And he's younger than us,' said Zasu Pitts.

'Younger, but in so many ways more senile.'

'He's what?'

'More senile.'

'Smile?'

'Senile.'

'Senile,' prompted Wislon.

'He's what?'

'I said he's younger but also more senile – in so many ways. More senile.'

'Senior. He's not.'

'Have it your own way. No, then. He's not.'

'Maybe so,' Zasu Pitts concluded.

Wislon had sat back for the first time during his visit. He could hear life going on outside the window, on the street two floors below them. Someone was making arrangements for a football match the following week, bellowing across Tailbush Road: 'Yam gooin' up the Villa Satterdee?' A motorbike without a silencer buzzed past. The sweaty tang of curry was in the room despite the sealed windows.

Wislon eventually left saying he had something to do. He went back to his flat and wished that he had something to do.

It was almost a relief to Wislon when he arrived back from the cinema that night. He had seen *The Client*; he wondered why so many films dealt with children who were more knowing than adults. Children never knew more than adults and that's why you could never fool them. Besides, as far as Wislon was concerned, knowledge was a curse. It dragged memory into play, kicking and screaming. Memory never came easily.

It was a relief to get back because he saw that the light on the answer machine was warning him that someone had called.

The message said: 'Wislon. You *still* haven't called me. Never mind. There's plenty of time. You've changed over the past few weeks. I've been watching. I wouldn't worry about that, either. That kind of change doesn't tend to last very long. Don't put too much hope in it. Anyway, I just wanted to let you know that I am still around. Goodbye.'

As usual, the tone was even and possibly friendly. Wislon played it back once more. There was something familiar about the voice. It was as if Armitage was speaking, but as a man. The voice was thin and whine-laden, reedy and with a vaguely masculine growl which acted as its bass line. Where had he heard it before?

The call had its desired effect and made Wislon question the assumptions that he had lived with over the past few weeks. Hope had proved more difficult than despair in this respect. It was reassuring to know that it couldn't get its way all the time.

When he went to bed that night, Wislon was neither happy nor sad. He felt that he was surviving – but not by choosing the right parents, or planning frequent job switches, or making long-term health provision for himself, or renting flexible accommodation. No. He was surviving inside himself where it was more complicated. Inside himself he was minimising debt, being suspicious of get-rich-

116

quick schemes and refusing to put all his eggs in one basket. Inside himself, happy and sad were playing out a goal-less draw. Nil–nil. And *that* was fine.

— 4 —

Killing

Wislon had been seeing Armitage for exactly six months. This was the kind of thing he knew about. He also knew that he had seen her maybe twice a week during that time; certainly no less than three times every ten days, anyway. That made it (say) nine times a month. Or sometimes ten, never more than eleven and definitely never *less* than eight, except for the time she stayed with a distant relative in Banbury around New Year. Wislon calculated around fifty meetings and thought he ought to have some idea about his feelings towards her. She ought to have had thoughts about him as well, of course, but somehow things didn't seem to work like that.

About one hundred and fifty hours of Armitage Time. Maybe one hundred and eighty. One hundred and ninety at the absolute tops. Where had all the hours gone and what did they amount to?

It was now April, the cruellest month. Not that Wislon noticed. To him, each month seemed as pitiless and murderous as the one before. Armitage's presence in his life had offered – *still* offered – some kind of hope, and that was really the problem. As yet, it was hope unfulfilled, unrequited expectation. Looking ahead became a painful but compulsive habit and one that he wasn't sure he particularly cared for. The relationship had stalled on a pleasant but unexciting plateau. It was all very well, but where did they go from there? Sexually, there had been little progress. Nor had Wislon actually tried to make any. He was afraid of losing what he had already acquired; a rush of blood or a sudden spasm of inexpedient lust might lose him everything. Without discussing it, without even offering the possibility of a negotiated settlement, Armitage had serenely seized the initiative. She seemed perfectly content with an assortment of chaste kisses, loving strokes, warm but unambitious caresses and tasteful, virtuous hand-holding.

At school, Wislon remembered that others used to talk about their Saturday night adventures using a simple numerical code that precluded the possibility of embarrassing and potentially lurid physical details. A 'Number One' was anything above the waist and a 'Number Two' anything below it. Long-term prisoners used to tell jokes to one another by simply giving each gag a corresponding number and then 'telling' it when an appropriate circumstance presented itself. Thus, Wislon's schoolfriends would only have to raise an eyebrow, state their number and leave the rest to the imagination. With Armitage, Wislon was stuck on 'Number One', and even then not all that securely. Maybe he could bend the rules and deal in fractions or decimal points.

In his more philosophical moments, Wislon wondered what love actually was. Whatever it seemed to be, whatever it amounted to, he was increasingly convinced that he didn't deserve it. Certainly, other people were too squeamish to approach him with it. He knew how they must feel. Wislon had also experienced what he imagined was the same kind of fastidious recoil. With him, it usually concerned dirty seating on public transport, the smell of beetroot or a determined and long-standing irresolution about public lavatories. That was how he felt others felt about him.

And now there was Armitage. For a while he had believed what he had been told at Sunday school. That is, only God truly, *really* loves us and everything else is lust and desire. He also remembered that his father had been particularly keen to reinforce the message, also (of course) mentioning 'one's parents' as being natural supplements to the religious order of things. Subsequent events, feelings and physical intuition had rendered such possibilities useless a long time ago – but that still left Armitage. She seemed to be dangling elusively, somewhere between divine abstraction and tangible flesh and blood. And Wislon thought he knew where he would rather be.

Over the years, he had sinned more in mind than in body. Still, he knew what his body was capable of. Including the treacherous Jane, he had (he supposed) fallen in love with several girls at school, even those who did not necessarily know about it. In fact, especially those who did not know about it. University, however, was altogether different.

Although he had risked more towards the end of his stay in Leeds, he had found the fact that 'girls' changed into 'women' something of a problem. Women seemed to know more. Worse, they knew too much. Their expectations soared and they became less experimental and more choosy. They had been through all 'that' and now they more or less understood what they wanted. Wislon knew they wouldn't want him so he didn't put them in difficult positions. In that way, at least, he was considerate.

But now. After (about) one hundred and eighty hours with Armitage, Wislon thought he might be in love. If that was what she wanted – maybe what she had *planned* – then she had succeeded. His resistance to it had evaporated. If he was honest with himself, he knew it was the kind of resistance that was just asking to be vaporised. Right from the start, despite appearances, it had lacked credibility. It was simply waiting to be mugged or vandalised by love, by a sweet heart – even by charity.

Now, he thought about Armitage most of the time. When he wasn't thinking about her, he was thinking about what she was doing to him. He could still remember the first time he had seen her in the Dog and Bitch. He persuaded himself that he had known all along, from the first glimpse, that there was something between them. It goes like this. After two people have been together for a while, they are allowed to ask each other about their initial impressions. Wislon dared not ask Armitage, even though he knew what his own were. At the first steady gaze, he had loved the symmetrical sheen of her hair and the tubular pout of her lips. He had adored her boyish manner and athletic figure. He had fallen for the whole thing, even the teasing naivety that now so perplexed him. Also, he was emphatically in love with the ways in which she was different from Dr and Mrs Small.

The worst thing about being in love was the sense of falling in with it, falling with it and possibly just falling *for* it. Wislon had usually been quick to recognise the absurdity of other people falling in love. Now, he seemed rather vulnerable to it. Neither was it any good feeling that your love was different to everybody else's, because everybody else was undoubtedly feeling the same way. That was the trouble with love; generically speaking, you couldn't argue with it. All the same, he wondered whether sex with Armitage might not change things. Not God's sex, either, but the sex everyone else in the world was after; selfish, clarifying, squashy sex. He would have to put it to her some time. Yes; but which some time?

Tonight, instead of their usual drink or film-watching or play-enduring, Wislon suggested an Indian restaurant in the centre of Birmingham. He thought that a meal might be the most convenient setting to sort out what had been on his mind. It seemed like neutral territory. The sense of dandyish exoticism that Wislon still associated with Indian restaurants – almost all restaurants, in fact – would, he hoped, rub off on Armitage. He wasn't quite sure how this would work. Vaguely at the back of his mind was the hope that some kind of extreme sexual liberation would make itself apparent to her at about

123

the same time as a plate of tandoori chicken.

The Indian Grill Restaurant and Crêperie was not much of a straw to clutch at. Wislon recalled his father's advice about restaurants, especially Indian ones. 'Before you go in, check the upstairs. Look at the windows. In particular, the curtains and the paintwork. If you can't trust it from the outside, don't go in at all.' Wislon had always followed this advice, despite the feelings of resentment it brought back. Now he found himself instinctively glancing up. He was angry with himself because the manoeuvre reminded him of his father. Still, he noted the good white paintwork and a triptych of windows which contained puffy, billowing layers of pink curtain.

Wislon had to consider his choices carefully when the menu was presented. He dared not venture much beyond naan or poppadom or rice. Occasionally, he would manage a small korma and a mild vegetable of some sort, but even then, only when followed by a large pitcher of furtive, lukewarm water. His stomach was certainly not up to spicy food. More alarmingly, his skin would always throb and his scalp tingle whenever he tackled something risky. It felt as if his body was ungumming itself. Meanwhile, Armitage was busy ordering what Wislon assumed was the most pungent selection available.

'You don't find it at all . . . uncomfortable?' he asked.

'Not at all. You should try some.'

'Well. No thanks. I'm not sure it would agree with me.'

'You don't know what you're missing.'

124

'I do know what I'm missing. You don't know what you're missing.'

It was a Saturday night and the restaurant was brimming with groups of men, all about the same age as Wislon. In contrast to his unmuscled slenderness, their gaseous bodies seemed swollen to the point of bursting. Chubby fingers attached to salami-like forearms delved and shovelled amongst the piles of yellow rice and fragrant stumps of meat.

'Christ,' said Wislon.

'It's really very nice,' Armitage confirmed. He recalled the evening spent with the Smalls and the strange stew he had been served that night. Since then, he had confided to Armitage that he'd imagined her father with a laboratory of some kind at the back of the house. 'The walls would be lined with shelves holding jars of preserved organs. You know, brains, eyes, hearts, intestines and so on – all floating in some kind of soupy fluid.'

Looking now at the splinter of chicken she was dealing with, he reminded Armitage of the fantasy. It seemed only a short hop from there to the main purpose of the meal. Jauntily swirling a tumbler of water around, Wislon put on his best unconcerned voice. 'Of course, I know that first impressions can be misleading.' In fact, his first impression was, for the time being, his *only* impression of the Smalls. He had not been invited back. And anyway, he firmly believed that it was difficult to argue with his first impression.

He wondered whether people wondered about his own parents in quite the same way. Perhaps, he thought, the wondering only started *because* of his own parents. That is, because they were the kind of people it seemed natural enough to wonder about, a habit of mind that discreetly extended itself to anyone else's parents. He supposed it was rather like comparing notes after a particularly bad examination – just to make sure that you hadn't answered the wrong questions, or responded to the right questions in the wrong way. More likely, Wislon thought, to ensure that everybody else had done as badly as he must have done. There was some comfort in that, at least.

There seemed to be some strange law that insisted on children being more than the sum of the parts of their parents. In fact, much more than the sum of the parts. Or maybe it just seemed that way. Even in his own weary case, Wislon felt that there was a point to be made. He considered himself. He looked at Armitage again. What had gone *right* with her? Maybe it was something to do with sex which erased all previous files. When mothers and fathers came together, did they simply become different people for a few brief moments, and was it possible that children were given their chances by being inscribed with that explosive neutrality? Of course, he knew all about genes and environment and so on, but maybe there was a small unaccountable something in the outcome of sex that legislated against absolute domination by parents. If that *was* the case, they certainly tried to make up for it later on.

Wislon didn't quite know how to say all this but thought he ought to have a go. First he told Armitage

126

about the way his father used to insist on him wearing particular clothes, on almost putting them on his back. 'You can't go among people dressed like that,' he would say. Then he would command Wislon to 'Strip!' before reclothing him from the 1930s' wardrobe in the small child's bedroom. Finally, his father would put a pound note in Wislon's pocket, smile, and say, 'You have to have a little something in your pocket. Don't tell your mother.'

Wislon thought it strange to think of parents as ordinary people, to try to fathom them as anything but parents.

He took a breath. 'I often wonder about my own father and mother and wondered whether you wondered about your father and mother, as one does.'

'What? In what way?'

'Whether you wondered – about sex.'

'Whether my parents have sex, do you mean?'

'Well, yes. In a nutshell. If you want to put it that way,' said Wislon, attempting to shift the emotional responsibility of the discussion.

'Of course. Everybody does, don't they?'

'I suppose so.' Wislon felt uncomfortable. The line of enquiry seemed as if it was about to rebound on him in unforeseen ways. He need not have worried, however, as Armitage continued.

'I didn't really have to wonder. It was all made pretty clear to me.'

Wislon asked how and she informed him about the advantages of being brought up in a medical family. She also told him that at quite an early age she

127

had found a picnic hamper in her parents' bedroom. It was full of fancy-dress costumes and, near to the bottom, odd pairs of rubber gloves, surgeons' masks and gowns, and so on. She had thought nothing of it until she came home from a party early one night to find her father and mother making love while dressed in a grotesque circus of clothes from the hamper.

Needless to say, Wislon was now deep in uncharted waters. He tried to understand. 'So your father would re-enact fantasies with your mother. Maybe fantasies he had at work, while in the gown and mask?' he suggested with an air of what he thought was learned panache.

'Sort of. But not quite. My mother was the one wearing the gloves and mask and what-not.'

'Bloody hell.'

'Yes. Daddy was wearing . . . what was it . . . a clown's outfit, I think it was.'

'With all the make-up? Big red smile, stars for eyes, white foundation . . .'

'Don't be silly. They're not that bad.'

'No. Of course not. I didn't mean to suggest . . .'

'You probably did, but it doesn't matter. It's quite easy to be broad-minded about these things, you know,' Armitage asserted with the sense of someone who probably did know. She was now spooning lime pickle on to her plate, somehow managing to make an essentially inelegant operation seem like a dainty tea ceremony. Wislon watched with gathering admiration, pausing only to gaze at the doughy pile of white rice and assorted breads which were now

128

marooned on his own plate. He was also hoping that Armitage's apparent broad-mindedness could be further exploited, and he was just about to say something to test the idea when she said, 'And how about your parents?'

'What? Sexually?'

'Sexually.'

'Sexually?'

'Yes. Of course.'

'*What* sexually?'

'You tell me.'

'Really?'

'Of course. I told you. It's only fair. What about them?'

'Well, they must have had it, I suppose.'

'That's no answer,' Armitage teased. And what must she have *thought* of such a half-hearted response?

Whatever, it was the only one she was going to get. Something strange had happened to Wislon. He was looking directly at and through her, an expression of discontented horror and sadness embossed on his features. Even without the spicy food, his body was beginning to play some extraordinary tricks. Inside, small blisters of misery had been activated. Wislon was seething.

The rest of the meal was completed in near silence. Wislon abandoned rather than finished the boggy contents of his plate. He only just managed to remember to pay the bill.

After the first few occasions when he had invited Armitage back to Winson Green, Wislon's hospitality had become infrequent. There were probably a number of reasons for this reluctance. Certainly the awkward memories of his bungled attempts to seduce her continued to engross him. Probably he felt ashamed at the neat but undeniably shabby state of his flat. He also wondered whether Armitage would be quite so keen now that she more or less knew what was waiting for her back at Tailbush Road. All true. But more than any of these, he realised that although he thought he 'loved' Armitage, he still resented her presence in his home. Initially, he had tried to deny these sensations, but the more he considered them (and he didn't particularly *want* to consider them), the more irrefutable they became.

The carpets that smelled of sawdust and cat food and traced a genealogy of ex-tenants back to somewhere near the beginning of Time. The tiny bedroom with its brown paintwork and unfathomably stained mattress. The low-slung tubular seats in the 'other' room, with their pendulous oatmeal sacks somehow slung and strapped between a clumsy arrangement of steel poles and metallic junctions. The kitchen's cracked lavatorial tiling and suspicious gas cooker that spluttered into ignition with a stubborn *Hhurh*! For Wislon, these rooms and their gear, their appointments, had a discrete life of their own. Whenever he walked around his flat, he was constantly aware of everything being appropriately arranged for him. His home was an agreement, a stealthy series of compromises that simply occurred whenever he was there. His milieu, his vicinity – his neck of the woods. Wislon's home was a point of repose for him, a stillness. Even Armitage's intrusion allowed doubts and anxieties to interrupt the calm, to muscle in on the party.

But now he had to deal with the situation. He had never actually had much difficulty in getting Armitage back to his flat. It was what happened when he got her back there that was causing problems. Or rather, what was not happening there. After a while, he had simply stopped asking. He didn't mind humiliation (that much), but not when it was so frequent. And predictable.

The stagnant relationship with Armitage demanded action. Back she must come . . . but for what? As yet, he wasn't quite sure. Sex was somewhere on the agenda, but certainly below talking about sex and a long way distant from simply thinking about it. Coffee was the only definite at the moment. At least, it was the only thing that Armitage had actually agreed to.

He hurried her out of the Metro which was now due, he noticed, for its fortnightly grooming at Soapy Sam's. They took the three sets of stairs at a brisk pace, briefly pausing outside Wislon's door while he fumbled for the keys. Behind Doughty's door, he heard a careful but unmistakable scraping which hastened him even more. Since leaving the Indian Grill, Wislon and Armitage had barely spoken to each other. He felt he knew what he had to do. Admittedly he also knew that knowing what he had to do did not necessarily mean it was the best thing to do, but it was the best he *could* do.

Pushing the door open, Wislon simply said, 'This way.'

'Mm?'

'This way. To my room. The other room. The bedroom,' Wislon spluttered and then finally and with something like conviction, '*My* bedroom.'

He pulled her through the doorway and sat her down on the bed. As yet, there had been no resistance. He bent over to switch on the bedside lamp. Its harsh light raked across the room and briefly discovered Armitage's poised but vaguely nonplussed face. This was more than Wislon could bear. Abruptly, he turned the light off again.

Still fully dressed, he lay down on the bed. Armitage now had her back to him. He felt the darkness muffling him and heard the flat's complicit series of mutterings and unaccented croonings. Wislon simply lay there and waited for a ruffle of duvet or the growl of hinges. Before he could think what the next move should be (or whether there was a next move), he felt the warmth of skin and silk nuzzling close. His nose became aware of Armitage's aromatic complexity. The rest of him made no move. Then she folded her arms around him and he sensed her legs drawing themselves into a fluid, smooth triangle against his body. Wislon responded and the two of them lay together in a possessive but chaste embrace which lasted until Armitage's soft breathing became deeper and more regular. She was asleep. Wislon hardly dared to breathe, afraid of unravelling the architectural snugness of the moment. He bent slightly forward to kiss the top of her head. Even that imperceptible turning of his axis caused her body to stiffen slightly and for the instant to be disturbed. He dared not go on. Inside his head he was urging her to do something, to do *it*, to do anything. However, the urging in him was all finished. Before long, he was also asleep. When he awoke early next morning, Armitage had gone. Later that day she phoned to say that she had taken a taxi. There was no regret in her voice, perhaps even some fondness. Maybe she likes me, Wislon thought. A pretty daring thought at that, he considered. Anxious as he was to calculate how these things worked, how life worked, he reckoned that this was enough to be going on with.

It was thoughts about this which preoccupied Wislon during the first few minutes at his desk. As usual, he had been the first one in. It was still mid-winter but the sun was already beginning to cut through the windows. On his way to work, Wislon had noted buds opening, premature daffodils complacently sunning themselves, confused squirrels darting around amongst dustbins, and a fat bluebottle pounding against the Metro's windscreen. The weather was definitely misbehaving, but Wislon thought it no more than that − a dose of elemental mischief. No doubt it would be snowing over Easter and fat-bottomed cricketers would be fleeing from fields in July, chased by hailstones. The weather was much as it had always been, it was just coming in a different order.

The flooding, the high tides and the bank-bursting had brought an unusual amount of business into the office. The mid-morning activity had become a din and had started up almost as soon as the waxy sleepiness of early morning reluctance had worked itself out. What was happening was something like bustle. Fat Mike trundled back and forth all day, unsmiling and serious. He was saying things like, 'Wislon, those Bristol estimates,' or, 'Simon, bring the Shrewsbury figures,' or, 'Virgil, have you worked out the thing for Norfolk yet?' And between all the carrying and exchanging and using of information, phone calls were being made to reassure, clarify and refuse.

'Maybe you shouldn't send the stuff yet.'

'There could be a problem.'

'Just the dining table. No. Not the car. Separate cover, that's why.'

'If you could send it back as soon as you get it – yes, by return if possible.'

The clamour subsided and became lunch, then the drowsy murmurs of early afternoon accelerated once more to become a mild hubbub.

'Where's all this sodding weather coming from?' asked Phoebe.

'Something to do with cold air and hot air colliding,' said Virgil.

'Colliding? Can air collide?'

'And does that mean that if there was no air there would be no weather?'

'Theoretically, yes,' offered Napoleon.

'Thanks, Nappy. What do you think, Matt?' Virgil said.

'Space is cold,' Matt grunted.

'So?'

'If space is cold, and there's no air in space, how can it actually *be* cold?'

'Interesting.'

'Surely even space is *something*, though,' said Phoebe, 'even if it's not air.'

'How can it not be air? That's stupid.'

'I read somewhere that the higher you go the colder it gets.'

'Even though you're getting closer to the sun?'

'Or the moon. It depends.'

'On what?'

'Which way you're looking. What time of day it is. Where you are.'

'The sun's always there, isn't it? We just can't see it all the time.'

'A bit like Needy,' said Virgil, slightly raising his voice.

'There or not, hot or cold, it's still raining like there's no tomorrow,' Phoebe announced.

'It's bloody well pissing down.' Virgil eyed the stack of letters and claims in front of him. 'Fuck,' he said. 'Fuck, fuck and fuck.'

Despite the odd jibes and moments of casual resentment, Wislon still felt accommodated by it all. There were so many places where he would not fit that not *quite* fitting didn't seem so bad. If this place didn't really want him, Wislon supposed, there were plenty of others which categorically didn't want him. He hadn't tried them or even looked for them but he knew they were out there.

Besides, he had begun to wonder what he could

learn here. In particular, and against his better inclinations, he was beginning to wonder about Virgil Young. He placated himself with the thought that inclinations were neither better nor worse – they simply existed. Furthermore, he seemed to spend most of his life doing something other than following his inclinations, so why stop now? Virgil Young's self-belief and confidence were probably a trick, but wasn't that the whole psychopathic point of confidence? And Wislon wanted to know what the trick was. He knew that he could lie, sometimes quite creatively, but that wasn't it. Confidence came from somewhere else and it made others pay attention. The others probably didn't *understand* the origins of such conviction. Not having it themselves, they believed in 'the trick'. Wislon understood this but he still wanted to know about it. He began to feel like old man Doughty and peered out at Virgil Young every time an opportunity presented itself. He watched the way he dealt with Phoebe, the manner in which he kept Fat Mike sweet, even the style which diverted any displeasure away from himself. 'I can't help being happy here, Mike,' Virgil would say, 'I'm here to do well. To achieve. I'm like a man with no past who is only looking ahead to the future. I want to be like this place, Mike, to have an identity.'

Occasionally, Wislon had overheard Virgil Young selling policies down the phone. His tone was invariably constant and encouraging. He talked up the softer message of insurance, giving peace of mind and the offer of public service. He played on the aversion to risk. They felt safe with Mr Young. Another thing that Wislon had worked out was that it was better to 'look' at other people rather than himself. You simply don't look at yourself. Rather, you scan and scrutinise everybody and everything else in the hope that they, somehow, roughly, 'stand' for you. And everything about everyone – Virgil, in this case – is actually quite good because you would like more of the same.

That was the theory.

Looking round at one or two of the others didn't help to reinforce the idea, but as a theory it was reasonably comforting. Wislon wrinkled his face. He supposed that at some point in life self-viewing was unavoidable, but there was no need to rush it. Pick your moment. Pick your mirror. Most of the time, try to pick other people.

Despite all this, Wislon realised that he could never be like Virgil Young. He may be able to learn a trick or two but life would find him out in the end. Virgil complained that the job was boring, a tedious dead-end. But Wislon disagreed. Surely, he thought, that was the wrong way round. Boring was good, and it was the other things that caused difficulties. The teeming variety of life threatened Wislon, the spectrum and unceasing choice of it all. Open your mind to it and you really do have problems. Wislon's mind was resolutely not open. Occasionally, he might wonder whether he was missing anything, but it was never long before the other thoughts overwhelmed him again.

Even though men, women, the sky and the clouds

might change from morning to night, Wislon was always and disappointingly *himself.*

During that week, Wislon need not have worried. The sky stayed more or less as it was; a translucent grey with random white scars. This was neither heaven nor hell, but some local variant.

Birmingham was trying to have no weather at all.

At work, the routine did not falter.

Wislon lurched back in his scientifically sprung office chair and pushed his mind around for a few moments. He knew that in a sense one never forgets anything. Not really. It was a frightening thought, but he had often come to the conclusion that he couldn't dis-invent memory. It was up there some-where – filed, tabulated, arranged, chaotically strewn, writhing, dormant – but (thankfully) much of it was simply not active for most of the time. Besides, remembering everything is a kind of madness, and Wislon needed memories so that he could forget.

He had heard that people always remember the good times, when it was always summer and trees were being gently bowed by aromatic breezes. If this was so, then why could he only remember the bad times? There must have been some good ones, if only to enable him to realise that the bad ones were *bad*. Maybe memories were like life. Both of them seemed to be getting nastier.

Sometimes Wislon wondered whether he had *any*

memories from childhood. On the other hand, he sometimes wondered whether memories from childhood were all that he possessed.

One of his earliest memories was of the dinner table. As he ate, Mr Needy would glance at him in a disapproving manner. Then he would say something like, 'Don't forget to chew your food. Chew it. We're not animals. We don't have the ability to digest without mastication. Chew your food before swallowing it. You'll also enjoy it more. Chew your food.' Sometimes he would say it and put a warning arm around Wislon's shoulder. Or pat him on the knee.

None of these rules really applied any more. He didn't suppose they ever had. It just seemed like it. He wondered why the world of his childhood was so fantastically removed from what he thought of as adulthood. He had been given very little apparatus to make sound decisions. At one time, he supposed that Mr Needy had meant well, but really he had been busy handing out the wrong equipment. He wasn't sure which was worse, but the result was that he was now comprehensively unequipped.

Apart from the daily routine at the dinner table and never going on holiday and always being badly dressed for school, Wislon had one other memory which he could not shift. He couldn't do away with it because he didn't quite know what it meant.

One night, he had been unable to get to sleep. Grandma Needy had been round for supper and he had been allowed to stay up longer than usual. He had seen *Dead of Night* on television and the episode with the ventriloquist's dummy which came to life had scared him, even though it was only in black and white. Darkness squeezes you inside yourself, so he had asked for the bedroom door to be left open and the landing light left on. Even its soft pink glow could not send him to sleep and he lay in his bed wondering if this was what it was like to sweat. His parents looked in and he lay on his side, eyes tightly screwed, pretending to be asleep. They turned the landing light off and went into their own bedroom. Wislon was still awake imagining what the bite of a ventriloquist's dummy must feel like.

After about half an hour, he heard his mother's voice from the room next door. It was soft and soothing but with a faint if discernible edge. She was singing in a quavering, uncertain falsetto. Wislon came out of his half sleep and listened more intently. He heard his mother sing, 'If you go down to the woods today, you're sure of a big surprise . . .' She managed about three or four more lines before coming to an abrupt halt. More noises came from the room, as if the furniture was being rearranged. Then Wislon must have fallen asleep.

Now, as he leaned back in his chair, he puzzled over the memory and went over the words inside his head. They were mechanical and struck him as being vaguely sinister. He could also remember his father telling him never to play in the woods. He said, 'There are plenty in there who'll do you harm.' Wislon tensed. Too right, he thought, and his hand instinctively located his groin. Too right.

The sound of a phone ringing reminded him that

there was probably too much work to do for anything else to matter.

At home, there had only been one more call on the answer machine (insistent but polite, and still the same message) and the voices had stilled to a companionable murmur.

He concluded that Amy must have recognised this equilibrium in him and resolved not to displace it. She and Wislon went almost ten days without visiting Henry's or anywhere else. That was Amy's charm for him; she was unchanging and made no demands. There was no attempt to infiltrate. For Wislon, Amy was like the weather – she was there, but not so that you would particularly notice.

It was surprising, therefore, that Wislon should have challenged the steadiness of those days. He had decided on somewhere different and away from the centre of town for his next outing with Amy. Through the Jewellery Quarter and across the main road that eventually led to the Soho Road there was a small place called The Lucky Dip. It could not be described as a café or restaurant, loitering indeterminately somewhere between the two. From the outside, having first seen it through the Metro's window, Wislon was reminded of his own flat; compact, neat, probably clean, but undeniably dilapidated and beggarly. The place lay amongst empty hulks of warehouses that once manufactured engine parts and other metallic bric-à-brac that was nondescript but no doubt essential to the running of any car. Now, if they housed anything at all, it was small retail outlets which sold cheap costume jewellery, mobile phones or traditional Indian clothing.

The owners of The Lucky Dip were most likely from the Middle East. They moved around their restaurant with a tolerant swagger and Wislon noted the almost accidental cleanliness of the floor and the tables. He inspected the cutlery for stains and glanced inquiringly at the ceiling. The food itself neither belonged to any country in particular nor bore much relation to the menu. Still, it was usually hot and came in large quantities.

As was normal, they walked from work. It was downhill to the main road and then up a steepish gradient on the other side. Amy's face was glowing bright red by the time they arrived. Neither she nor Wislon had said very much since leaving the office. It was as if both understood that the progression from drinking to eating was in some way significant. When Amy saw The Lucky Dip she realised immediately that any development was minimal. Or rather, that Wislon probably preferred that it should be perceived in that way.

Now, she elbowed her way behind the small Formica-topped table they had been offered. Not that it particularly mattered, as there was nobody else in there. As the table scraped and screeched and gently rocked on its fragile legs, Amy said, 'Any bigger and they'd have to get a crane and winch me in.' Wislon curled his lips and moved the table forward a few inches. Amy smiled back and sat down heavily on a chair that warped to the right as she

142

settled. *Wislon* wondered what such a joke against *himself* would entail. Probably more than a one-liner. Probably a hefty soliloquy full of put-downs, demolitions and disablements.

The service in The Lucky Dip was quick and efficient, though too unpleasant and unsmiling to make it worth very much. Amy and Wislon talked of the strangely frenetic week at work and the unexpected fact that over a quarter of a million people lived in areas threatened by flooding of one sort or another. The idea of floods held a natural appeal for Wislon and he told Amy of his childhood obsession with swimming.

'I could imagine it,' she said.

'How do you mean?'

'Well, you're pretty sleek. There's no real heaviness to you. It doesn't look as if it would take very much to propel you through water.' She made the word 'propel' sound intriguingly mechanical.

A large plate of cheese omelette, rice, boiled potatoes and a mongrel salad was hammered down in front of Wislon. Amy thought she had ordered something different. She got something that looked much the same until she spotted half a mushroom poking out from the omelette's side. Her dish was also garnished with something like chives.

They talked about floods and risks and the misleading small print in some policies. Amy thought it wouldn't be long before the Pacific Rim countries did to insurance what they had already done to manufacturing. That is, take it over and do it better. Then she asked where that would leave them.

Wislon's mind didn't really operate on that scale. They sat and stared at each other for three or four uncomfortable minutes. Then Amy spoke again as if trying to put the other moments behind them.

'Do you know why I like sitting here at the window looking back up the road we've just walked down?'

'No,' Wislon replied. The thin monosyllable chimed self-consciously in his ears.

'I like seeing things from a different perspective, from an unusual angle.' She looked at Wislon's doubt-ful face. 'From the kind of position you don't normally live it, I mean. Do you know what I mean?'

'Of course.'

'It's only a small thing. This restaurant. That hill. The place we work in. I'm up there every day. Just coming here makes it different. That's all. Probably better,' she concluded, and then more softly, 'that's all.'

'That's why I come here,' said Wislon, half begin-ning to believe it.

Then they lapsed into silence once more.

A little later, Amy said, 'I've been meaning to say something to you.'

In Wislon's experience, when people said that, it usually meant that there was something uncom-fortable on the way. Usually it involved what his father would have called 'home truths'. Wislon had never fully understood what the phrase meant. Did it have to do with truths which were so personal (i.e. so damning) that they could only be spoken of at home

144

and were simply not fit for wider and more public consumption? Or was it to do with a kind of truth that was only applicable *at home*? Either way, he did not feel that Amy was qualified to tell him one. Something heavy turned over inside him. For the first time since they had began to meet, Wislon braced himself for her next words. That was the other thing about home truths; whoever was going to tell you one was not likely to be brushed off by a squinty expression. That was the least of their concerns.

'Oh yes,' said Wislon.

'It's just a thought,' she continued, 'and it may be of some use to you. At least, it could make things *easier* for you.'

'I'm not sure that I want things easier. I quite like them being hard.'

'No you don't. You're just saying that.'

Wislon observed Amy with a look of plundered innocence, but she pushed on anyway. She told him that the others in the office were not 'so bad' and that, even if they were, Wislon shouldn't (what was the word she used?) 'glower' at them. Apparently, it was this glowering, this angry gawping and sullen feasting of the eyes, that made others behave towards him in the ways they did.

'So you think it's all my fault?' Wislon started, speaking with what he hoped was an impressively casual shrug of the shoulders. In fact, it felt more as if invisible strings attached to his elbow were being yanked skywards by an incompetent puppeteer.

Wislon wanted to tell her the bits about staring at other people because of the ways in which they

145

seemed to represent him, or at least give him context. He used to watch his father shaving, getting dressed, setting out the croquet hoops, going off for work every morning, the way he drove his car, the assertive grip with which he held the telephone, and the shape of his mouth as he talked. He even watched Virgil Young and he could never take his eyes off Armitage. He wanted to say something about it being easier than looking at himself. However, he could not deny the general truth of what Amy was saying. Maybe she was on to something and maybe this was seeing things from an unusual angle. It couldn't *all* be a question of angles, though – could it?

'That's not what I'm saying,' she answered with a slow, mournful shaking of the head. She went on to inform Wislon that although she quite understood his difficulties with 'the others', it did not make things any easier to dislike them so actively. 'I mean, I don't exactly get on with them but there's no need to advertise the fact.' Wislon thought of her virtual invisibility in the office and wondered where it had got to now that he needed it. Amy assured him that she was saying these things for no one's benefit but his own. She was sure that he might find working easier if he ignored the others. 'Don't give them a point of focus. Don't give them an excuse to go for you. It can't be very pleasant. And look how much better it's been the last week or so, simply because nobody has had the time to be vindictive.'

Wislon watched Amy's face while she spoke. Her eyes didn't blink, which he assumed was some sign

146

of integrity. Her soft features were temporarily hardened by the urgency of her words and Wislon was aware of taking in the writhing network of her hair as it sloped down her shoulders and disappeared behind her back.

At first, he suspected that she might be blaming him for a crime he was unaware of committing. However, even Wislon realised that Amy was not capable of such premeditated trickery. He felt sure that she was speaking for what she saw as his best interests and was only doing what she could for him. He remembered a phrase his mother often used – 'We all do what we can. You can't ask for any more.' Now Amy was doing what she could. In a way, this was worse. Maybe a lot worse. Now he had to bear the burden of her good intentions, perhaps respond and co-operate in the whole benevolent scheme.

Finally, Wislon just wanted to get the business of differentiation sorted out. While Amy was in the process of confirming that he was indeed '*completely different*' from everybody else at work, another couple wedged itself awkwardly into the next table. Their sudden entrance created an immediate gust of self-consciousness on Wislon's part.

The man was red-faced, slightly overweight and turning to fat. By contrast, his companion was pale and pencil-thin. Her body was composed almost entirely of angles, a recurring series of Formica surfaces. There was so little meat on her that her pinched mouth didn't look capable of a smile. Wislon shot them a look of intense malevolence. Then, remembering all too vividly what had been said only a few minutes before, he became whey-faced and grim. What should he do? Without thinking, he reached across the table and grasped Amy's hand. She smiled artificially at him before patting the top of his knuckles with her free hand. It was an affectionate, entirely non-sexual smile. The heaviness inside came back. He looked down at their two hands lying together like a piece of elementary origami and repeated the question to himself: what should he do? What should he do?

About half an hour or so later, time enough to refuse rice pudding and strawberry ice cream but to drink a cup of scalding coffee, Wislon and Amy were heading back towards the Jewellery Quarter. Although the area had been more or less depopulated for the last hour, both had their cars parked near to the office. Because he arrived early, Wislon usually managed to acquire one of the occasional spaces on the weedy blot of scrubland heroically called 'Car Park'. Amy, however, had to find somewhere further away. The distance was dependent on what time she arrived in the morning, which was variable. She often ended up in the multi-storey, which was actually just two storeys. Wislon had only seen Amy in her car once but had often seen it parked somewhere in the vicinity. She drove a vivid green Fiat Panda which was always piled with miscellaneous junk and seemed to have been the epicentre of a recent paper storm. He didn't think she ever cleaned it. Ever. Rather, she would constantly rearrange what was already there.

This in contrast to Wislon's Metro which had a regular shampoo and was routinely purged of any unnecessary scraps. He wasn't in any way mechanical and worked on the principle that as long as the car was moving and looked all right, then there was nothing to concern him. He even had a roll of black sticky tape that he could use to cover any of the warning lights on the dashboard that flickered to life when he least wanted them to.

They crossed the main road and began the trudge back up the hill. Neither was speaking, although Wislon assumed that this was because both were conserving energy. Whatever, it seemed the simplest thing to think and he left it at that. A lone tramp sat bunched in the doorway outside a building where a sign boldly announced a specialisation in metal pressing. He did not say anything, but Amy instinctively reached inside her shoulder bag and dropped a fifty pence piece in the man's lap. His grizzled, bearded face looked up and muttered thanks. He seemed more surprised than grateful, Wislon observed. Further on up the road, they saw an old lady struggling with the gradient. She was about seventy yards ahead of them. Her gait was classic granny, a shambling and parodic quick-step. It was painful to watch. Wislon was about to say something like, 'There but for the grace of God . . .' when suddenly, a youngish man shimmied out from between a watch repair shop and a kiosk which sold charm bracelets. He moved with some urgency, seizing the old lady's handbag, and tore down the hill towards Amy and Wislon but on the opposite side of the road.

Without having to be prompted, Amy broke into something resembling a gallop and went towards the stricken woman. Wislon, meanwhile, had taken root. His strong inclinaton was to stay exactly where he was. Even at about twenty yards he could see that the thief would be too much for him. He wasn't particularly big but he looked like the kind of man who was thick-skinned, for whom pain was only a distant rumour. He also had the accoutrements of hard-core tenacity: denim jacket, toilet-brush hair and a sandpapery face. Wislon could not be sure, but he thought he also detected small silver hoops through both his ears, his nose and an eyebrow. Before the man tilted past, Wislon just about had time to consider and reject the possibility of a chase. He raised his right arm limply in the air and croaked, 'You. Hello. Stop!'

The utter feebleness of his response was just beginning to sink in when something else happened to dishonour him. The tramp who had been slumped and inert only a few seconds earlier was now up and after the thief. More than that, he was gaining. A crumpled hat toppled off his head and rolled drunkenly into the road as his spidery legs began to devour the ground ahead of him. The thief was perhaps more surprised than Wislon. Instead of increasing his speed or turning to confront the beggar, his gears jammed and he got stuck somewhere between the two options.

Wislon turned back up the road towards Amy. He expected to see her tending to an old lady, kneeling down, half-whispering words of comfort, telling her to lie down for a few minutes, propping her head and being benevolent. That sort of thing. Doubtless this was what Amy also wanted and expected to be doing. Instead, she was standing up and looking as irrelevant as Wislon. Meanwhile, the old lady herself was now rampaging after the tramp and the thief who had snatched her bag.

Wislon felt some sympathy for the mugger. The tramp soon had him on the ground in an impressive-looking arm lock. The muggee was clamping his wrists with a set of handcuffs. As he came out of shock, the thief started to shout, 'Bastards. Cheats,' before being led away by two uniformed officers, the tramp, the old lady (now minus wig and obviously not elderly in the slightest) and someone Wislon presumed was yet another policeman, this time dressed as a vicar.

Next morning and Wislon was at his desk. In front of him was a copy of the *Birmingham Post*. It was open at the headline, 'Police Use Grannies To Trap Muggers'. The first paragraph read, 'The frail old woman struggling with a shopping bag on the streets of Birmingham may look like an easy target for muggers, but any assailant could be under arrest in seconds.'

Wislon was grappling with appearance and reality as, he supposed, he ought to do at moments like this. Scribbled in the dry margins of the newspaper were 'And Mutate Yourself' and 'Any Mucus Yielded'. He now added 'Appalling Murder Yarn'. He glanced across at Amy who was stacked up behind a tumbling mass of papers. In her usual way, in the way that only women knew how, she was pretending not to be there. She looked over at him.

He looked back at her and felt completely sick.

He reviewed what had happened the previous evening. When Amy got back to him, Wislon had still been standing in exactly the same spot where she'd left him before bowling up the hill on her mercy mission. Not just the same spot or about the same spot or even more or less the same spot. *Exactly* the same spot. He had not necessarily done anything wrong. He had done nothing at all. The police did not even need him as a witness. Maybe, Wislon thought, you had to do something to be a witness, whereas he had given a good impression of not even being there. Not so that anybody would notice. Not so that it particularly mattered.

Wislon had always thought that, roughly speaking, men do things and women have things done to them. It was probably more complicated than that but the formula had a persuasive symmetry about it. So what did that make him?

He had been glad to get home where he could stand in front of the mirror and nip and knead his flesh. Outside, it was no longer even cold. The dusty weather and wind's warm rushes had reactivated his skin. He had looked at the reddening sky and could tell there was more on the way. A whole week of it looked down on him.

And what of Amy? Once again, he thought of The Lucky Dip. Rather than reaching across the table and taking her hand, what else should he have done?

Wislon blinked and reminded himself that he was a bungler. Everybody's fool. He had already shown that he was no good when it came to love's complex paraphernalia. He understood women even less than other men. At least they seemed to have a scheme, whereas he was merely guessing. There were times when Wislon thought that this blankness was the single most significant fact of his life. He wanted to blame circumstances, his mother, Armitage . . . but these areas were also void. His soul seemed to lack even the most elementary understanding and was, at best, insubstantial. Maybe the absence had been inside him right from the start.

For the moment, Wislon contented himself with the thought that men often remember how they should have acted or what they should have said after the damage has been done. That was the rule. The image of Amy's hand lying inertly in his own still troubled him. What *should* he have done? He still did not know. That morning he had wanted to cry – possibly a sign that something was deeply wrong, although you could never be sure with crying.

Wislon looked up from his desk. Napoleon Jones was just about to fail to bring him a coffee. Everyone else was intent on the work in front of them, or talking on the phone or gazing through the window, and he scanned the room with eyes of sullen incoherence.

This is better. Now you are getting somewhere. Well might

you cry. If there is something wrong – really wrong – then that is exactly what you should be doing. There's nothing to be ashamed of. After all, it's all you've got left at the moment. Remember what you were taught: women can cry about most things if they put their minds to it. Bad dreams, good dreams, dreams they can't even classify. Especially the ones they can't classify. But men need something altogether more aggravating and inexpressible. It's something like a last resort. Something like.

Well might you cry.

I hear you. It means something. It's not nothing.

I hear you – but remember that time is running out. There is still some way to go.

You can remember the first time that you cried. Or rather, the first time you can remember crying, which is not quite the same thing. There had probably been many involuntary tears before that, but somehow they don't count. Willing them to come is altogether different because it is a conscious, deliberate response – and that is probably why you remember them.

It is something to do with your father pushing against a door. You recall that it was a bedroom door. Your mother is on the other side of it. He is saying that she mustn't be silly and ought to let him in. He is saying it quietly but you seem to remember that a few moments ago he had been shouting. Then you can tell that your mother has released the pressure on her side of the door while she thinks about it. Your father, however, does not stop pushing and with a violent motion the door suddenly swings inwards. The small gap between the bottom of the door and the old blue carpet had accommodated your mother's foot which had also been pushing against your father. Now, the door's movement

takes your mother's big toenail off, leaving it marooned
about six inches away from her foot. Underneath, the toe is
red and white, a kind of mottled crimson. From your
position on the stairs you have seen all this and begin to cry.
Great watery boulders throwing themselves down your raw
cheeks.

When your father eventually gets to you, he says what
he always says: 'Careful, or you'll drown in your own tears.'
Your mother is also crying and you wonder if she will
drown as well.

Wislon drove to Agnes Tunnelle's little brick house.
As usual, he was two minutes late.

Agnes Tunnelle and Wislon had been doing business for almost three years. After university, he
thought that he ought to give it a go. Besides, all
the doctors he had seen said it was 'necessary' or
'important'. Or usually both. There was nothing
really complicated about *how* Wislon began seeing
Agnes Tunnelle. Probably it was the reasons which
were complicated. Nor was Wislon embarrassed about
going. She was a stranger who took his life seriously.
Probably more seriously than he did, if he was
honest. Even when she was wrong about something,
Wislon usually thought that somehow it was all his
fault.

And what did Agnes Tunnelle offer? A service? A
treatment? Hope? A renewal? Possibly all and none of
these. Maybe he just wanted to be told that he was a
patient who took himself seriously. That would be a
start. Wislon thought that most people forgot they

were patients so soon as they left the doctor's surgery or were discharged from hospital. They simply shuffled the fact to the backs of their minds. But not Wislon — he was serious about being a patient, serious about being ill. Wislon thought that she encouraged him to think about some things so hard that there wasn't any room left to investigate the things that really bothered him. It was a good trick.

'I don't want to have to do it,' Wislon was saying.

A pause. Then Agnes Tunnelle said, 'Do what and to whom?'

'To her.'

'Yes.'

'To her. To me.'

'Go on.'

'That's all there is.'

'Yes.'

'Do you understand?'

'Do *you* understand?'

Wislon considered. It was something that had come to him in the middle of one murderous, feverish night. It had woken him so he hadn't had a chance to forget it all. Agnes Tunnelle was wearing a lot of wool today, most of it the colour of lightly browned toast.

'No. I don't think that I do.'

Usually the night left Wislon alone. It was peculiar to be woken by it and to find himself in bed. Something bad must have happened while he slept. Something had got in and messed Wislon up good and proper.

'Right and proper,' as his father might have said. It had forced such a vindictive, distressing entrance that it must have meant business. Maybe it bore a grudge and hated Wislon's life and wanted to murder what was left of his soul. That was the way these things probably worked. There was no doubt it did mean business, but what did 'business' mean? He had struggled for long enough to keep these thoughts away. Now his mind was striking out on its own. It was doing more or less as it pleased. At first stealthily and now more graphically the past was getting its own back.

Did he have to do what he was told? With horror, Wislon realised that he probably would do what he was told. He asked for it and he continued to ask for it.

He didn't want to have to do it to her.

But he knew that he would.

During the next week, Wislon took an afternoon off work and went to the cinema. He sat in muffled seclusion towards the back. The foyer had been full of under-agers trying it on, a trickle of failed students and a hard core of pensioners taking time off from riding the buses. Together, they had watched *Frankenstein*. Wislon only had half a mind on the film and was unable to make narrative sense of the images. The air tasted of stale velvet and dust. Wislon felt resolute and that he was moving up in the credits. Best boy, gaffer, key grip. Before long he would be producing and directing.

On the way home, he checked the sky again. At home, Wislon's doubts and anxieties were temporarily stilled. He took a long bath and lay in the water, fearing the sleep that would come afterwards.

Friday. Wislon thought there was no time like the present. There *used* to be a time a bit like the present. He no longer had time for it now that the nights had been so effectively violated by the past. And still he wanted to cry. And still he didn't want to have to do anything, but knew that he must. In a sense, he already had.

'Well, I thought it might be quite nice.' Wislon sensed Amy's reluctance, though as with most things and Amy, it was neither forceful nor insistent.

'Yes, it might be. But – listen – we don't have to go out to wherever it is. Henry's is fine. It would be fine. Really.' Amy was only just able to look Wislon in the face.

Meanwhile, he was doing nothing else. He fixed her with his own fat eyes.

'But it would be nice.'

'Yes.'

The idea of a restaurant out towards the Black Country had seemed to break all the established rules. Wislon knew that Amy understood about him and rules. He also knew that she would eventually yield.

'Nice.' 'Quite nice.' 'Fine.' The vocabulary of

innocence and eventlessness. It seemed absurd to him that something so important should hinge on such uncomplicated sounds. Words suddenly seemed a bad idea and Wislon wished he could do without them altogether.

Another deviation was the use of his Metro. Again, initial resistance had collapsed under the promise of an early return to the Jewellery Quarter. Besides, Wislon had argued, Amy's Fiat would be perfectly safe in the multi-storey. It was wedged between an open-top coupé and a new BMW. 'If anyone's going to try something they won't notice yours,' he said. 'And what would they want with all the stuff in the back?' he added with especially poor timing.

They drove in silence. The Metro crossed the canal near Winson Green. Here it was wide and featureless, a black, charmless ribbon that gently bucked under the moon's steady glow. Disused warehouses nuzzled the road and seemed to stare carefully, inspecting the car as it accelerated past them. The beams from the headlamps picked out a grainy atmosphere rendered fantastic by the lambent orange flicker from the street lights.

Amy said, 'There's really no need for all this, Wislon.' It was clearly something she had wanted to say for a while. 'If it's about the other night . . . it doesn't mean . . .' It was the first time that she had mentioned it. Wislon made a determined show of being interested in the Metro's dashboard. Soon, he activated the windscreen cleaner and sluiced the glass in front of him with foamy water.

Wislon peered through the windscreen and

159

thought how like a cinema screen it seemed. Perhaps all drivers perceived life as a film — never repeated, never ending, but always a film. People and small events crowded in for a few seconds at a time before diving off the screen, usually for ever. It was not a case of liking or disliking; it was simply and unalterably 'there'. And coming towards you were all those other people watching their own films. Wislon realised that he was both viewer and transient star, mostly at the same time.

'Filthy night,' he said. It was a long way from the truth. The weather was mild and dry. Amy spent the journey watching the route as if she was worried about having to find her way back. Her under- standing, her compliance, made Wislon tense. It was exactly that kind of thing which demanded a response. He felt her volume next to him and noted the ambrosial perfume she was wearing. He estim- ated its contrast with the acrid vegetable dampness outside.

Then they turned off the main road and were amongst a series of low modern buildings, apologetic, like recently promoted bungalows startled to find themselves in an industrial estate.

Wislon brought the car to a halt and turned the engine off. Amy sat still, apparently unmoved, looking straight ahead of her. There were no street lights here and the damp roundness of her face caught some distant reflections and glinted faintly. Above the slow murmur of faraway traffic the Metro ticked with uneven contentment. He put his hand into the small plastic tray on the side of his door and pulled out what had been concealed there. Amy turned to him with a half-irritated grimace before settling back and rearranging her hair so that it once again fell over her shoulders.

She turned to Wislon with an understanding smile and said, 'Look.' She probably meant to say a lot more. Later, he reflected, that was almost certainly only the beginning of a longish sentence. Probably the start of a fairly decent paragraph, in fact. When people had something they wanted to get off their chests they usually started with 'Look'.

The silver hammer hit Amy somewhere on the top of her head. Wislon used all his strength but the Metro was a small car and it was difficult to get much leverage. She didn't say anything and the two continued to gaze at one another for several seconds before a thin trickle of blood started from her nose. He watched, fascinated, and then drew the hammer up again. Wislon saw that along its side were the words 'Made in China'. It used to be his father's hammer and he could sense his strong hands around the wooden handle that still carried traces of oil and sweat from twenty years ago. He wanted to avoid hitting anywhere close to Amy's face, and waited until she had slumped forward before easing her back into the hollow of the seat with the flat palm of his hand. Now, with the side of her head turned towards him and vulnerable, he picked a spot and brought the tool down swiftly and precisely. This time, there was a distinct cracking sound and her expression changed significantly. She was no longer smiling or looking startled. Clearly something inside had simply collapsed and her face now responded by registering a look which was devoid of human intention. Her mouth was simply a shape. She made no sound other than a faint sighing, rather like a small boiler igniting: *whhummf*!

That was it. Wislon had feared having to launch a frenzied attack and there being a great deal of shouting and scratching. But no. As with her life, Amy had been reasonable and willing. Her death was a clever pastiche of that life. Apart from his charged breathing, Wislon could now hear very little. There was an unsettling but clear silence. He reached up and clicked on the Metro's interior light. There was a small cluster of blood spots on the passenger window. Other than that, everything seemed remarkably clean. The gore issuing from Amy's mouth was being soaked up by her dress. It was an old favourite; crushed velvet and purple. On top of her head there was a crimson dent and a slight matting of the hair.

Wislon settled her in the seat and observed that she had not even unbuckled her seat belt. It clung tightly to her expansive, limp body. He climbed out of the car and wished that he smoked. The air was cool against him and he noticed that he had been sweating.

Was this what he did not want to do? Was it what had to be done? Now he might cry. After all, now there was something to cry about.

Leaving

Wislon stood next to the Metro for a few moments trying to take in what had happened. Now, something had clearly changed in his life but it was difficult to define exactly what difference it was making. He looked around and patiently absorbed the wounded silence. Then he held his hands up and inspected them carefully, at one point turning the palms deliberately down towards the ground. Everything was changed and then again nothing *seemed* to have changed.

Next, like an actor who had momentarily forgotten his lines, Wislon jerked his eyes open and took in several deep breaths of damp air. Mechanically, he scanned the area immediately around him. Nobody had witnessed the incident. There wasn't even a boozy tramp or a teenage solvent abuser skulking ominously in the shadows. He forced his body to hold still for a few more moments, to cease its inner mumbling and surging. There were no sounds and no movements.

Completely satisfied, Wislon turned to the Metro

and considered Amy. He could not leave her in this place. His sense of decency also recoiled against merely dumping her body next to the road or leaving it in the middle of some dreary field. After all, she was dead – and that was bad enough, wasn't it? As it was probably such a long way off, Wislon wasn't sure that he could embrace the idea of dying. But Amy was a start and he knew that if someone had killed him he wouldn't like to be left out here. Where was it? A deserted industrial park somewhere near or in the Black Country. Wislon didn't particularly *like* what he had done, and liking himself a little more for not liking it he decided to make the most of a good thing and be civilised. He owed her that (at least), and besides, it was one of the few decisions he could make by himself. He could and would choose.

And anyway, the police always seemed to find those kinds of bodies quickly enough. Then they would come to the office and Wislon was not sure whether he could manage another set-piece. Maybe later, but not now. He decided that he needed time to think. It was Friday night. Presumably he had until Monday morning before anyone would even begin to miss Amy Facer. She lived alone. He could probably rely on other people not to start worrying until Tuesday. Really, he knew what he had to do. He felt that he had always known. There was no need to ask any of these questions. The safest place to hide her would be in his own flat in Tailbush Road. Or rather, the least dangerous. No one visited him. Not now. And old people didn't really notice dead people. Not very much, anyway. They couldn't afford to.

Wislon did not consider that this was a gamble. He was not a compulsive risk-taker. Like many others, he preferred to play it safe. Never insure a gambler. He knew the figures from work. For example, in every deck of fifty-two cards there are 2,598,960 possible five-card poker hands. The bad news is that you can only be dealt one of them. Normally with those odds he would not even join a game. However, in this case, Wislon felt that he could choose his own hand. The 2,598,960 possible permutations could work *for* him. Nobody would discover Amy until he allowed it. Only he would know where to find her. Yes. The discreet stillness of his flat was the only place. That was the hand he dealt for himself.

Wislon went back to the car. First, he found the fat Chinese hammer. It was lying between his seat and the brake handle. He must have dropped it there just before clambering out through the door, although he could not remember the moment. Now he closed his left hand around it, leaned back behind Amy and replaced it neatly under her seat. He noted that there was not even any blood on it. Next, he considered what to do with Amy on the journey back to Winson Green. A part of him wanted to gamble: he thought about leaving her in the front seat. Who would know that she was dead? Then again, when Amy's absence eventually became known, someone might remember having seen a white Metro with her in the passenger seat. Wislon resisted the temptation to bluff and opened the small boot at the back of the car.

The space did not look very large. He unfolded

the sheet of plastic which had been neatly stowed for an unspecified emergency. It had been bunched in the corner since he'd bought the car. Then he went back to Amy, unbuckled her seat belt and with some difficulty manhandled her to the boot. It was like moving a sack of oatmeal. Her bulk shifted around inside her skin in an increasingly unhelpful manner and there didn't seem any way that he could manipulate it into a more manageable volume.

Again, an intuitive sense of etiquette forbade him from simply piling her in. Besides, to get her in *at all* needed a certain amount of cautious manoeuvring. For a few irritating moments, he thought about the geometrical difficulties that Amy presented, and then pull-pushed her bulk into the waiting space. Her legs dangled woodenly over the side. Wislon thought how pretty she now looked. He was grateful to her for having kept the inside of the car so clean. Now he noticed that her blood and the other strange fluid that had been streaming from her nose had more or less ceased. Her dress was sopping but Wislon calculated that the plastic sheet would be more than able to do its job. He stepped back and remarked to himself that Amy looked like a crumpled puppet or a doll about to be returned to its box.

He pushed her head to one side of the boot and swivelled her body around, using her bottom as a kind of pivot. Then he half-turned Amy on to her side and neatly folded her arms into a position about half-way between her breasts and her stomach. Next, her legs were arranged and bent so that they also fitted the snugness of the boot. He moved a small cardboard box containing an atlas and an A–Z of Birmingham to accommodate her more easily. He could not understand why he had persisted for so long with such a large box and so few items. It was clearly inefficient.

Moving Amy's body around and processing its curves and ramps of flesh stirred Wislon's memory. As he gently guided her legs into place and ran his hands along her leg and thigh, he recalled Armitage. He sensed a rhythm beginning to emerge: shove the body–move an arm–treat the leg. He put the parallel out of his mind as quickly as he dared. Amy's eyes were tight shut. The patch in the middle of her head glistened. It had become drier and was now dark red. Eventually, when everything else was ready, he twisted the head slightly to the side so that it was propped more comfortably in relation to the rest of the body. Not that it particularly matters where her head is, Wislon considered. Still, it was a thoughtful touch.

When the operation had been completed, Wislon walked slowly around to the front of the Metro, climbed in, pulled the door shut and reached for the ignition key. For the first time, he felt the heightened importance of the moment. He could not turn the key for fear of something happening. Probably, he was only afraid of the sound the car would make. Over the last few minutes he had become accustomed to the near-silence which had closed around him. To disturb that, to pierce it with the engine's agitated whinny, might change everything.

Wislon paused for a few seconds before

aggressively wrenching the key clockwise. The engine shuddered and then caught. He had expected this brief moment to be a defining one. It should have signalled his entry into another life, a different one than he had woken up to that morning. He could have been sick. Possibly, he could cry. He thought of Agnes Tunnelle; there was no box of tissues in the Metro either. Wislon decided not to cry. He released the handbrake, depressed the clutch and did something quite normal with the gears. The car moved smoothly away. As Wislon turned sharply back on to the main road a few moments later, a muffled thud at his back told him that Amy was fine.

On the drive back to Tailbush Road, Wislon made sense of what had taken place. He wondered whether Amy Facer had meant to make such intrusive demands on him. Probably she didn't know what she was doing but that was not his concern. She'd asked for it, even if she didn't mean to. Wislon wished there had been another way. Maybe something altogether more acceptable. But he was sure there wasn't. Not really.

The Metro retraced its route with a reassuring calm. Wislon remembered that he had run out of milk and decided to buy a couple of cartons from a corner shop. On the pavement outside he noted an old red telephone box and breathed in its mustiness as he walked past. Once he was in the shop he could not find his wallet and fussed about the thought of having left it at the scene of Amy's death. At one point, he thought he would be unable to pay. Walking back to the car he wondered whether he should open the boot and borrow a pound from her. He knew her handbag was in there as well. With relief, he found his wallet which had somehow got wedged down the back of his own seat. In the event, he only bought one carton. After all, tomorrow would be Saturday and he had places to go.

As he turned into Tailbush Road Wislon estimated what he ought to do next. He couldn't very well throw Amy over his shoulder and carry her up to his flat. He wasn't sure he could carry her at all. He would deal with that when he came to it. He toyed with the idea of leaving her where she was. But that wasn't solving the problem, just moving it around. Besides, there were so many dogs and so many *types* of dogs in the road that one would be bound to smell Amy before the night was out. Whatever happened, Wislon did not want to be woken by a snuffling canine frenzy.

Wislon drove carelessly, his mind elsewhere. A proud Indian in a blue A reg Astra almost slithered into the Metro. He was sitting in what appeared to be the back seat. His arms were fully extended and parade-ground straight, gripping the steering wheel with a determined panic. As he sailed past, he jerked his head temporarily sideways and barked a fleeting obscenity before quickly reassuming his lordly position.

Wislon pulled up the Metro. His mind had started to drift during the last few hundred yards and now he was glad just to park the car safely. He tried to get to his feet and then sat down again. There was a heavy reluctance in the bottom half of his body to do very much at all. It had had enough. Then, somehow, he became upright more or less at the same time as hustling himself out of the car. He glanced back at where Amy was before deciding to go on up alone. Unusually, he took the scruffy stairs very slowly – Raymond Doughty speed. What it must be like to be old. During his funereal trudge he hoped that some idea to do with carrying a dead body up three flights of stairs would come to mind. Wislon wondered why these things had to happen to him. *Him* of all people. What had he done to deserve it?

When he reached the landing he did not hear the scuffling that meant Raymond Doughty. One of the reasons he did not hear him was that it was almost impossible to hear anything. The scratchy sounds of early Duke Ellington were boomeranging around the cramped space. Disturbed and dangling precariously on its plaited cord, the light bulb was managing a mildly epileptic jig. The music was rushing from the belly of the weird sisters' flat. The hubbub was occasionally punctuated by other strangled noises from inside. Wislon thought he heard a chair going over followed by an accusing rant. Then there was a suggestive thump, followed by silence, followed by some high-fidelity cackling, followed by the wheezing outbreak of 'Haunted Nights'.

Wislon had his key ready and pushed through his door into the relative quiet of his own flat. He walked slowly over to the sofa and sat down heavily. Once more he inspected his hands. He paid special attention to the pronounced ridges of blue vein which had apparently formed themselves into new patterns over the past few hours. In almost total darkness, Wislon looked around the room and noticed that the red light on the answer machine was flashing. He wandered over and pressed the 'Replay' button. If it was another one of 'those' messages he decided that he would give himself up. 'We're all in it together now,' the polite voice chimed. 'I understand what's going on. Unfortunate, I know, but those mitigating circumstances are somehow very persuasive. We should talk about it some time . . .'

Enough, thought Wislon. He reflected that it was just as well he hadn't told the truth about giving himself up. No doubt the message still troubled him. He stood uncertainly in the hall and considered its smug knowingness. On the other hand, at least people were still interested. They were calling him up. But if Armitage was also involved, what would *she* be thinking?

What was he saying? These thoughts had to be pushed to the back of his mind. It was dark there, a place where other unwanted thoughts were coiled and ready for use.

A furtive creak on the landing outside his door told Wislon that Doughty was now pottering about. Then there were three sharp insistent raps. He did something knotty with his brows and opened the door. As he did so, the music from the other flat bubbled across the landing. Doughty's face was very red. He clearly wanted to say something but couldn't manage the words. Wislon wondered why it was that words were so plentiful only when they weren't needed. That was partly the trouble at work. All those things that the others managed to say which didn't seem necessary or even particularly useful. Whatever they were, Wislon couldn't manage them. But now Doughty had begun a sentence. It didn't start very well. Wislon was reminded of a First World War bi-plane spluttering reluctantly into life. There was a lot of breathless gasping and phlegmy expectancy before his throat finally caught and whizzed the words around.

'Could you . . . could you . . . could you . . .'

'Yes?'

'Speak with.'

'Could I speak with?'

'Could you speak with . . .'

'Yes? Could I speak with *who*?'

'Those bitches next door.'

Ah, right, thought Wislon. Is that all? 'What would I say? What do you want me to say?' he asked.

'Tell them to be fucking quiet.' Doughty's face contorted at the word. It had obviously been lying around for a long time. Now it had been dusted off and brought out for its rainy day. And once started, there was no stopping him. 'It's been going on all fucking night. I get to bed regular these days. But those cunts. They've brought on my asthma.' At this he opened his mouth and pointed back down his throat. Without another word, he turned, shuffled back through his own door and slammed it with a deeply symbolic bang.

Wislon had nothing else to do. His mind could not start dealing with Amy. The committee in his head decided that he should, like Mr Micawber, wait for something to turn up. Besides, he was curious. He semi-strode over to the weird sisters' flat. He did not knock. Somehow he knew that the door would be open and he pushed it gently before heading in.

As Zasu Pitts and Tempe Pigott saw Wislon they waved him in. There was a lot of young-fellow-me-ladding and attentive, breathy cooing. Zasu Pitts was attending to what seemed like a new music centre. A pile of records lying in a fan-like heap cluttered the floor. She said, 'How about some Bix? Would you like some Bix? I think I would. I could just do with a bit of Bix.' Scuffing in the pile, she found something by Bix Beiderbecke, pointed to its Scalextrics of grooves and shouted, '"I'm Coming Virginia".'

Before long, Zasu and Tempe were bobbing up and down like a pair of highly coloured blancmanges. As far as Wislon could tell, one was dancing a version of the hornpipe and the other a species of fandango. The sweet-sour smell of gin hung in the air. On a table, Wislon noticed several empty bottles of the stuff arranged in parodically licentious ways. Both the sisters had their Joan Crawford mouths on. Zasu insisted that Wislon take a glass of brandy; the gin had long gone. He took the glass. Even before putting it to his lips he felt his body starting its routine of dissent. Something like acid was happening in his stomach and unaccountably his neck began to itch.

As the two sisters bounced across the room they occasionally collided with and manhandled each

other. Tempe Pigott's white body was already beginning to poke out from behind her clothes. Her
corsets had been loosened and her flesh was on the
move. The pale prairies of liberated skin contrasted
grotesquely with the urgent colouring her make-up
provided above the neck. Zasu Pitts was wearing an
orange bandana around her head. 'What sort of a day
have you had?' she asked.

'Fine. You know. Nothing,' said Wislon. He took an
imaginary sip of brandy.

'Well, we've had a shit day. Haven't we, Tempe?'

'Yes. Absolute shit.'

'All day. Nigger music from across the road. Dogs
barking. God knows what else. Well, now we're
getting our own back.' She pointed to the music
centre with some pride.

'Do you know what we saw? Do you know? Go
on. Guess.' 'I'm Coming Virginia' had come to an
end. Tempe Pigott lowered her voice for a moment
and stumbled over to the music centre. She found
'For No Reason At All in C' and the room once
again filled with a loud distorted fuzz.

'Guess,' she insisted. But she did not really want
Wislon to say anything. 'A wog wedding. Just over
there in that back garden.' Her fragile hand waved
vaguely in the direction of the window. Each finger
had a ring and each ring had a different coloured
stone set in it. 'A big vat of curry. You could tell it
was curry. It stank to high heaven. Then the bloody
dog went for a sniff. Then the bloody thing fell in.
And do you know what? Nobody did anything. They
ate out of that vat not five minutes later.'

174

'The country's going to the dogs,' added Zasu Pitts, leaping with laughter while staring absent-mindedly at the ceiling.

Sweat and tears were now running down both sisters' faces, streaking their heavy make-up and distorting their features. Soon their faces would become indeterminate blobs of black, blue and scarlet.

Wislon continued to watch. Sensing an audience, the two sisters jigged on. Tempe Pigott said they were going to 'Bix the night away'. After a while, their words became less coherent but a general rattle of discontent could still be made out.

'Fucking sickening. It disgusts me. It does. I'm sorry, but there you are,' proclaimed Zasu.

'Vile. Absolutely vile.'

'Wicked.'

'Filthy.'

Watching them was like seeing footage from another age. Wislon pictured the sequence of numbers that counted down all old movies, then the untidy sequence of insect twitchings and blurred hairs before the picture proper. The only difference, he observed, was that in this film *he* was the colourless grey one. Wislon felt monochrome. Still, he took a peculiar satisfaction in watching the spectacle in front of him. In the next few minutes he also picked out an argument about a film star with whom both Zasu and Tempe were claiming an ancient liaison.

'They come and go,' Zasu shrilled, 'they fucking come and go.'

'Mostly go,' replied Tempe.

'Anyway, he was a faggot. Everybody knew that.'

'A clear faggot. A celebrated faggot.'

'We didn't need him,' said Zasu, lolling clumsily across the room to embrace Tempe Pigott.

Then there was a brief lull in the drama. The record was changed to Count Basie and the two sisters sat down to begin cataloguing their differences and similarities. Wislon heard about the state of their teeth, the size of their feet and the respective frequencies of their ear wax. Soon they were into constipation and menstrual flow. 'Mine was always copious. Bursting. But yours – meagre. At best.'

'It doesn't matter now though. Dry as the Sahara, both of us.'

While all this was going on, Wislon thought impatiently of Amy. *What should he do?* He had anticipated that some pretext for leaving would turn up, although the last thirty minutes or so had produced nothing. After unsuccessfully trying several ploys to replace his first vain efforts to make a polite and unnoticed exit, Wislon thought again about trying to make a polite and unnoticed exit. Then, for the first time, he noticed that there was a blood spot on the sleeve of his shirt. It was no bigger than a small button but he thought he ought to clean it off. Leaving the sisters, he wandered towards the kitchen. He nodded, manufactured a grin and held his glass up to them by way of explanation.

The sense of normality he had experienced during his previous visit now evaporated completely. Wislon stared at the washing-up that lay in, around and quite far away from the sink. The cups and saucers and plates and glasses needed gathering, organising and then some muscular wiping. A part of Wislon – quite a big part, in fact – wanted to give form to this awful collision. His mind's eye ran ahead and could not help witnessing the last tea cup cheekily glinting with a new cleanliness before being lovingly placed inside the kitchen cupboard. He had been sympathetic on his other visit but now he saw that this place devoured orderliness. Everything contained the potential for spilling, leaking and breaking. This in contrast to his own fortress of order where knives, spoons, bowls and potato scrapers all did their regimented duty. Most houses probably used up order, he thought – they couldn't really help it. But not his. If Wislon could have his way, there would be nothing in his flat to give chaos a foothold. If he could work it, there would be nothing *at all*. No furniture, no floors, no walls. A small, comfortable vacuum would be fine. Where would entropy be then?

With a start, Wislon realised where he was and what he should be doing. He washed the blood spot from his shirt, using only cold water as his father had instructed him many years before. He turned his back on the formless pile of deflowered crockery and utensils. It pained him, but it had to be done. He walked back through the other room where Zasu Pitts and Tempe Pigott were singing quietly to one another. They had found a bottle of cherry brandy and were giggling at slurred or misremembered words. Count Basie was still going: 'One O'Clock Jump'. They hardly noticed Wislon as he surged past

177

them, through the front door, on to the landing and into Raymond Doughty.

'Oh. It's you,' said Wislon, rather obviously.

'That didn't do much good,' Doughty replied.

Wislon sensed a confrontation. 'Not really. They're too far gone.'

'I've taken some sleeping pills. They'll see me off all right. As a rule I don't like them – but needs must. Anyway – I'll be off then. Leave them to it. Poor sods. Goodnight.'

'Goodnight,' said Wislon, his voice a mixture of relief and gratitude and now, he noticed, mounting panic.

He took his key and hesitated for a few moments before re-entering his own flat. Again, he gave himself up to the sofa's cut-price sponginess. If he'd had any drink, he might have even poured himself one. *Any* one. His stomach was still being ironic at the thought of the brandy he had just drained. However, he needed something to unscramble his head. The situation needed some lateral thinking. Ordinarily, Wislon knew he wasn't really up to it. Amy Facer was still down there in his boot. How should he deal with it? How should *anyone* deal with it? He closed his eyes and gradually a kind of order was restored to his buzzing mind. Doughty would be asleep before long. Zasu Pitts and Tempe Pigott were, he thought, in the last stages of their decrepit defiance. He glanced at his watch. It was now well past midnight. If he hung around for another hour or so he could probably risk bringing Amy upstairs. Yes. That was the only thing he could do.

Wislon stretched out on the sofa and considered whether or not he could ever be the person he had been before driving Amy towards the Black Country a few hours earlier. At the moment he was holding steady. He did not feel any different and supposed that this was somehow significant. As an involuntary precaution, he once again held up his hands for inspection and peered at them through the prismatic gloom. He remembered *Macbeth*. All right; so he had washed a blood spot from his sleeve, but he did not think that counted. It was not the same thing. He wondered whether happiness could ever be more than a lack of *un*happiness and the absence of suffering. If that was so, he was home and dry.

He shuffled these thoughts around his head for a while before easing himself to the floor. At the last moment, he slowed his movements and allowed his feet to take his weight in an exaggeratedly reluctant manner. He did not want to wake anyone and eventually brought them softly down. Feet and floor behaved as two like magnets. Moving towards the front door, he brought his thighs up comically high with each step and only pushed down on the pads of his feet. Once he was on the landing, he stopped to take off his shoes and then left them neatly outside the door. Every step down the stairs seemed frustratingly slow and mechanical, but it was a pace he must maintain. His teeth grimaced and his neck muscles tensed as he descended. He wondered whether he ought to check the weird sisters' flat as he tracked past their door. The lights were still on but everything else was silent. He had decided that on the way down to the Metro he would tread with great caution but maintain a deliberate, steady rhythm. What woke people up in the middle of the night was the irregular and the unfamiliar. Well, Wislon thought, that and the other things – fear, loneliness and pain. Crying and bad dreams do the trick as well. Not to mention guilt. Really, there was quite a lot to wake people up in the middle of their nights. Wislon treading around was not likely to be high on their lists. But the others? Yes, certainly. They didn't bear thinking about, so Wislon silently willed people not to think about them. Stay asleep, he concentrated, stay asleep. It's just bad dreams. Or fear. Or whatever. We can all cope with that. *Stay asleep.*

He considered who else would be up at that time of night. Sleepwalkers? Junkies? Insomniacs? The blind? Then, before he had time properly to register the fact, Wislon was outside and at the back of the Metro. He juggled with his keys for a few moments and looked back down Tailbush Road. This was a reflex. If anyone was watching they would hardly make themselves apparent to him. He turned the key and clicked the boot open. The sound of the yielding lock and whoosh of compressed air broke the night. Wislon thought he heard the exaggerated snap of breaking twigs and the comic whistle of Hammer Horror wind. Amy Facer was still lying there. He hardly glanced at her before rudely lifting the body out, leaning her against his own frame and shutting the boot again. This time the sounds came in reverse order and ended with a contemptuous crack. Amy was larger than him and now her dead weight became a factor. He grappled with her for several moments and tried to bundle her over his shoulder. His hand slithered and skidded over the rolls of flesh and her wet dress. He could not bring himself to pinch her skin so simply picked her up in his arms once he had rotated her into the right position. Abandoning all caution, Wislon ran back towards his flat. Wheezing and breathing heavily, he took the stairs as quickly as he could. Although Amy seemed to be slipping, his fingers developed an existence of their own. They gripped tight while the rest of him floundered. He had shifted her as far as the landing outside his door when he came to an inexplicable halt. These last few moments were to be savoured. He breathed in, drew up his arms one last time and marched Amy triumphantly over the threshold. Now they seemed be involved in some kind of hysterical dance. They did not stop until they had reached Wislon's bedroom. Once there, he lowered her gently on to the mattress and flexed his numb fingers. Pumping his arms in hydraulic fashion, he managed to bring feeling back to them once more. Turning on the bedside lamp, he craned his body over Amy and for the first time noticed the sunken, jowly look of her face. Her dress was badly creased and the surge of blood had caused a dark but essentially colourless stain. Wislon drew himself up and surveyed the wreck of her body. The velvet dress was still gamely clinging on, covering, defining and making the most of a bad job. He boiled a saucepan of water and brought some paper towels. Soon he was swabbing Amy's face, rearranging her hair and collapsing her arms back across her chest. Her make-up came off in uneven patches and Wislon decided to leave alone what was not bloodied. When he had finished, her face was clean but looked as if she had eczema. 'Now you're more like me,' he remarked to himself. Smiling, he patted her head, plumped up the cushion she was lying on and pulled the duvet across the point at which the top of her neck met the dress. She would be all right for the moment and Wislon didn't mind sleeping on the sofa. After all, it would only be for the night.

That night, Wislon remembered his first dream for several years. When he thought about it next morning, it made him stand still and place his hands over his face. At one point, he looked around shyly to see if anyone was watching. He had not yet grown fully used to the idea that Amy would not be watching. He even began to realise that remarkable things could happen to him while he was asleep.

But this was later on, the morning after his dream.

Wislon entered his flat. It was strangely familiar. The dimensions were as he expected but there was also an alien modernity about it. Everything seemed newer, cleaner and brighter. He noticed a set of white blinds, for example, which hung in place of the clean but drably patterned curtains. These were certainly an improvement. Now, Wislon felt that he could shut out everything more completely. He walked over to his tape deck and selected Duke Ellington's 'West Indian Pancake'. This surprised him as he could not recall owning the piece. Come to think of it, he did not know what it should sound like or even whether Duke Ellington recorded it. Still, there it was now, rollicking along in the way that Wislon assumed it ought to. Who knew what might happen next. Maybe a few phrases of Russian or the low-down on molecules. Dreams were pretty good once you managed to have them. He had half a mind to spend more time with their flaws and illusions. The only trouble was, dreams were also what you woke up from.

Then, before he knew why, Wislon found himself too excited to merely *listen* to the music. He stood in front of the deck and, awkwardly at first, began to shift his weight from one foot to the other. It only took a few minutes before he was actually in time with the music. In increasingly inflated bursts of ambition, he then took turns with the various solos; restrained with the clarinet, less so with the saxophone. In quieter moments he chugged along in a steady equal four on the piano, smiling at his band and occasionally mopping his brow with an invisible handkerchief. Soon he was managing all the instruments at once and set off around the small room in a clever, syncopated heel-and-toe shuffle.

After a while, and through an unnatural tiredness, Wislon stopped dancing. He mopped his face but felt as though he wanted to mop his whole body. Having ground to something like a halt he gingerly took in his surroundings. His flat was no longer his flat.

Come to think of it, it hadn't really seemed like it all along. If anything, it resembled a room in a hospital. It wasn't one of those long wards that smelled of phlegmy-sweet orange juice and was full of coughing octogenarians, but one of the private ones not ordinarily available for public use.

He saw that the light in the room was multiple and uneven. One kind was a pallid glow which oozed through the blinds even though the narrow slats seemed to be firmly shut. Another one found its way in through a couple of broken slats and flooded the room with a sadistic artificiality. Finally, a bank of lights similar to ones that he had seen at the dentist's hovered over a bed he assumed that he had once slept in. Even though it wasn't 'his' bed, he knew that he had been *in* it.

Wislon felt vaguely excited by these mysterious intrusions, at not-quite-knowing. But he'd got no business to feel that, had he? His mind recalled Grandma Needy's death in a hospital a few years ago. Apparently, the doctors had just given up on the old woman and stopped putting stuff in her. In any case, she probably didn't want it. The point was, the room Wislon was in had an obscure medical smell in it. It was the kind of smell that he associated with trying to disguise what would otherwise be a much worse smell. The conjunction of the two bred a fuggish, distasteful neutrality.

It was then that Wislon noticed he was wearing a white smock-type thing that seemed to be manu-factured from toilet paper substitute. He noted that there was no plastic bracelet around his wrist, but the

184

awareness of smock, bed and Grandma Needy suddenly made him feel dreadful. Worse than all this was a sharp, throbbing sensation in his groin. No. It was probably more than a sensation if not yet a constant pain. The way things were going, however, he didn't feel that he could reasonably discount anything. Especially anything bad.

He dared not look underneath the smock although he knew that something was seriously wrong in that department. There was a pulsing and a slow vibration that Wislon could not recall having experienced on previous occasions. There was something foreign down there and, on the whole, he really didn't want to know what it was. Consciousness; awareness; knowledge; these were the things he wanted to avoid. His mind was burdened with a compulsion to understand it all, and a compulsion to get away from the compulsion to understand it all.

He stood paralysed by the half-knowing (or was it the half-not-knowing?), too afraid to move, his feet as useless as a couple of smashed crabs. The wiring inside him was suddenly all wrong. The various sources of light hurt him, but at least they stopped him looking at anything worth looking at.

A twangy thudding in his head brought him to a more stable consciousness. The music to which he had been listening drifted quietly back and his feet decided they could manage something like a dance again. Wislon's body rocked awkwardly for a few moments and then the spasm in his groin subsided.

It was then that he became aware of a faint noise from the other side of the window. He broke his rolling gait and walked carefully over. Before he touched the blind he knew that something was wrong. However, it did not prevent him from twisting it open. A clean light immediately bored into the room. The blind's slats broke it into a series of symmetrical rays. The atmosphere was noir. Once his eyes became accustomed to the light, Wislon could make out a number of faces crowding at the window. He recognised Zasu Pitts and Tempe Pigott. Raymond Doughty was there with Virgil Young. Fat Mike, Tony Tuesby and the rest of the boys from the office had also come along for a look. No Amy, of course. No women at all, apart from the weird sisters. They must have witnessed the whole performance of 'West Indian Pancake'. He snapped the blind shut. That was when Wislon woke up.

Glancing at his watch as he woke, Wislon noticed that it was seven a.m. He always opened his eyes at that time no matter what he had done the night before or what time he had gone to bed. In truth, of course, he had rarely ever done anything the night before. And he went to bed at more or less the same time. Whatever, it was good to know that his dream was entering into the spirit of things and co-operating with his biology.

He lay on the sofa for a few more minutes listening to the rain that had started up some time during the last hour. He imagined the apocalyptic sky waiting outside and gently mauled the cushion his head was resting on. His body was trying to deal with a number of sensations which were all happening at the same time. Its internal kicks and shudders told him of its discomfort. The sound of thunder made up his mind and he rolled energetically from the sofa and on to the floor.

Wislon walked to the bathroom and sat delicately on the toilet. He tended to sit whenever he could, disliking the view from a standing position. In theory, he had a choice of views, but in practice it never worked out like that. Anyway, here again everything was functioning normally. He was so regular that Wislon occasionally wondered whether it might not be abnormal. His movements were as reliable as the equator.

Back in the main room he checked the curtains but did not open them. He preferred the dark – they were only torn apart on dark winter afternoons. Summer was nightmarish.

It was at this point that Wislon remembered his dream and placed his hands over his face. In part, he was overcome by the fact of the recollection and that the reality of the dream even existed. In part, he cringed at the thought of having been discovered. Then, he stood and listened to the rain again.

Normally, he would now have made his bed, scuffing and rumpling his duvet into freshness. Today he avoided the bedroom and neatly folded the blanket on the sofa before stowing it in a cupboard in the hall.

Wislon made himself a bowl of muesli and poured himself a tall glass of chilled mineral water. He didn't go near the taps. The stuff you got from them tasted like bile. Nor was this surprising, he thought, when you knew where it had been, where it had come from, who it had been through. Before taking his austere tray from the kitchen into the other room he went to the bathroom again and ran a bath. Although the water was scalding, it drained from the tap in a dissenting, unwilling dribble. It would be twenty minutes before he could clamber in.

He sat on the sofa eating his breakfast and watching early morning television. Saturday morning and there was a repeat run-down of this week's chart-toppers. Wislon saw a group of four boys called something like Boys Galore or Boy Party. They were bouncing around to a dumb mechanical thump and wore white shirts which flapped loose to reveal a quartet of corrugated wash-board stomachs. No matter how violently the boys thrashed their bodies, those stomachs stayed rigidly in place. Their faces were pretty to the point of being feminine and their skins were black, but not emphatically so. In all aspects of their existence – gender, race, colour and dress – the Boys were busy having it both ways. Wislon switched channels and watched as a nondescript fashion disaster pointed to a squadron of rain clouds banking over Scotland before shifting down to Birmingham. 'That's all, so have a nice day,' he eventually said. Wislon concentrated on his muesli and searched in vain for a currant.

He used to have a pair of scales in the bathroom. That was when he *knew* what his weight was going to be. These days he wasn't so sure. He certainly didn't want to know if he wasn't sure. His thin, obscurely paunched body had not been behaving itself recently. It looked the same, but sometimes he wondered where all the weight had gone. At other times, he wondered where he was hiding it.

Wislon slipped out of his dressing gown, ducked the mirror and climbed into the bath. The tap was still slobbering and spitting. He surveyed the small collection of pots and tubs on the shelf and then lay back in the water, welcoming its elemental, scorching heat. His body shrank and raged against the temperature. This was true indomitability. The act of stretching brought thoughts of Amy. He had done what he could for her and now she looked peaceful enough. Still, it continued to bother him. Here was the past, slowly descending on him like black smoke. He had ignored it before so why should it bother him now? Wislon did the only thing he could and thought of Armitage. To one on his back in the dark it seemed the only thing to do. Even now, he supposed, *she* would understand.

Since the time when Armitage had fallen asleep and not stayed the night, Wislon's relationship with her had continued much as before. True, the handholding was perhaps more firm and the kissing was occasionally on the ardent side – but that was about it. Armitage behaved as if nothing in particular had happened, suggesting neither willingness nor reluctance. Perhaps *nothing* was exactly what had happened. He didn't like to make too much of the incident for fear of being tiresome. He wasn't sure that Armitage liked the idea of issues being raised. Besides, Wislon knew that he was a trundler and a loper, a lethargic mover in the wake of circumstances and a determined non-shaker. He reckoned he could get away with calling her 'a girlfriend'. But *his* girl-friend? And what about all the other things – being a couple, a pair, an item? He knew that she saw other men who were always referred to in evasive ways as 'colleagues' or people who were met 'through work'. He rarely discovered their names and even when one was offered he was never certain that it was the truth. Armitage did not lie, she simply concealed. Wislon realised that this elusiveness was one of the things that kept him interested. Of course, there was also her vigorous beauty and apparent perfection. After all, if you didn't know very much about someone why *couldn't* they be perfect?

It was the plateau thing again. The relationship was stuck and needed small prods and tugs to knock it on to other levels. Actually, it needed a lot more than tugs and prods, especially small tugs and prods. But he had to start somewhere. Wislon didn't mind the idea of a plateau and felt sure it was just a matter of finding the right one. He cut down on the number of films he took her to and built up the meals. He rang the changes and tried varieties of Indian, Chinese, Burmese, Mexican, Spanish, North Ameri-can, Thai, Vietnamese, French, Polish, Italian and Japanese. He followed this up with some unlikely dishes from Finland, trips to an Australian restaurant and a café that served specialities from the Faroe Islands. Finally, when all else had failed, he tried

British food. And when food didn't get him anywhere he moved on to ballet, then jazz and finally sport. He started at what he thought was the safe end of the market – volleyball, netball, basketball and, when Torville and Dean were doing 'Favourites on Ice', ice-skating. Going up-market, he experimented with horse-racing and show jumping. Then down-market with speedway, cycle speedway and roller hockey. He considered and rejected angling. Mostly it was Wislon who paid, though occasionally Armitage would not only buy the tickets but also take him for a meal afterwards. Wislon noted that these occasions invariably coincided with his own restlessness about the money situation. He reasoned that she knew exactly when and how to placate him.

With some desperation he asked her to a football match. Surprisingly, she agreed with enthusiasm. 'Oh yes. Daddy used to take me all the time. Let's go on Saturday.'

Wislon had been a few times when he was at school. He didn't like the game very much, though aspects of his liking for low-life now made the going seem less of a chore. And with Armitage accompanying him he indulged in a rare feeling of optimism. He even began to look forward to it.

Sitting in the new stand, Wislon searched the programme for Birmingham's results during the season. He found that their fortunes were at a particularly low ebb. Despite some good wins over the last month or so, they were in a lowly division. He saw that all the games seemed to be against teams from northern towns associated with important railway junctions or those from seaside resorts in the south. He certainly didn't recognise any of the names as being those of football teams.

'Yah roobish. Yah fookin' roobish,' someone shouted. The voice was sitting behind them and Wislon gave a cautious glance to see that it belonged to a large man with a stack of chicken pies and a plastic beaker of Bovril.

Wislon leaned across to Armitage and put on a jovial voice. 'He'll have fun at half-time.' He flicked his neck backwards with what he hoped was a jocund flourish, willing it more or less in the direction of the pies.

'No. No he won't,' replied Armitage impassively.

'Oh. Why not?'

'Because he's a she.'

Wislon glanced round and took in the short hair, bomber jacket and scarred face. He looked again. Other than the top of the head, there was certainly no stubble or any other real evidence of shaving. Both ears were pierced and a pair of reasonably delicate horse-shaped earrings dangled from them. The voice came to him again. Not high, but not low either. Difficult to say. In any case, the voice had lost its purity and was curdled by large quantities of mucus. No doubt the lungs were well and truly kippered.

'I'll take your word for it,' said Wislon peevishly.

Whenever Birmingham attacked everyone stood up. It gave the illusion of expectation and generated excitement. Soon it became clear that the people at the back only stood up because the people in front had already done so. Perhaps they were genuinely excited, but it was difficult to tell. No one seemed to get upset with the people who had stood up so Wislon kept quiet. Birmingham did quite a lot of attacking and he found himself standing up, sitting down and then doing nothing and becoming irritable.

'Want some pie, mate? I got too many.' Wislon turned round and offered a watery smile.

'Yes. Please,' said Armitage, before he could refuse. The girl with the shaved head broke off a large segment of damp pastry and handed it over.

'Thanks.'

'Yam welcoom.'

There was something sticky on the lip of his seat and now it was stuck to him. At half-time, Wislon went to the Gents, but only to wash his hands. As far as the other thing was concerned, he had organised himself very carefully about an hour before meeting Armitage. He had strict rules about public urinals and never used them. In the Gents, he found sinks routinely ripped from the walls, paper towels lying in puddles of urine and an orderly row of smashed mirrors. Meanwhile, Armitage had simply given up her trip to the Ladies. A slow-moving queue at least forty yards long slithered out of the entrance. Wislon and Armitage beat a path back to their seats. She pointed to a shortish man on the opposite side of the ground. A small section of the ground had been partitioned off from its surroundings by a low wall. 'That's where the directors sit. The managing director's a woman.'

'It doesn't seem to be very full,' Wislon observed. 'Don't they like football?'

'Not all of them. See that one there, in the middle.' Wislon nodded and peered across dutifully at a unit of sheepskin coats. The man in the middle was noticeably smaller than the others and had a luminous orange tan. Wislon thought of Faith Dawkins. 'He owns the club,' said Armitage.

Looking around the ground, Wislon was aware of the depth of the divide between the outside world's toughness and the softness he felt was inside most people. A long time ago, he had believed that the closeness and closedness of the home was also soft, but he had learned that this was not so. His home had eventually given up trying. The stadium's heaving, violently packed multitude was both hunched and loud. Its unhealthiness was picked out by the stern glare from the floodlights in the bloody-minded, thundery, slushy brown afternoon air. One section was set aside for the elderly, and from his seat Wislon could see their beaten-up old domes, vulnerable and fragile and bony and liver-spotted, and their sinewy necks which bred the wispy out-crops of careless shaving. Something had happened to the scaffolding of their faces. Some flopped half-heartedly forward on their walking sticks, vaguely attending to the football and the rest of the crowd. It was clear to Wislon that they had simply stopped trying not be soft and had retreated hopelessly and terminally back inside themselves.

After the game, Armitage insisted on buying a blue and white scarf and a large T-shirt with a blue bulldog printed boldly on the front. As they walked back to his car, Wislon took in the sheer diversity of the crowd for the first time. A pungent lot they are too, he thought. Old gummy men, clusters of suited estate agents, early seventies bovver boys, ex-convicts, fat suburban businessmen, junkies, taxi-drivers, men in blue wigs, small girls and pubescent boys all thronged through the gates together. There was claustrophobia but no panic. He observed a group of about five hundred particularly foul-mouthed supporters as they poured into the foyer of a nearby bingo hall. Wislon thought it a strange choice until the group launched a sudden attack on an unsuspecting pack of 'away' supporters, clattering and whooping through the double doors and fire exits. For a few seconds, Wislon thought he heard the undeveloped chants of 'Zulu-Zooolu-*Zoooloooo*.'

'Better hurry,' he said nervously, and guided Armitage by the arm.

The Metro was parked safely enough about a mile from the ground. A small boy was standing next to it when they arrived. 'That's five pound, mister,' he said.

'What for?' Wislon asked.

'Minding your car. Me and me mates.' Eight or nine other boys then hove into view. They were aged between eight and eighteen. Wislon worked out that even the youngest would probably be too much for him. He observed a tattoo on the boy's arm depicting a dog devouring what looked like a small rat.

'Thank you very much,' said Wislon. He fished a crumpled five-pound note out of his back pocket and did a quick calculation about the cost of the whole trip. He winced slightly as he handed it over.

On the drive back to her flat, Armitage asked Wislon whether he actually liked football. The question caught him off guard. 'Yes. Of course. I mean, bits and pieces.' And then, 'No. Not really. Not at all.'

'So why did we go?'

Because, thought Wislon, it's my way of cheating and inventing, of producing someone who can stand in front of you. It was part of a plot in my heart which was designed to disguise the fact that I am one of those people who feels no strength in himself and who has to become an artist, an inventor of the self. Because, after all, isn't this what everybody else does? Aren't we all architects and authors of bearable performances, desperately attempting to enrol everybody else in the make-believe? The strongest and most successful are able to out-cheat and out-perform the rest of us − and they sign up the most people. That's how they become powerful. That's what it's all about − to get others on your side, to enlist others into a version of 'yourself' and what seems to be real. Because I thought you might like football and might like me. Who cares if I don't like it? In terms of the world − with its banks and theatres and organisations and institutions and politicians and cities and armies and prisons and so on − it's not a big cheat. You can't even call me a successful inventor or artist. I hang around at the edges.

But Wislon dared not say any of this. Instead, he looked guilty and made a point of avoiding Armitage's glance.

'Didn't you like it?' he said moodily.

'Yes. I like football. But you weren't to know that. You don't even like crowds. I'm not sure that you like people.' She opened her eyes rather wider than usual. For a few moments, she seemed like a teacher about to tell him off for being mischievous. He quite liked that look.

Maybe he should tell her all about low-life. There was something compelling about the simultaneous allure of and resistance to the unwashed, the tarnished, the uncivilised and the sullied, the jazz of humanity. In this respect, disgust was actually attractive and even necessary, Wislon thought. Instead, he made up a lie about atmosphere and said something about the notion of a crowd denying the possibility of people. 'It's just a crowd,' he said, 'just a crowd. No more than that.'

They had reached her flat. Wislon brought the Metro to a steady halt beneath the cool glow of a street light. Armitage looked at him for a few moments and then reached for the top button of her coat. As she did so, she picked up Wislon's flaccid hand and tucked it neatly inside the opened flap. She guided it underneath the blouse and then held it under her breast with a gentle cupping motion.

Wislon smiled artificially. 'Does this mean you like me?' was all he could manage.

'What do you think?' Armitage replied.

He felt a gentle thud from behind his forehead. 'I'm not sure.'

'Oh, Wislon. Bloody hell.'

'What?'

'Nothing.'

She kept her hand with his for a few moments longer before taking it back, opening the car door and disappearing into the gloom.

After the bath, Wislon dressed and listened to the radio. Bombs were exploding in the West Bank and there had been an air crash somewhere in eastern Europe. An unidentified plague had broken out in southern India and there were the usual famines neatly spread around Africa. A part of Wislon re-joiced in these reports. They confirmed his own well-being in the universal run of things. In Bir-mingham, probably even in Tailbush Road, his stock was not that high. But *globally*? You could probably put your money on him when you considered the wider picture. Just listen to what was going on out there.

Alternatively revived and ashamed, he had not yet been through to his bedroom. It was unusual for him to wear the same clothes for a second day but he didn't feel quite ready for Amy. At least he now knew where he would be going. It would probably only be for the weekend. After that? He would see. He wanted routine, but who knew what would happen before Monday.

Quickly and efficiently, he made ready to leave, moving around the small flat like a nervous rat. He considered and dismissed the absurd possibility of a disguise and rummaged through the contents of the kitchen cupboard before reassuring himself that it was only for a couple of days. He picked and rejected an old leather suitcase that had acquired a strange smell.

Soon, he marched confidently into his bedroom with two plastic bags and carefully loaded them with an assortment of socks, underpants, shirts, jeans and a spare pair of shoes. He didn't look at Amy and held his breath for the thirty seconds or so that the operation took. The room was still in darkness. On the way out he glanced down momentarily and picked out a pale oval face. Its features were inanimate and strange. It was no longer Amy.

Without hesitating, Wislon made for the front door. He had gone past the telephone and was considering the answer machine when the phone started to ring. Ignoring its plaintive urgency, he bent down and unclipped its lead from the connecting socket. It was now exactly seven-fifty a.m. and time to be on his way. He opened the door and looked out on to the landing. There was an uncharacteristic and total silence. Nobody was up. The sleeping pills had clearly done for Doughty what Zasu Pitts and Tempe Pigott had done for themselves. As he turned back to close the door cautiously behind him, Wislon took in his flat with a single disarming gaze. He was both cheered and repulsed by what he saw. Its homely shabbiness, the toilet base's tendency to leak, the odd stains on the tiled kitchen surfaces, the disquieting patches and chips on the paintwork. Such imperfections were both familiar and unsavoury. They reminded him of his own body's dirty load.

Whatever, he knew where he was going and turned to start the journey.

Wilson arranged his cargo in the Metro's boot and was immediately impressed by the complete absence of Amy. He pulled away and drove with some sedateness. Although it was barely eight on a Saturday morning, the roads were already swollen with eager learners and large German cars pounding with inner music and being driven at high speeds. Wislon resisted the horn, gave way, waved on, and politely asked himself what they were all *doing* on the roads. What he wanted to do, of course, was something entirely different. He wanted to wind down his window and holler obscenities, cut up, fuck up, and beat away. *Come on!* But not this morning. He kept calm and as the traffic thinned he depressed the Metro's indicator and turned on to the Soho Road. The shops and market stalls were getting ready for the day. Crinkled shutters were being hoisted with a grating clatter. When the shopkeepers weren't worrying about theft or vandalism, they had to contend with starting up, going bankrupt and changing hands. Rents and rates had doubled, trebled and quadrupled over the last few years. The rapid changeover of shops and the giddying variety of goods, foods and religions made the road mutable, plastic and even sexy.

A blast of truck horn vaporised Wislon's thoughts. He slowed, did the thing with the gears and timed it to roll across a set of traffic lights at the instant they greened. The Hockley Flyover took him past the Jewellery Quarter which lay below and to his right.

200

The Metro churned towards Snow Hill Station. Once a glamorous homage to steam, it had been turned into a Gothic car park before being demolished and then brutishly rebuilt when the line to Smethwick reopened. It was now surrounded by a cluster of glass towers that were still only knee-high to their Manhattan uncles. Buildings appeared, were modified, abused and taken down. It was difficult to relate to the city other than as a series of objects and surfaces. Wislon thought he rather liked this renewable strangeness which had a logic and sexuality all of its own. For him, it was better than nostalgia and permanence.

He swung the car to the left, past the fire station and the complex of underpasses that oozed between the high-rise chaos of Aston University. A little further and he came to the loop of roads that surrounded the Bull Ring. Wislon remembered his father taking him there, buying fish and chips and lifting him on to the merry-go-round that could be seen from the road. Neither shop nor ride now existed. The Bull Ring motif was a large but ill-conceived mosaic of a charging bull. As a child, Wislon had read it backwards, perceiving its whiplash tail as a head, the ensemble as a dinosaur. He could just remember a thirty-foot King Kong with abnormally long fingers being placed in the Bull Ring. It was meant to emphasise the similarity between Birmingham and New York where the film *King Kong* was shot. Wislon supposed that it was this statue, with its red eyes and absurdly grasping arms, that had initiated his own interest in the cinema. The fibreglass monkey had been routinely smothered with graffiti, attacked with steel bars and set on fire. Dogs regularly relieved themselves on it. Eventually it was hauled off to a car showroom on the Stratford Road: 'The King Kong Kar Ko'. Its move signalled a loss of hope. Wislon had been upset at its disappearance but it prepared him for the regular displacements in his life over the next fifteen years. He learned not to trust. A letter in the *Birmingham Post* had suggested that 'maybe we are like gorillas, shy, retiring, living in dark tunnels carved out of the jungle but immensely dangerous when roused'.

From the Bull Ring, Wislon headed the Metro towards Edgbaston, passing the county cricket ground, Armitage's flat, and then following the route to her parents' house. Instead of turning into that road, he continued on to King's Heath. He recalled the words of a Cliff Richard song, from a film he had made in Birmingham. It was the only film he had made there. It was probably the only film anyone had ever made there. 'Now I believe that you're a tough town and that's the way I like 'em/Concrete City I'm not easily thrown.'

Wislon also remembered that King's Heath was where Jeff Grossman – a haemophiliac and HIV carrier – had allegedly infected a number of local women after unprotected sex. He wondered what Cliff would have made of it. He reached forward for the bag of wine gums he kept in the glove compartment.

Two years after the Jeff Grossman incident, Wislon had spent a week reviewing life-insurance policies for women in south Birmingham. Even though he was well known as an HIV carrier, women had still been queuing up to sleep with him. The story had only become newsworthy because someone from South Birmingham Health Authority had telephoned the *Birmingham Post*. The *Sun* had published a family tree of potential victims encompassing thirty people. The number of requests for AIDS tests in the West Midlands rose by a third. A number of women who had slept with someone called Jeff around that time contacted an AIDS helpline and the name 'Jeff' took on almost mythical proportions. For a short time King's Heath had been of national interest. Jeff-postman, Jeff-bus-driver, Jeff-salesman, Jeff-police-man, Jeff-teacher, Jeff-labourer, Jeff-cashier and Jeff-jeweller all had their moments. Then, at least for a month or two, they had had their moments and would subsequently have to work very hard to have any more of them.

Now, and especially at that still time in the morning, King's Heath had reverted to middling towniness. The High Street was all Argos, bingo and Boots. By way of dignified and nostalgic remembrance, the Hare and Hounds offered evenings of jazz, folk music, real ale and no Sky TV. Jake Thackeray always seemed to be playing there. Next to the blue circles and squares that patterned the new shopping centre, it amounted to little more than an awkward conscience. Jeff Grossman probably wouldn't have drunk in the Hare and Hounds. Even Cliff Richard would most likely have avoided it.

Once, Wislon had been taken to one of the

family-owned clothes shops along this stretch. His father had been keen to economise. About every six months, usually coinciding with a birthday or Christmas, Wislon's wardrobe of shame was speedily and crudely replenished. Cheap and baggy rectangles of brown wool and fearsome lengths of cotton had been scooped up and quickly bought. Later on, Wislon was somehow squeezed into the various purchases. Either that or they were folded and clamped around his body. He was never allowed to try them on for size first. He often felt that he was hiding in the middle of a badly made paper dart. The shop was called Dudley's. Then it became a Job Centre, but that had been boarded up for the past six months or so.

Chewing contentedly on a fistful of gums, Wislon did not allow the memories to affect his concentration at the wheel of the Metro or his resolute sense of destination. Away from the managed heat of the city, King's Heath seemed no more than a place of cold bustle. Bringing the car to a sharp halt at a red light, Wislon sat back in his seat. A neat woman with a canvas shopping bag looped over her arm glared and shouted as she crossed in front of him. He wondered at the manners of some people.

Sitting there, he recollected a sci-fi story where everyone lived underground in a controlled environment. There were shops, restaurants and offices like everywhere else, but you never needed to come up. Wislon rather liked the idea of an absolutely institutionalised existence – a calm, discreet place away from probing eyes, changing weather and harsh lights.

In the story, one man *never* came up. He maintained that so long as he stayed down, 'they' couldn't get at him. Down there, there would certainly be no need for traffic lights.

The lights changed and the Metro accelerated away, out of King's Heath and into the Maypole. Here there was a golf course and a green field which sometimes contained a horse. It was what local people called 'the country'. At a large roundabout, Wislon took the dual carriageway towards Evesham and Stratford. Most of the street lights had turned themselves off although a few still radiated a faint orange glow. Somewhere the sun was out. It wasn't very satisfactory but it was having a go. Some birds were also up and about, swooping and bending before becoming suddenly invisible. Wislon felt vaguely expectant and even began to wonder how his mother was. About another hour and he should be there. He leaned over to check the wine gums and took another handful, cramming them nervously into his mouth. He switched on the news and hoped for something bad.

— 6 —

Returning

Rumour had it that the city would go on for ever. Certainly Wislon was finding it difficult to shake off. It clung to the landscape, occasionally thinning for a few moments before reasserting itself. It was there in the noxious grass at the sides of the road and the buildings that gathered themselves together every mile or so. The ever-widening rings of tile and brick castles were serviced by giant foodstores and could be reached only by car. Wislon's mother had tried to put Birmingham behind her, but now it seemed to be reaching out to reclaim its own. She was safe for the moment, but for how long? Wislon steered the Metro along the dual carriageway that was required to hold everything together. He was not quite in Birmingham and not quite out of it. Really, he was not quite anywhere.

It was a landscape which seemed to move beyond the human scale, not built to be inhabited. Those who did the inhabiting, Wislon thought, did so almost by accident. Each housing estate eventually became an industrial estate, whether it wanted to or not. Soon, there would only be 'estates'. Endless repetitions of nondescript buildings merged solemnly into each other. Each had a forecourt for parking. Roads had been straightened out and nobody walked for the pleasure of it. No dogs met other dogs, no children ran into the road after other children, no women passed the time of day over gently rocked prams or buggies. The only grass around was on the verge beside the wide dual carriageway. There was no rural calm to be shattered. No sharp urbanity to wonder at and mischievously envy. Only the banal and the dull, occasionally interrupted by gawdy unimaginative logos drilled on to the corrugated shanks of commercial buildings. Even a bit of industrial soot would have been welcome, but this grey, casual jauntiness was numbing. Life – or what seemed to pass for life – was now conducted on the margins. And in each margin a few saplings struggled to get noticed and initially confident floral displays had given up or were in the process of giving up. Wislon knew how they felt and pressed the accelerator to the floor, not actually increasing his speed a great deal but causing the Metro to shudder and vibrate in a reassuring manner.

He watched the road and the fields and the buildings around him and found himself wishing for an accident or a fatality through reckless driving. Only something like this could put things in perspective. He knew all about the figures and statistics and distribution of accidents and the knowledge made him feel better.

He had not seen his mother since his father died,

but he still could not remember exactly how long ago that was. He knew where she lived now but had never visited her. As he thought about her, Wislon remembered that she had always seemed to be on the run. Although she had been quite well educated, a series of small-time jobs ensured that she never gained a proper foothold in life. She had worked as a secretary, a shop assistant, a research assistant and a cook. Wislon's father had been a manager in a car factory for twenty years and demanded that his wife always be available. She could not afford to do anything that might take her away from him. In many ways, she reasoned, she had been lucky to get out at all. She had to cook and sew and clean and open the door for him when he arrived home from work. At least he took the dog for its walk and fixed the cupboard in the kitchen. No, she could not be anywhere else that might take up too much of her time.

Sometimes, he would set her a test by not telling her that something should have been tidied away or cleaned. Then, over the next few days, he would watch her failing until his increasingly sullen mood indicated that something was wrong. He observed her failing at making the right kind of dinner or failing at mending the tear in his jacket or failing at getting up in the mornings. At that point, she would search frantically, trying to discover what had been left undone. Mr Needy never told her. When she did 'put things right' he would simply say, 'About time, too' or, 'I suppose you think that makes it all fine?' or, 'What about the times you haven't worked it out?'

Over the years, Wislon's mother had begun to assume that everything in life was an examination which she was bound to fail.

It had not always been like that. When his parents met they had fallen in love. Even though he could not swim, Mr Needy met Wislon's mother at a swimming pool. He enjoyed pushing her in and watching her swim strongly back to the edge. Occasionally, he would not allow her out of the pool and would hold her head under the water until it seemed wise not to do so any longer. She would come up gasping for air, desperate but smiling and always making a joke out of the betrayal. Wislon discovered all this from photographs and the stories that his parents sometimes told him about their courting days. They didn't tell him everything, but he soon learned to work out the rest. Mrs Needy loved to swim. Mr Needy never learned to swim. Soon, they stopped going to the pool altogether.

As a child, Wislon had wished that Birmingham was a city of water and that its inhabitants would have to find ways of living with the fact. He had often been told that he was born during a tremendous thunderstorm which had speeded up his mother's labour. Then and for the rest of his life Wislon had been punctual, impatiently forcing his head into the world at precisely the estimated time. It had been an easy birth, but when the midwife spread Wislon out on a pink towel to show Mr Needy he had turned his back in disappointment. Although it was impossible, Wislon felt he could still remember the moment and often reconstructed his father's blank, enraged face. Wislon did not understand his father's dismay. Maybe it was another test his mother was failing and nothing to do with him at all. Maybe it was the first test she ever failed. He wished he had been born with webbed hands and feet, even a mermaid's tail. Then his father could have thrown him back into the water and the two of them need never have seen each other again. Perhaps, after all, that would have been best. When the midwife had taken out her knife to sever the Gordian knot she could have stuck it into Wislon instead. He had revived the scene in his mind many times. The midwife would show the thick blade to his mother and she would nod tamely, imagining that the act would be painless and that it was what Mr Needy wanted. She couldn't be sure, but even then she was learning not to take chances.

After driving through Stratford and turning down a series of ever smaller roads, Wislon came to what he supposed was the village in which his mother lived. It was exactly the place that someone who was running away would come to. There was no railway station and, as far as Wislon could make out, no bus stop. The village was poorly signposted and hidden amongst a sprawling arrangement of other more obviously attractive neighbourhoods. Apart from the church, and in spite of the Cotswold stone, the buildings were drab and anonymous. Nearby was a waste disposal plant.

Wislon knew the address and eventually found

Honeysuckle Cottage where his mother lived. It was at the end of a row of squat terraced houses, a prosaic rebuttal of its picturesque name. He was not surprised. This was in keeping with his mother's character. Now, Wislon had also ceased to trust promises. Beyond the house, the road dipped and bent alarmingly before disppearing altogether around a corner. At night, it must be completely dark as the last street light was almost ten houses away. During the winter, Wislon thought, the dark probably came down like an axe. Even now, the disappearing road seemed gloomy and otherworldly. Without their leaves, heavy branches were still able to sling themselves across the road and cut out much of the light. In one of the unfenced fields running parallel a herd of deer shuffled about in an apologetic manner. You could not see them from the road as each side was bounded by a sharply rising bank of nettles and grass. Now and then, a low rumble could be heard as the deer stampeded across one field and into the next. There they would continue their silent grazing until another car or sudden sound startled them back in the opposite direction.

Wislon parked the Metro outside Honeysuckle Cottage. It almost seemed to be an offence to lock the door in this place but he did so out of habit. He knocked on the front door and waited a full minute before knocking again. There was no answer and he repeated the action twice more before accepting that his mother was not at home. Why should she be, he thought; I haven't told her that I'm coming.

Knowing that his mother was also a creature of

habit, Wislon made his way around to the back of the house and looked underneath the base of the dustbin. The spare keys were there, and he wiped the damp off them before going back to the front door and using them to gain entry.

Once inside, he looked around but did not turn on the light. Although the day was overcast and it was still raining, Wislon preferred to accustom his eyes to the dimness rather than break the mood by using the lights. Some say that people often take on the look of the furniture that they surround themselves with. Wislon recalled a neighbour in Birmingham who pushed weights and had a broad, powerful chest, yet whose legs remained strangely thin. Mr Needy always made a joke about drinking off that man's chest, but Wislon thought he resembled a heavy sideboard with ornate, curving legs. He needed a vase of flowers more than a decanter or a bottle of spirits. His mother's furniture, however, was plain and anonymous. It all harmonised together so that nothing impressed itself on the visitor. All was functional and unnoticeable until it was actually used.

Wislon wandered around the house for several minutes. It was not large and there were only two rooms on each floor. Curiously, the kitchen and dining room were below street level in a kind of converted cellar that gave on to the back garden. He reasoned that this must be to take account of the slope which the road immediately outside traced so dramatically. He also noticed that there were no photographs, no pictures and no telephone. He wondered where she called from on the rare occasions when they had spoken to each other over the past few years. In all its aspects, this was a house that was clinging to the edge of things. His mother did not want to be seen or disturbed. It seemed that she was as close to extinction as the living could possibly be.

Finding a chair in the small front room that opened on to the road, Wislon sat down and closed his eyes. For the first time that morning he began to feel tired. He dared not sleep but for thirty minutes or so his mind moved in and out of consciousness. Even now, he did not think very much about his mother. He was too self-obsessed to be particularly curious about other people. Nor did he feel es-pecially burdened by guilt when he thought about the last twenty-four hours. Contrary to what he had expected, guilt seemed to be light rather than heavy. It was also, he thought, important to keep guilt to yourself, to keep it inside. To release it would be like expelling air and he was even afraid that he might laugh.

While he was thinking, Wislon heard a key in the lock. He refocused his eyes on the door, sat up in the chair and prepared himself. Underneath his shirt, skin buckled and itched. His mother glided unobtrusively in, snapped on the light and immediately saw Wislon.

'You,' she said.

'Yes.'

'A surprise . . .' She walked over and bent down while Wislon strained his face up towards her. His lips brushed against her cheek which was moist and slightly cold to the touch. As she stood up again and moved away from him, he saw that she was dressed in shapeless folds of creamy linen which neither emphasised nor belittled her body. They simply shielded what lay beneath. Her eyes were set far back into their sockets and Wislon noted that despite their withdrawn hollowness, they were still black and alert. They darted about with a restless, febrile anxiety.

'I should have contacted you,' said Wislon, 'but you don't have a phone and I only really decided to come at the last minute.'

'Oh. I see.'

'So I couldn't write.'

'No. Of course not.' Her eyes fixed him with a violent intensity. It was clear to Wislon that she was not prepared to take anything at its face value. 'And are you staying?' she continued. 'I mean, staying for the night?' Her tone was neutral but dutifully considerate.

'If that's all right. And tomorrow – if that's possible.'

'Yes. Of course. I'd better go and air the bed.' Her mouth twisted slightly in the attempt to form a smile. The rictus was familiar to Wislon and he watched as she turned, fussed with something in her handbag and then silently ascended the stairs. Once she had gone, it was difficult to imagine that she had ever really been in the room. There was no trace or smell of her. Whilst actually there, she had been functionally present but had never impressed herself.

Over a cup of coffee about twenty minutes later, Wislon and his mother talked about nothing in particular. She did not ask why he had arrived. He told her he was still working in insurance. 'That's good,' she said. 'By the way, did you know I'd had my thyroid out?'

'No. Why didn't you tell me?' he asked, and looked with some concern at where he thought her thyroid might have been.

'Not worth it. It's not as gruesome as you might imagine. They do it with electricity or something, like burning it out. Lasers probably – they all are these days. Whatever. I was radioactive for a month or so, you know.'

She took a mouthful of coffee and snapped a digestive with a dramatic flourish. 'The cat knew. She wouldn't come near me for weeks. Funny that, isn't it?'

'Where is she now?' said Wislon, suddenly turning his head in all directions to see if she might appear.

'Dead. The dog up the road disembowelled her.'

'*No*,' he replied, without quite knowing why. His mother ignored him and seemed for a moment to be talking exclusively to herself.

'That's nature for you,' she went on, 'you can't blame the dog. He was only doing what was natural for him.'

They talked on for a short while before Wislon felt he ought to have a look at his room. His mother stayed downstairs attending to a series of domestic chores which took their cue from the neatly tabulated list pinned to a cork board above the fridge. She had already ticked off the first item, 'Go for a walk'. This accounted for her absence when Wislon had arrived.

As he walked up the stairs carrying the bag of

clothes that had been in the Metro, Wislon wondered if it was unusual that he and his mother shared the same lack of curiosity about each other's lives. It was true that they were primarily concerned with themselves but how had this happened? Had it always been this way?

She seemed less resigned than before, but this steeliness (if that's what it really was) had only been achieved at the expense of something else. Probably something quite important, Wislon thought. Curiosity? Compassion? Sympathy? Softness? *All* emotions? Mmmm. On second thoughts, he wasn't so convinced that his mother hadn't got it right. Or at least, was on the right track.

The bedroom was spartan except for a few objects which had the effect of stirring Wislon's memory. It was the first proper memory he had experienced for several years, powerful, embracing and somehow loaded. He stood still and put the bag down carefully on the floor. On the wall was a reproduction of a painting of Adam and Eve. It showed Adam offering an apple to Eve. Surprisingly, the background was a pinky-grey and not the usual luxuriant green. As a young child, Wislon had nailed the print to the wall of his own bedroom. He remembered Mr Needy entering the room with a brown paper parcel and offering it as a gift. Once unwrapped, he had asked, 'How can you tell which one is the man and which the woman?' and held it directly in front of Wislon's eyes. He had considered carefully, then offered, 'I can't tell. Neither of them is wearing clothes.' His father had taken the picture away and told him he could only have it back when he was able to supply the correct answer. Eventually, Wislon had passed the examination, retrieved the print and tacked it neatly on to the chocolate-coloured wall above his bed. Later, he learned that there were others in the series. *Elohim Creating Adam*, *Satan Exalting over Eve* and *God Judging Adam*. He had often asked for them as Christmas or birthday presents, but his father had always said, 'He who asks does not receive.' The trouble was, even when he didn't ask, Wislon didn't receive. Now, Adam and Eve were immediately before him again.

At university, he had once been in an audience watching a hypnotist. Some people were more susceptible than others. The hypnotist soon found out who they were. Once on stage, he asked them to regress and act as they would have done fifteen or sixteen years earlier. One immediately wet his trousers. Two suddenly became left-handed. Another was quickly sick. At that moment, as Adam and Eve stared out at him, Wislon remembered his own childhood. Was this how it came back, Wislon thought? Was this how the past caught up and got back at you? He saw himself surrounded by adults. It was something like a party except at parties you were meant to have a good time. He wasn't having a good time. Everybody was dressed strangely and there were no other children present. Either that or they had all gone home. They were safe eating their tea in their parents' houses. Wislon wanted to go home with them. Even though he was in his own home he didn't much want to be there. If he had been on stage with that hypnotist he would have followed home the person standing next to him. He didn't care if they wet their pants or wrote with the wrong hand.

Wislon stood by the bed and dropped his hands to his sides. He tried to imagine what it would have been like to go home with other children. He wanted to look in through the windows of their houses and see the uncomplicated cosiness of their lives. Closing his eyes, he tried to trace their steps through small streets and across locked parks. Soon, the images seemed less bright and began to fade from his mind. But the way had been shown and Wislon's mind made itself vulnerable to other reflections. He collapsed his legs, fell sideways on to the bed and allowed his mind to roam while the thick gloom of sleep closed around him. Maybe now he was concerned to find his place. If that was so, he also knew that, in time, he would find it.

Mr Needy arrived home from work clutching three small oblongs of paper.

'Guess what these are,' he asked Mrs Needy. 'Go on. Guess.'

Wislon's mother detected the note of confrontation behind the affable question. She did not want to disappoint her husband, so she smiled accommodatingly, even with a practised coyness, and said, 'I really don't know.' She tried to say it in the sort of way that suggested that she did know and was just playing a teasing game. She looked nervously around and took a step backwards as she spoke.

'Have a go.'

The last thing she felt like doing was having a go, but the order was sharp and unambiguous. She noted that her husband's suit needed dry-cleaning; there was an oil stain somewhere near the pocket.

'T-tickets,' she stammered.

'To the pantomime,' he confirmed. Mrs Needy was grateful to be spared the ordeal of a fuller grilling and managed what she thought was a genuine smile. It was a smile of relief and fear. The day was going well for her. During the afternoon she had sold a pair of expensive shears at the hardware store in which she worked.

'I knew you'd be pleased,' said Mr Needy, advancing across the living room and slumping heavily in his favourite green chair.

Wislon was also pleased when told the news. Apparently, there had been a chance of more tickets but Mr Needy had turned them down. He told Wislon, 'I thought a family outing, just for the family, would be best. We don't often go out together, do we?'

Wislon suspected that the real reason was not his father's sense of family. Certainly he had never considered Wislon or his mother at any other time. The Sunday afternoon drives with Grandma Needy wedged dolefully in the back seat of the blue Allegro were an obvious case in point. Over the years, they had covered most of the West Midlands with her unsmiling face staring uncomprehendingly out of the car window. She had a weakness for bubblegum and the only time Mr Needy ever stopped the car was to buy her more supplies. When they got home, it was always Mrs Needy who had to scrape the gum off Grandma's dentures with the fish knife. Nobody except Wislon's father wanted to go on these excursions, and that included Grandma. Still, nobody dared to complain and the afternoons usually subsided into an atmosphere of sullen politeness and near silence. Occasionally, Mrs Needy would say something like, 'That's a big factory' or 'I don't remember that being there last time we came this way', but she need not have bothered. Nobody else was really listening.

The real reason for the 'family outing', Wislon guessed, was his father's mean-mindedness. The car had been 'governed' so that it would only turn over at a rate which would guarantee the maximum mileage per gallon of petrol used. Wislon had seen the equation, carefully worked out in his father's book of mauve Basildon Bond notepaper. The other result was that nobody else was capable of driving the car without stalling it every fifty yards or so. His mother was a good driver, but since the Allegro had been neutered she had lost her nerve and had now given up driving altogether. Also, the heating in the house was set at a barely tolerable level. Likewise, the hot water had been fixed so that you could comfortably bath in water taken only from the 'red' tap. At every turn, Mr Needy headed off extravagance and waste, assuming (thought Wislon) that the restraint would be good for them all.

At the time, Wislon was friendly with a boy called Gerald who lived two doors away. He mentioned his friend's name to his father as somebody who could have taken a fourth ticket. A while ago, Gerald's parents had taken Wislon to see *Star Wars* at the New Street Odeon. As yet, the favour was unreturned. 'Not Gerald,' his father had replied. 'Oh no. Not Gerald. Not after what he did to that cat.' Wislon knew he was referring to the fact that Gerald had thrown next door's cat Jinx into a water barrel three years earlier. Although Jinx had been rescued, her front and back halves had moved independently of each other ever since. 'Absolutely *not* bloody Gerald.'

Thus, the gloss seemed to have been taken off the trip to the theatre before it had even started. Another thing worried Wislon: the pantomime was *Peter Pan* and yet a woman was playing the title role. She was well known as a mother of three in a popular sit-com in which she was always getting herself into scrapes. 'How can a woman be Peter Pan?' asked Wislon, 'she's not even a man, let alone a *boy*.' Mr Needy had taken it upon himself to explain that small boys weren't 'good enough actors' to take the part of Peter and that women were more like boys than men.

'Oh,' said Wislon.

'Nobody would believe it if a man pretended to be a boy . . . but a woman? That's different,' said his father expansively, staring nervously at the thermo-stat. It was cold outside and the boiler seemed to be making too much noise. 'I'll just go and check that,' he said, waving in the direction of the plastic disc on the wall.

While he was poking around in the cupboard underneath the stairs, his mother, who was in the kitchen, scribbled a note on some greaseproof paper and held it up. Wislon could only just read it from the other side of the room. 'DON'T BOTHER YOUR FATHER,' it said, and 'COME AND DO THE SPROUTS BEFORE HE HAS TO TELL YOU.'

On the evening of the pantomime, Wislon made an effort with his appearance. 'Don't be too long in that bathroom,' his father ordered. He washed his hair with a cheap brand of washing-up liquid and spent rather too long rinsing out the oily suds. He heard his mother fussing outside the door and imagined his father in the green chair pretending to read a book. He wiped the bathroom window thoroughly and then took a piece of toilet paper and dried the plug in the sink. On this occasion, he did not have to, but felt that it was a thoughtful touch. If his father should notice it might put him in a more compliant mood. One of Mr Needy's tricks to check that nobody had run any hot water without his permission or 'out of hours' was to check all the plugs for tell-tale droplets. Likewise, he would look for condensation on the window that even lukewarm water would cause as it rose into the cold air.

After he had finished with his hair, Wislon pulled it into some kind of shape, although the washing-up liquid generally caused it to bunch and dry in uneven clusters. He looked around the bathroom to check he hadn't left anything behind. The only toiletries were the multi-purpose washing-up liquid and a bottle of Hai Karate aftershave which he had bought for his father at Christmas three years ago. It

remained stubbornly unused although Wislon occasionally unscrewed the lid and patted the liquid on
to his face. He wondered what it would be like to
shave and thought it might be somehow ennobling.
He slipped into his clothes, which were various
shades of brown; the bottom bits were too tight and
the top flapped loosely like a sail. He somehow
engaged the two halves and worked them into a
presentable shape before going downstairs.

As they drove to the Alexandra Theatre at a steady
twenty-eight miles per hour, Mrs Needy pointed out
the landmarks. She always did this and, since there
was never anything new to see, Wislon suspected she
did it to fill the heavy silences. Mr Needy was not an
accomplished driver; even at a little under the legal
speed limit, he needed all his concentration. As they
went past the end of the road where his parents had
rented a flat immediately after their marriage, his
mother became nostalgic and regretted the changes
that had occurred. 'Those houses they put up in their
place. I'm sure they're very comfortable but they just
don't look like homes.' Mr Needy said something
about slums and how he thought it was a good job
that the old houses had been put out of their misery.
Mrs Needy could remember fishing on the canal, but
Mr Needy said there had never been any fish there.
Never. He was quite certain of the fact. 'Besides,' he
scoffed, 'you've never been fishing. You've never done
anything.'

They lived in Handsworth Wood which Wislon's
grandma had once described as 'the un-unposh bit of
Birmingham'. Although it bordered on Lozells and

Handsworth itself, Handsworth Wood had more trees, fewer dogs, fewer tramps, no students, no Blacks, no Indians and slightly wider roads. One of the houses had ivy growing up its side and there was even an antique shop nearby. People in Handsworth Wood were proud of not being in Handsworth and they certainly didn't go fishing in the canal.

When they arrived at the theatre, Mr Needy drove heedlessly past. He didn't like parking the Allegro in full view of other people and always made straight for the multi-storey. It involved a mile-long walk back to the Alexandra but at least parking was free after six p.m. The three of them were wrapped up tight against the flurries of snow which plunged and swooned around them. Wislon's top began to come away from his bottoms and he pulled his coat even closer about his body. His father told him to stop dawdling and nobody else spoke as they eventually trooped into the foyer with almost a minute to go before the curtain went up.

Although he wanted to go to the toilet, Wislon thought better of it. He certainly wanted to avoid anything like the disaster at *Mother Goose* three years ago when his father had vowed never to take him to a pantomime again. The year after that he had been asked whether he would prefer a Christmas present or a Christmas tree. Out of a wincing idealism he had gone for the tree, thinking it would be selfish to suggest anything else and deprive others of a seasonal atmosphere. No. He would not be going to the toilet before the interval.

There was a fair amount of seat-swapping when

225

they eventually found their places at the back of the stalls. A woman with a large amount of hair had taken root in front of Wislon and Mr Needy didn't like sitting next to a small boy who kept asking him how many 'half-times' there were likely to be.

'One, I expect,' he eventually replied.

'That's good because then I'll be able to get an ice cream. Do you think they got ice creams?'

Mr Needy beckoned to his wife and told her that she was better with that kind of drivel than he was and that she would be better placed in his seat. They changed over with some awkwardness. Wislon was now on the left, his mother on the right, with Mr Needy clumsily spliced between them.

The first act of *Peter Pan* came and went. Throughout, there was a constant line of children making their way to the toilets, treading on and pushing through and over the Needys' legs. On stage you could see the ropes and wires and pulleys whenever someone was meant to be flying. Sometimes the apparatus didn't work properly and one of the children on stage would skid and hop before eventually taking off vertically into the wings. One of the doors fell down. Wislon saw that his father was giggling to himself, his hand hiding his mouth in case anyone should see him.

During the interval, Mr Needy had a brandy and Mrs Needy a Babycham. Wislon's father liked to spoil himself on these occasions and even stretched to a chocolate tub when Wislon asked for one.

'Are you enjoying it?' he asked.

Wislon knew the routine. The question was another kind of test and he had to manage the correct response. There should certainly be immediate appreciation but the smile and the 'Oh yes. Thank you,' had to be fulsome rather than gushing. There was no doubt that Mr Needy could spot a fraud.

'Oh yes,' said Wislon, showing only a few teeth and pausing for thought just before he spoke. 'Thank you,' he added thoughtfully, and with what he hoped was just the right amount of emphasis.

'So what do you think it's about?' his father continued.

'Pardon?'

'You heard,' said his father. Mrs Needy picked at her pork scratchings and took another swig of Babycham. Her eyes fixed on a point in the middle of the ceiling and held it with a determined stare. Wislon thought she looked very symbolic. He wondered about the pantomime. There was clearly a bit about the wonderful world of childhood that was coming under threat. Tinkerbell and all her shining represented something indefinable about the life force. Captain Hook looked like the hippy across the road who had once got stuck in a wardrobe he was treating for woodworm. He had the same long curly hair. 'I don't trust him,' Mrs Needy had said. 'Each to his own,' Mr Needy had replied, partly to contradict her and partly because there was a part of him which fancied itself as unconventional. Mr Darling was obviously being played by the same actor as Captain Hook. Wislon could tell by his ears which were kidney-shaped and completely undisguisable. This was what really intrigued him.

In the end, he piped up, 'It's about good and evil.'

'Go on,' said Mr Needy suspiciously.

'Captain Hook is evil and Mr Darling is good and yet they're really the same.'

'Mmmm,' Mr Needy replied, and furrowed his eyebrows dramatically.

They took their seats for the second half. Wislon worried about the pantomime. It seemed to suggest that as Darling and Hook were the same then it stood to reason that *all* fathers were out to kill their children. On the other hand, perhaps all bad men really wanted to be good fathers. It was an impossible dilemma. Wislon looked at his father. His impassive face betrayed no emotions except boredom. Wislon, however, knew that a lot was happening backstage. He didn't yet hate his father but he wondered if he disliked him. It was an odd feeling.

Towards the end of the pantomime some Indians began to thump a set of tom-tom drums. Tinkerbell started to die but was then brought back to life as the audience cheered and clapped for her. By this, they were supposed to express a belief in fairies. Even though Tinkerbell was clearly just a powerful torch light that was being shone by a fat man dressed in black, everybody joined in, even Wislon's mother. He supposed that she embraced any opportunity to be happy or animated. Peter Pan said, 'She says . . . she says she thinks she could get well again if children believed in fairies.' Wislon closed his eyes and wished while children and parents all around him hooted and clapped. He also closed his eyes when he prayed at night, though he would say his prayers very quickly and in a whisper as if afraid that someone might be listening. He thought of Captain Hook, ticking clocks and a hungry crocodile. He also thought of The Never Land. Most of all, Wislon concentrated on the fact that his father had had his hand near the top of his leg for several minutes. The grip of palm and thumb was tight and unyielding, but the fingers caressed and smoothed his thigh.

Wislon looked at his mother who was clapping and smiling and full of Babycham, pretending to be happy. Mr Needy's fingers were dancing and Wislon was confused. He knew something was wrong. The fingers went higher and their movements became less abstract and more deliberate. He imagined his father's hand as a hook about to work its way under-neath his skin, piercing and ripping it open. Peter Pan said, 'Clap your hands and Tinkerbell will live.' Wislon clapped his hands once or twice in a fumbled attempt at the real thing. He kept his eyes tightly shut. A small girl behind him shouted, 'Don't let Tink die!' and started to cry. Wislon held back the tears but couldn't look at his father.

Wislon was nine years old and didn't much care for pantomimes. He smelled brandy and listened to Peter Pan's continuing exhortations. 'If you believe clap your hands.' Wislon and his father were the only people in the theatre not clapping.

When he woke up, Wislon saw that the room was semi-dark despite the curtains still being open. He looked at his watch. It was half past two. He must have slept for nearly five hours. As his eyes grew more used to the dimness, he noticed a neatly cut square of paper on the bedside table. The words on it said, 'WHEN YOU WAKE UP, MAKE YOURSELF A CUP OF TEA AND HELP YOURSELF TO BISCUITS. I'LL BE BACK AT ABOUT FIVE O'CLOCK.' There was also a note on the other side of the paper which read, 'YOUR SKIN HAS GOT NO BETTER. I'LL BRING SOME FRUIT FROM THE SHOPS.'

As he brought his body upright and perched himself on the edge of the bed, Wislon was aware of the skin on his back expanding outwards once more. After being packed tightly against his bones it was now resuming its normal shape and texture. He felt its pockets of grumbling and discontent at the disturbance.

Wislon kept the lights turned off, alert to the darkness outside caressing the cottage. In the dark, he felt as if he was in disguise. Sometimes he wondered whether he depended on the darkness, which contained whatever you cared to put into it. For the second time since he had arrived in the village, he thought of Amy. From Dr Small he knew something about the body's functions after death. What was it he had said? 'Even when people are dead, they never do what you want.' But Amy had been so accommodating and he was certain that she would not be too difficult now, either. All the stuff about eyeballs liquefying and skin blistering and discolouring surely wouldn't be happening. Not just yet, anyway. He recalled a television programme which had shown the processes of deterioration in a corpse over a period of several days. Nails and hair still grew, but everybody knew that. Then, odd gases moving about in the body might lead to burping and farting as they made their ways out of the carcass.

Wislon understood that he had killed Amy, but he could not think too directly about what he had done. It wasn't that the fact was incomprehensible, more that certain aspects of the enterprise were difficult to grasp. Wislon was not sure what it all signified or how it represented him. As yet, he wasn't getting the whole picture. There was something else at the back of his mind. It writhed and squirmed but was kept from full consciousness by a curtain of fine gauze which had descended through his head. The Never Land. What had happened was no more than a piece of florid fiction, persuasively descriptive but some-how distant. He didn't feel that it was not *not* wrong. That was about as far as he could stretch it. It wouldn't quite do, but then again, it wouldn't quite not do, either. For the moment, it was the best he knew. Wislon screwed his eyes tight and rubbed his scalp. He was suddenly reminded of how he'd felt at the theatre with his father's hand rubbing the inside of his thigh and touching the extremity of his crotch. And yet, he could not bring himself to admit that these things contained 'intention'. Now he was no longer himself again. Difficult to think but easy to feel. Wislon was no longer himself. He lay down on the bed once more and brought his legs close up to his chest. His eyes stayed open. They watched the inky, empty air around him whilst his ears paid attention to the silence outside. He controlled his body and grew afraid of any sudden surges or unexpected tremors.

On Sunday, Wislon and his mother walked into the village. His mother had been to church earlier in the morning. Wislon could not remember her ever going when they lived in Birmingham. His father had dis-approved of religion and he had never considered that his mother might believe differently.

The village contained a small number of shops, including a general store and a cobbler's. Its main street was framed by two pubs. One (his mother assured him) was for the local working men while the other was for tourists and city people who were staying for the weekend.

They walked side by side through the village before looping back behind the mill pond, a row of cottages and a scruffy bowling green. His mother barely spoke. Once, she pointed to a large cat that she claimed was almost twenty years old. 'He still catches things, you know. Last week, I found him rolling a squirrel's skull around the school car park. I think he even ate the brains. Only the tail and the two back feet were left and he'd lain them out in a kind of symmetrical pattern. At the time, I wondered what he'd done with the front feet. Maybe they just taste better.'

Wislon congratulated himself on visiting his mother. He thought that she was no longer curious about people or events. The energy needed for such interest had long gone. Occasionally, she would recount a story which showed the lengths she would go to in order to make the most trivial discoveries about people or animals. But this was not the same as curiosity. The cat and the squirrel was a case in point. After the initial sighting, she had watched the cat obsessively for several weeks, determined to discover what he did with squirrels' front legs. After almost a month of catching nothing, the cat had lain down in front of the school gates, panting heavily and looking as if he was about to die a quick and un-explained death. Soon afterwards she saw him trotting up the lane with a large rat clamped between his teeth.

His mother also knew all about the woman who used a vacuum cleaner to remove the dirt on her driveway and the man who thought he was Winston Churchill. She knew about all these people without actually being *curious* about them. Neither was she happy or unhappy. Wislon recognised that in his mother, motivation was a spent force. In her quiet house in the hidden village, Wislon's mother had successfully disguised the fact that she was alive. Life had been reduced to function and become a wholly mechanical business.

As they rounded the bowling green, Wislon's mother told him about the retired journalist who had stripped naked last winter before doing four circuits of the green while the club social was in full swing. Then he had bitten Mrs Thrift who did Tuesdays and Thursdays at the post office. Her

233

shoulder had ached for a week and the teeth marks took a while to go away. Although she'd kept an eye on him for a couple of months after the incident, Mrs Needy said that he'd never repeated the be- haviour. She marked it down as a 'strange occurrence' and said something about there being no explanation for some people and that it was better left at that.

Wislon looked across the bowling green and saw a series of grey clouds scudding towards them. A note outside the tea rooms said that they were shut between November and April. Inside, unused bottles of salt and pepper stood ready on green plastic table cloths waiting for spring. A man with slightly hunched shoulders moved around heavily inside.

You start believing yourself when you tell yourself things. You even begin to trust yourself. If you look hard at your reflection in the mill pond you will see distortions of your face. You need not worry. The distortions are what you might become in the future. You belong to your mother and father. You don't like it, but what happens to you is foretold by them. Their past will become your future.

You seem to understand that.

The surface of the pond has the appearance of polished jet, like a black mirror.

When you ask yourself how it is that order and contentment have turned to uncertainty and panic, that is where you must look.

You believe it and begin to trust yourself.

Back at his mother's cottage, Wislon went into the bathroom and locked the door behind him. Of course, there was no mirror in there but he could just make out his reflection in the bathroom window. On one side, it looked out to a sloping sequence of fields that were stapled together by sinewy rows of fences. To the right, a nest of council houses brooded uneasily, a thin rope of greyish smoke struggling up from three or four of the chimneys. Inside, the window seemed to transpose Wislon on to the land-scape. The end-of-day's pinky incandescence brought his features into a soft relief. Being with his mother again had stirred him and compelled a rudimentary self-examination. In front of the window, he took off his clothes. Standing slightly back, he gazed at his body's harsh angularity. It looked adequate but incongruous. The light was kind to his skin's texture. In these circumstances, it amounted to something pleasant enough. His eyes were firmly fixed on his face. Although carefully focused, the outline of the top half of his body blinked into Wislon's view. He could see his shoulders, his neck and the awkward diagonals which jagged down towards his boggle-eyed navel. Some people had a squashy, demure eye-lid, but he had always had a cartoonish bulge. He had never liked it. Still, his eyes did not venture any further; he knew what was further down and it was mostly bad news. All the hair and bone in the world could not disguise its true nature. Rather than looking, he merely imagined, and what he imagined was terrifying. The reality, he knew, would probably be worse.

He looked out past his superimposed self and into the pale sunset beyond the window, beyond the fields and the council houses. 'Red sky at night, shepherd's pie,' he remembered his grandma saying. Now he could only see blood. Wislon felt a little mad. He reasoned that a little madness never did anyone any harm. People who didn't think they were a little mad must be losing their minds, he thought.

'Are you still in there, Wislon?' his mother called. It seemed strange to hear her calling his name, using it. At least she didn't push any notes underneath the door.

'Yes,' he replied, 'just coming.'

He pulled and tugged his clothes on to his body and managed to wrestle them into some kind of shape. He unlocked the door. His mother was standing outside.

'Just going up for a lie down,' he said.

'Have you seen the sunset?'

'No,' Wislon replied, 'have you?'

He walked up to his room, lay on the bed and absorbed the sky's intimate pink as it pulsed and fluttered far beyond the window. It had stopped raining and the sky was busy reforming itself.

Since watching *Peter Pan* nothing much had happened. Three months went by and Wislon began to wonder whether he had imagined the whole thing. Neither did his father show any sign that something odd might have occurred.

Then, some time in April, Wislon noticed some

small changes in Mr Needy's behaviour. He began to insist that Mrs Needy cook him increasingly exotic meals every evening. In the space of a month, dinner necessarily developed from marinated pork with coriander and oxtail with haricot beans to Goan-style mussels or Royal lamb in a creamy almond sauce. Bread was baked at home and mayonnaise manufactured in the kitchen. Mr Needy was also quick to point out when something was not exactly right. He would eat the meal with a persistent sighing and look around the dining room as if aware of some plot that was being hatched against him. Half-way through a fried aubergine slice he complained that there was not enough cayenne pepper and that the lemon wedges weren't up to the mark.

'I'm sorry,' Wislon's mother said, 'maybe the lemons aren't fresh.'

Soon he was making it difficult for her to work at all. He came home early some evenings and late on others. At all times, he expected Mrs Needy to be waiting with his supper. In the end she went part-time so that she could always be on domestic duty.

Wislon's father also became morose and withdrawn. He would sit in an armchair listening to old Beatles' records, his disappointed hump turned slightly away from his wife and Wislon. At other times he would inspect the kitchen for signs of grease or dirt, making unreasonable demands on Mrs Needy and blaming her for the apparent breakdown in domestic order. Gradually, Wislon saw that his mother was buckling under the pressure. She had gone beyond the desire for argument. The impetus had drained away from her and she became resigned.

At school, strange things were also happening. In September, Wislon moved up to a new class. He was proud to have a desk to himself for the first time. His teacher was Mr King who dressed only in smart suits, pursed his lips when he was speaking and rapped you on the back of the head with his knuckles if you misbehaved. He put Wislon nearest to a girl called Maureen, who sat at the desk opposite. At first, he was very suspicious of her. Seeing him staring, Maureen turned and looked down before majestic-ally arranging her new coloured pencils on the desk. Wislon looked down at his old, chewed set and grew depressed.

At break, he came back into the classroom early to sneak a look at the pencils. Maureen came back sooner than expected, surprised him and offered a nervous, watery smile. Wislon scowled back and then looked away. Although he tried to ignore her after that, he became increasingly aware of her presence just across the aisle. When Mr King turned his back, he tried to look at her. He noted the long black hair that flooded over her shoulders, the maroon cardigan that clung to her back and the white bloodless skin stretched tight against her bones. Her eyes were large and a curious grey colour. Maureen caught him watching her and made the beginnings of a fairly prolonged smile. Her lips curved upwards at their edges and her face became slightly creased. Some-thing moved in Wislon's stomach and he quickly turned his eyes to the front, his body sticky and tingling with an uneasy, unidentifiable thrill. Mr King

238

gave him a dark look and clenched his hands. Wislon saw his knuckles whiten and stared directly ahead of him, unable to move a muscle.

During the rest of the week, he thought he began to understand that Maureen was beautiful and that she was different and that he was probably in love with her. He wanted to smell her hair and touch the lobe of her ear. He found himself inching his foot into the narrow aisle that separated their desks just so that he could *feel* near to her. He felt both guilty and exhilarated and often pulled her elbow just so he could ask, 'Can I borrow your black pencil, please?' He had one all right, but it was safely hidden at the back of his desk, behind the history text book and a copy of *Julius Caesar* which had last been used in 1957.

'Of course,' she said. 'Any time.'

At home, his father continued to be difficult. Mr King gave the class a geography test in which Wislon scored eighteen out of twenty. 'What happened to the the other two marks?' Mr Needy asked. He didn't even look up from the *Evening Mail* and was listening to 'I Am the Walrus'.

Once, when Wislon was helping with the washing-up and his mother had gone to check the boiler, his father suddenly appeared behind him in the cramped kitchen. He didn't say anything but as he leaned forward and reached up to the cupboard above his head, Wislon felt his father's free hand steadying itself against the hinge of his hip. Without understanding why, Wislon stopped washing. His whole body tensed and became motionless. He felt the material of his father's trousers rubbing rhythmically up and down the small of his back. Mrs Needy arrived back before Wislon could say anything or properly absorb the moment.

'The pressure's down again,' she said, and 'I don't think the chocolates are up there any more. Try the fridge.'

Without hesitating, Mr Needy's body folded itself in two. He found what he was looking for and strode silently back to his armchair.

Wislon looked at his hands. They still clung to something and were covered in suds. A small pool of water had formed at his feet and the plate was still dripping.

As Christmas drew closer, the atmosphere in the house intensified. Mrs Needy became almost invisible, little more than a domestic function who answered only to her husband's demands. She did not even question the fitting of a water meter as Wislon's father sought further economies on an already lean budget.

'It will save us money,' he announced, 'so long as you're careful during the day.'

'So how many times do I have to use the lavatory before I'm allowed to flush it?' asked Mrs Needy helplessly. Wislon noted that she was rubbing her hands together as she spoke. Her body was craned slightly but submissively forward.

'Three times; unless, of course, the unthinkable happens.' Wislon wondered what 'the unthinkable' could be. 'Then, I suppose, you had better flush it. After six o'clock, we're all in the clear.'

The situation in the bathroom was equally unfortunate. Before six in the evening, baths had to be shared. Even after the curfew had passed, Mr Needy was able to indicate a point in the bath above which the water should not pass. To make it clear, he daubed a small amount of black metallic paint on the exact spot. He was nothing if not suspicious and after a few weeks of poorly concealed doubt, he unscrewed the lock on the bathroom door and instigated a series of checks.

At first, he gave plenty of warning, knocking before he entered and glancing casually at the water level. Then he would rummage in the cabinet for an aspirin and walk out again. Soon, though, he abandoned all elements of pretence and came into the bathroom whenever he felt like it. Often, Wislon sat in the bath, the tepid water lapping pathetically around his young child's thighs, his knees held up nervously in front of a white chest. His father never said anything, and simply stared at him. Mr Needy was meant to be checking on water levels, but Wislon began to suspect that his father was actually staring at him. The visits made Wislon uncomfortable. Soon he was down to one bath every ten days or so. Attempting one before six o'clock, when his father generally arrived back from the car factory, could not even be contemplated. The water meter would certainly find him out. Wislon felt dirty and it was becoming a wretched, cold winter.

What most distressed Wislon during these months were the simultaneous feelings of revulsion and excited fear he felt towards his father. There was something enthralling about the manner in which he had subdued the household and brought it entirely under his will. Rather than sympathising with his mother, Wislon began to resent her timidity and lack of resilience. He would watch his father from the dining-room table where he was doing his home-work and be proud of their close association. There was something in his certainty, his intent, that captivated Wislon. He could think of no other rules he would rather obey, no creed he would more willingly follow. Of course, he never actually under-stood what that creed was, or meant, but whatever it was, whatever it could be, it would be the one for him. It would be enough. To be part of it would be enough.

One evening, when his mother and father were at the pub with a group from the factory, Wislon ventured into their bedroom. In the large wooden wardrobe which smelled of dust and mothballs, he found one of his father's two suits. It was a soft brown colour with a darker check discreetly imposed over the top. He took it off a hanger which had the name of a Swedish hotel printed importantly along its stretcher. The hanger was a souvenir from his parents' honeymoon. As far as he could tell, it was the only time they had been abroad. 'Never again,' his father often said. 'Abroad is disappointing. It's not all that it's cracked up to be.'

He tugged the suit off and it fell to the floor in a crumpled, ill-shaped turban of cloth. Then he picked it up and pulled the trousers and jacket on over his own clothes. Catching glimpses of himself in the mirror on the back of the wardrobe door, reflections of himself in a man's suit, Wislon felt a little blood stirring beneath his pre-pubertal skin. He identified it as the same sensation as when he reached out his foot towards Maureen's desk at school.

One night, about a week before Christmas, Wislon's mother visited a friend in hospital. She did not leave until about seven o'clock, and not until the family had eaten a meal of pears in cream dressing, Italian fennel casserole and rum and raisin cheesecake. Mrs Needy watched nervously as her husband picked his way through the various dishes. She wondered whether she had overdone the grated cheddar cheese in the casserole or perhaps underplayed the tarragon in the cream dressing. She need not have worried. Mr Needy consumed the food with a grudging but obvious relish. He even helped with the washing-up, and then stacked the plates neatly into the cupboard above the fridge before arranging the cutlery drawer so that the knives, forks and spoons were symmetrically aligned.

Mrs Needy headed out into the raw night. Splinters of cold rain fell on her shoulders and spattered against the small maroon umbrella which she held doubtfully above her head.

In the living room, 'Yesterday' was about to play and Mr Needy was opening a bottle of Chianti. He poured two full glasses of red wine and gave one to Wislon. 'There you are,' he said, 'try this.' Wislon took the glass and sniffed it cautiously. It was only a year since he had drunk a mug of sherry in one unsuspecting gulp after assuming that it was a soft drink.

After that, he had once managed a weak shandy.

'Cheers,' his father said, and swallowed two sizeable mouthfuls. As much as anything else, it was strange to see Mr Needy so cheerful. Wislon did not wish to contradict him. Besides, he was still in thrall to his father, even if he did not quite trust him.

He stuck his tongue into the wine, shuddered at the sour-sweet taste, closed his eyes and took in a mouthful. Most of the wine disappeared down his throat before he had time to register its taste, but the last few drops stayed up. Their furriness caused the rest to jolt violently on the way to his stomach and his body went through a series of mild convulsions. Immediately, he felt dizzy and had to sit down. He wasn't sure where the middle of the chair was and steadied himself carefully before eventually sliding into it. His father walked over, refilled Wislon's glass and said something like, 'That's the spirit,' even managing an embarrassed grin at his pun.

Mr Needy sat on the arm of the chair, occasionally sipping his wine and encouraging Wislon to do the same. Although he did not want to take any more drink, the few polite swigs he did take soon had an effect. His head began to drift and he felt as if his feet were somehow floating a few inches above the ground. He thought of Maureen and closed his eyes again. He asked if he could borrow her black pencil to do some outlines and then laughed at his cheek and boldness.

'Poor thing,' his father said, 'you've had too much. Poor thing. Poor thing.'

Wislon felt his father's arms under his armpits.

244

Then he was lifted out of the chair and carried upstairs. Mr Needy's hands dug into his ribs but he no longer knew how to complain. Once more, his blood stirred. Somewhere in the back of his mind a small voice of protest tried to make itself heard. Outside, he could hear rain spitting against the window. He was supported as far as his bedroom and then dropped gently on to the side of his bed. Then there were a few minutes of silence as Mr Needy simply cradled Wislon in his arms, rocking him slowly back and forth.

'We had better get you ready for bed,' he said at the end of the quiet. He peeled Wislon's jumper off, taking his time and folding it neatly over a small wicker chair in the corner. Occasionally, Wislon opened his eyes and made out the chocolate-brown walls of his room and the small blue lamp that stood on his dresser. All the time, he was aware of his father's shooshing noises and a faint smell of car oil and metal. At some point, Mr Needy stood him upright again.

After being loosened, the rest of Wislon's clothes unwound themselves from his body and he was left standing naked in the middle of his cramped room. He looked down and saw that the garments res-embled a large twist of ice cream. They had collapsed on to each other and gathered into a vertiginous coil of cheap cloth. He stared at them for several moments as his eyes accustomed themselves to the gloom. His concentration was only broken by the sudden sound of his bed gently wheezing behind him. He turned round to see his father slipping beneath the sheets. Mr Needy's own clothes had been abandoned in anarchic piles around the bed. Clearly they had been discarded in some hurry. Wislon could not recall having heard the soft rasp of his father's undressing. Now, he listened to his voice as it came to him through the dark. It was strangely lenient yet still unmistakable. 'Come and give your dad a cuddle, then,' it said. Mr Needy pulled the top sheet slightly back and Wislon glimpsed his father's nakedness. 'Come on. Just a cuddle.' Wislon walked unsteadily over to his bed and climbed in. There was not much room and he could hear nothing except his father's breathing. Even the weather was hushed.

7

Letting Blood

Wislon heard his own breathing. It made a rattling sound as if it snagged on each emission. A voice came to him in the dark. But apart from the voice and the faint catching noise of his own breath there was no sound. The voice dwindled until there was absolute silence except for the sound of a vacuum cleaner somewhere else. Through a window, Mr Needy could be seen in the garden. He was turning over thin strips of soil that bordered the grass. He didn't know that someone was looking at him. In parallel gardens, other men were working on their own thin strips of soil. No doubt, out of sight, it was the kind of thing going on all over the place. Or something very like it. It struck the young child looking through the window that here was a real inertia of the soul. A future of boredom comprehensively mapped out, compartmentalised and packaged. Maybe a Small Heath or a Digbeth or an Edgbaston of the soul. And 'soul'? Now there *was* a funny thing.

Did it have to be like this? The voice remained

silent. But at least it had been company for a few short moments.

Wislon thought he was spending too much of his time asleep. It was thinking this that woke him up. When he opened his eyes again, he didn't know what time it was. He even wondered whether it was still Sunday. Reason told him that tiredness and the strain of the past few days were catching up with him. Had *caught* up with him. He had sleep-need. He had been tired before, but never quite like this. Regularity and promptness were not appealing in themselves, but at least Wislon could usually rely on them. Now, it was all changing. It was all going wrong inside his head. He was inclined to make excuses for what had happened there while he slept. Because there was no doubt about it – s*omething* had happened. Something had come and clawed him while he slept. Whatever it was seemed to hate him and wanted to do serious damage. This was clearly how things got back at you. They waited until you closed your eyes and then skulked in. The worst thing about it all was that Wislon wanted this dislocation. He had brought all the twisting and the jolting on by himself. It excited him. Now that he had started, he did not know where it would end. All he knew for certain was that he probably wanted more.

He shook his head as he supposed he ought. If anyone was watching it would at least give the impression of having been in an authentically deep sleep. His eyes picked out a note from his mother on the table next to the bed. It read, 'SUPPER IS READY WHENEVER YOU ARE.'

Wislon took the stairs carefully, went through the living room and then took the second set of steps down into the basement. The table was set and his mother was in the kitchen putting the last touches to a large omelette and salad. He noted how plain her cooking had become now that she no longer had to please Mr Needy. She must have heard him getting off the bed as the meal was exactly timed to coincide with his entrance. Mrs Needy turned to Wislon and said, 'It may only be the light, but I was wondering whether you ever used moisturiser. It's only a thought, but skin *is* skin.'

She brought the food over, sliced the omelette neatly in two and slid equal portions on to the plates. 'And if you think about it, the skin of men and women is really the same.' She looked up apologetically. Wislon was busy with the tendrils of melted cheese which had snaked out from the side of his omelette. He tried to scoop and plait them into a more coherent shape. Finally, his mother said, 'I mean, there's no need for a *man's* skin to be like it is. A bit of Nivea every night should do it.'

Wislon nodded. He recognised his mother's good intentions but recoiled at their meaning. There was no need to tell Wislon. He knew all about skin. It held him together and stopped him getting out. Best of all, it stopped most other things getting in. Skin tended to intervene at just the right moment. But – Christ – if he looked like *that* on the outside, what was happening underneath? Nothing, clearly, that a

249

few daubs of moisturiser wouldn't put right.

While they ate, he stared impassively at the small expanse of table in front of him. Everything was precisely as it should be. The salt and pepper pots were set equidistant between them, both filled to capacity and wiped scrupulously clean. A small basket of brown bread was settled on his mother's side of the table. It was balanced by a small plate which contained four symmetrical oblongs of butter. This, Wislon saw, was closest to him. A small china-blue vase with two starchy cornflowers completed the arrangement. Both Wislon and his mother had a large tumbler of chilled orange juice which had been poured from a brown pitcher. Mrs Needy returned it to the fridge after it had been used. Apart from some mumbled comments, Wislon and his mother ate in silence. At one point, Mrs Needy wondered whether Mr Beresford the greengrocer, who had provided the ingredients for the salad, was a homosexual. The word sounded strange on her lips. She pronounced it 'holme-oh-sexual' and said that, of course, she didn't mind if he was. However, for some unspoken reason, her suspicions no longer allowed her to buy mushrooms from Mr Beresford's shop. It was, she continued, all the attention he was paying to young George that was the crux of the problem. George came in on Saturdays. It wasn't natural, she said. And what did George make of it? He was, after all, only seventeen.

Wislon nodded and gingerly absorbed the illusion of normality which the layout of the table suggested. He contrasted it with the disturbing bluish tinge he had noticed in his mother's complexion. It was a light from another world – a light shining irresolutely from an agitated mind. His mother's state of mind was not as it seemed. Both finished their meals without further comment.

Afterwards, when the two of them were sitting together in the living room, Wislon decided that he must go back to Birmingham early on Monday morning. Initially, he had found his mother's obsessive neutrality a timely asylum. Now, he was unnerved by her inertia. He also found that he was increasingly blighted by what he had left behind. Although he did not feel guilt for what had happened to Amy, he was nevertheless bewitched by the images of her which cruised around his mind. He wanted to know what she looked like now that she had been by herself for a couple of days. Wislon hoped that no one had discovered the body and violated its poised serenity. He hoped that she was still lying comfortably on his bed.

When his mother spoke again, he found himself becoming more irritated. He clenched his fists and the skin on his cheeks glowed with an impatient anger.

'The woman two doors down is trying to start a Society for Ancient Wisdom in the village,' she said.

Wislon stared back at her.

'She's always complaining about her stomach. Something to do with having flowers in there. Or flora. Flora and fauna, I shouldn't be surprised. I'm sure I don't understand it. The sort of thing your father might have got a handle on.' And then she added, 'No doubt.'

It was the first and only time that she mentioned Wislon's father during his stay. He blinked and tried to pretend that he hadn't noticed anything. However, he felt that the room was checking him over, looking him up and down. The fabric of the place was colluding with Mrs Needy. Surely she must have felt *something* after what had happened. Wislon concentrated his mind and tried to remember what *had* happened. Immediately, darkness and a thick web of gauze mixed in his mind. He could only think that it must have been something unforgivable. Regret and sorrow suggested the hope of forgiveness. Maybe Wislon and his mother both knew that all their reproach and anguish could do no good. What was done could not be undone. Still, in his case, Wislon wanted to know what would happen next. In killing Amy Facer, he had destroyed something which could not be replaced. What came in its stead? Surely there had to be some kind of balance. Wislon thought about his mother's table downstairs and felt a surge of sympathy. No. It was no good. He must go back to Birmingham. At least there he could find some kind of choice. He could make his own decisions. But first he had to leave.

He forced himself to focus on his mother's words. Now she was talking about the Carpenters who lived further on down the road in the village. Last August, they had suddenly become Muslims. She could not remember where she had learned the information, but she knew that Muslims had to shave their pubic hair. Moreover, husbands and wives had to co-operate with each other in what she called a tricky operation. 'I wouldn't trust Rodney Carpenter if I was her,' she was saying. 'From what I saw of him in the newsagent's last week, he's got the beginnings of Parkinson's.'

Wislon beamed artificially at his mother and she smiled back. But it didn't count for anything. No matter what happened now, he would soon be back in Birmingham.

After Wislon first climbed into bed with his father, there had been a short respite before it happened again. But then it occurred more often until it became a habit. Wislon tried to keep a record of the number of times his father approached him. He would always say, 'Give your old dad a cuddle then,' or, 'Have you got a kiss for your father?' But it never stopped there and Wislon grew ashamed and perplexed, especially when he was asked not to tell Mrs Needy. 'A good woman, but she wouldn't understand,' said Wislon's father. 'She can be quite highly strung, you know.'

Wislon kept a table of the meetings with his father, but he could not find any real pattern in the figures. He was glad they were doing graphs and elementary statistics at school because that made everything easier. Wislon had a skill for this kind of work and often helped Maureen when they arrived early on Thursday morning, the night after maths homework. The numbers did not tell him very much apart from the fact that his father had approached him, on average, twenty-three times a year over the next three years. During the fourth year, it went up to twenty-seven, but then over the following twelve months it mysteriously dipped to nineteen. Wislon compiled more figures about the average per month, per week and per day. The last, excluding leap years, worked out at a miserly 0.063013698 times every day. Put this way, things didn't seem to be too bad and Wislon took heart from his calculations. He kept all the papers under lock and key in a smart turquoise wallet which had a tiny gold padlock attached to it.

There was no doubt, however, that things were changing in peculiar and unaccountable ways. Wislon decided that he didn't actually like what his father was doing, but remained powerless to do anything about it. Worse (or maybe better?) than this, he found that there was a part of him which responded to his father's neediness. At times he felt compassion for him and tried to help by holding his hand or stroking his hair. This was what people who were close to one another did, he thought. He remembered how older boys and girls acted towards each other at the swimming pool. A large sign had been placed at the deep end. It said 'No Petting' and featured a crude line drawing of a man and a woman holding hands and looking at each other in a strange, intense manner. Little red hearts fluttered playfully between them.

At school, he wondered whether Maureen or any other of his friends were in the same difficulties. Although he still liked to look at Maureen, he had begun to lose his nerve. He used to take pleasure in it, but now he succumbed to feelings of guilt and shame. Whenever she looked at him, he turned away and pretended to be doing something else. Although they remained in the same class for the next four years, their friendship did not develop. Maureen still smiled at him, but now it was a sad, resigned smile. Although the corners of her mouth made the right movements and shape, it didn't seem to be a proper smile at all.

Wislon's reports told Mr and Mrs Needy that their child was becoming a 'day-dreamer'. He could not deny it. During classes, he found himself fantasising about being rich, about being at a fabulous funeral, about being an acrobat, about living underneath the water. He dreamed about living in a place where everybody went about in disguise and where nobody knew the identity of anybody else. Each day, the inhabitants of this city of disguises would reinvent themselves, walking the streets in the confidence that nobody would recognise them and that they could be anybody or anything they pleased. Sometimes, the streets would be filled with water and the sun would never come up. Everywhere there would be darkness and ornate black boats skimmed purposefully through the choppy waves. There was a rumour that diamonds and gold could be found at the bottom of the water, but when the streets returned to normal there was never any sign of them. Nor had anybody ever managed to dive to the bottom of the water. It was blue on the surface, but quickly turned to an inky black and seemed infinitely deep.

While he was thinking these thoughts, Wislon began to bite his nails. Soon, he reduced them to gnarled splinters and began to chew the skin on his fingers, turning each one to a cratered pulp. Then he created scabs on his face by scratching his cheeks. It was only a matter of time before he picked and scraped them off, leaving a spongy, uneven, weeping complexion.

One Sunday afternoon, during a lunch of lambs' kidneys in red wine, potatoes boulangère, broccoli fritters and spiced apple and raisin crumble, Mr Needy suggested that they hold a fancy-dress party for the New Year. Wislon's mother was not enthusiastic. Although they usually 'had people round' at that time of year, the ambition suggested by fancy dress seemed threatening and difficult. Nothing more was said for another week, when Mr Needy's tone of voice turned a suggestion into an instruction. Wislon found himself hating his mother's reedy, uneasy argument. As in most things, she had now become the focus for his fear and anger.

He could smell oil and machinery on his father. He discreetly inhaled some air through his nose and exulted in the metallic tang that came to him. He watched darkly as his mother fussed with the washing-up. Every movement she made implied assent and a kind of weak, cringing conformity. Full of contempt, he felt blood surging through him. Then he reluctantly pulled himself out of his seat and went to help her in the kitchen. He only went at all, he decided, because his father would be pleased. Or rather, he would not be pleased if Wislon did *not* go.

In all his actions, he now found himself increasingly absorbed in Mr Needy's requirements.

The party was therefore bound to happen. The phrase that most appealed to Wislon was Mr Needy's, 'Even best friends won't be able to recognise each other.' He could not believe that this would literally be true, but it was something to aim for.

Although each disguise was meant to stay secret, Wislon had little difficulty in discovering that his mother would be Cleopatra while his father thought he might make a good Napoleon. When they asked him who he would be going as, Wislon used a phrase he had often heard his grandma use: 'Never you mind. That's for me to know and you to find out.' He had his ideas, but for the moment he was keeping them to himself.

The invitations were sent out and Mrs Needy set to work on the food. Whatever she produced, Wislon knew that it would have to be extraordinary to avoid failing Mr Needy's critical scrutiny. In the end, she went for a traditional roast turkey, roast stuffed goose with prunes and apple sauce, Yugoslav kebabs, creamed potatoes with nutmeg, gratin dauphinois and a range of vegetables. In addition, there was a lemon suprise pudding, St Stephen's pudding, cara-melised apple flan and a large traditional trifle. Wislon watched his mother with disdain during the days that led up to the party. It was little wonder that his father treated her in such an imperious manner. Who wouldn't? Wislon understood what was happening and felt privileged to be so closely associated with his power and authority.

On the day of the party, Mr Needy researched a special recipe for punch. He bought the necessary ingredients from Aziz's Off Licence at the end of the road and mixed them in a large bucket. Wislon observed the procedure with pride and drew closer to his father, who rewarded him with a thin smile.

'Who are you coming as? Have you decided yet?' He asked the question and then idly ruffled Wislon's hair.

A spasm of pleasure shot through Wislon's body, and he hated himself. He glanced out of the window at the moon which was glowing softly in the dark sky. He could not help what he felt.

'No,' he replied. 'I mean yes.'

'Which one?'

'I mean yes.'

'I haven't seen your costume. Have you hidden it?'

'Sort of.'

'Very mysterious,' said Mr Needy. He looked up from the bucket for a few moments, giving out a muffled gasp as his back took the strain. 'I hope so. You've only got a few hours left.'

When the guests started to arrive, it was not quite as Wislon had anticipated. In fact, it was nothing like it. For a start, he could tell exactly who everyone was. He watched them from the small landing at the top of the stairs, keeping himself in the shadows. He wanted to make sure that nobody could see his own costume until he was ready. Mr and Mrs Needy still looked like Mr and Mrs Needy. A hat and a cream dress edged in red made some difference, but they hardly suggested Napoleon and Cleopatra. A man with a patch over one eye wandered in. He was also carrying a telescope and Wislon supposed that it was Gerald's father trying to be Nelson. The couple from two doors down on the other side came as Batman and Robin. The costumes were plausible but weren't able to disguise the identity of their wearers. Nor did anyone else succeed in not being themselves. All this was a great disappointment to Wislon who had expected an evening amongst virtual strangers. He began to worry about his own disguise. Would the guests walk by, nodding politely, without even registering the fact that he was wearing fancy dress?

The time passed slowly, but after about thirty minutes Wislon was able to take in all the other guests. Down below, they thronged and drank and laughed in the Needys' cramped living room. As well as Napoleon, Cleopatra, Batman, Robin and Nelson, there was an Al Capone, someone's grandmother as Churchill, a Charlie Chaplin and two vicars. For no apparent reason, Mr Dobson from up the road had come as Hitler wearing a kilt. The costumes were generally accurate, but the guests didn't fool anyone. Certainly not Wislon. If the costumes allowed it, the men walked around with their hands thrust deep into their pockets, occasionally halting for a few moments to share a joke with someone. The women clustered together, all of them talking at once, their eyes sparkling and urgent. Wislon saw his mother detach herself from one of the groups. She seemed flustered and scuttled off to check the food. He felt anger and pity mixing in his stomach and was aware of the muscles in his neck tightening at the reaction.

Wislon went back into his room and put the finishing touches to his own costume. He arched his back as he surveyed his image in the mirror and shuffled round 360 degrees to ensure that all was well. Then he pulled himself smartly to attention and stood front on, immediately before the mirror. He made some adjustments to his hair before setting off down the stairs. As he came into view, he was aware of several guests discreetly nudging one another and quietly gesturing towards the descending figure. One or two even stopped talking. As some of the general noise abated, Wislon was able to pick out snatches of some individual conversations. An elderly man with liver spots on his hands was asking someone how much padding he had used for his Quasimodo. Another man, this time with black, oily hair, was commenting on the punch and Mrs Needy's buffet.

Wislon's mother looked up as she saw him nearing the bottom of the stairs.

'Ah. What a surprise,' Wislon heard her say. He saw her trying to manipulate her mouth. As he walked fully into view, it was clear that the young child had somehow transformed himself into Mr Needy. He was wearing his father's brown check suit, pinned and folded to hang in exactly the same proportions in which it dressed his father. Most startling, however, were Wislon's posture and facial expression. Here were smaller replicas of Mr Needy's slightly self-conscious manner, his weary tread, the suspicious eyes and the severe mouth. Someone made a joke about Mr Needy having shrunk. Wislon's mother was now blinking uncontrollably. The talk in the room started up again and Wislon made his way through the din towards his father who, he now saw, was standing behind a table serving the punch. The two of them looked at one another. Mr Needy tried a tight smile, but it didn't fit and slid quickly away from his face. There was fear and ignorance in his eyes. In exactly the right voice, Wislon said, 'I would like a soft drink, please.' The glass was filled and passed over without comment. Then Wislon walked heavily to the other side of the room. He stood alone and observed the circles of talkers, listening to something by the Moody Blues on the new record player.

Wislon spent the remainder of the evening quietly with his mother. In the absence of a television, there was mostly silence. Wislon was more settled than he had been during the rest of the weekend because he now knew where he would be going. At that moment, he wished his mother might show a little more interest in him. In the beginning, he had been glad for her lack of scrutiny, but now things had changed. She read through a small pile of neatly stacked magazines, made comments on more of the villagers and offered Wislon several cups of tea.

A part of him wanted to be discovered. It was the least that Amy deserved after what had been done to her. He did not want his name splashed across the front pages of newspapers. Nor did he want to witness a courtroom trying to suppress its collective disgust towards him. Or to stand in front of a jury. He could have told Agnes Tunnelle, except that would have been more like telling himself. And he *already* knew. He could have told Armitage – long ago. Not now. He wondered whether he could tell his mother. He wanted to tell his squalid secret to her, to be found out. He was tired of being so precariously situated in the world. His pretence had to be revealed and the intoxicating pain of instability yielded in order for something *certain* to emerge. Only then would Wislon be truly himself. But it needed his mother's co-operation. He glanced up from the magazine he was looking at to see that she was still reading. He made to speak, but no words came out. Still, the barely audible sound of someone intending to say something is often more appetising than the real thing. People never seem to miss it. Thus Mrs Needy looked up barely a second after the dry but strangled click had escaped from Wislon's lips.

'What? Mmmm?'

Wislon thought for several seconds.

'Nothing,' he replied.

As a plaintive darkness grew around the cottage, Wislon became increasingly restless. He did not want to leave his mother, although he knew that this was probably more for his own sake than any good it might do her. The temptation to confess weighed heavily. She asked him if he wanted to go to the pub.

'No,' Wislon replied, 'thank you.'

'Are you sure?'

'Yes.'

'Well. If you're sure. I don't suppose you know anybody.' She looked up, her face non-committal, before continuing, 'You seem a bit agitated. Stretch your legs. A walk will do you good.'

Wislon turned his head and looked outside. He thought that a walk would be the last thing to do him any good. He couldn't see anything apart from the black velvet of the night sky and a medley of stars. He tried to remember the names and positions of the main constellations. He recollected his father explaining about them one night, and the memory brought an involuntary shudder which startled his neck into a momentary shake. Wislon tried to remember whether his father had placed a hand on his shoulder while he imparted the information. He had to admit that he could not remember, but in his mind he still felt Mr Needy's operative presence close behind him. Now, all he could think about was how many stars there appeared to be in this sky in contrast to the flat featureless one that hung so sadly over Birmingham. He was not sure whether this made things simpler or more complicated. Not that it really mattered. He considered the dark. Definitely the last thing that would do him any good would be to walk in it. Didn't his mother understand anything? He controlled his contempt and composed his features before replying, 'No. I think I'd rather stay in. Early start tomorrow.'

His mother nodded without actually seeming to agree. She turned back to the shiny woman's magazine in her hands and Wislon started to burrow through a bulbous Sunday newspaper. He had already been through news, sport, leisure, style, business, fashion, cars and arts. He was now deep amongst reviews, critics and features. After that, there was only 'Life'. Spread out around him were the previously read and now unhinged sheets of newsprint. Wislon glowered at the wreckage and reflected that it seemed to be a condition of readership that once you had finished with the news, it finished with you. The forlorn pages had already whorled themselves into an alien and inaccessible sprawl to either side of his armchair. He had just finished articles on the habitual life of the giant octopus and another on the recent revolution in Belgian pâtisseries when something else took his eye. It was headlined 'Genital Tax' and reported an American book which advocated that one hundred dollars should be added to each man's tax bill. It argued that Genital Tax should be imposed because, in the USA, ninety per cent of murderers and ninety-four per cent of prison inmates are male. Wislon paused uneasily at the information. Did that necessarily mean that *all* murderers were caught? The article went on to say that sperm counts were falling at the rate of two point six per cent per year. Did that mean that in about forty years sperm would cease to exist? Wislon looked thoughtfully out through the window once more and cursed his luck. Why did he have to be a man? Things were clearly not going well for men. For *him*. Given the statistics, the trends and the forecasts, did he really stand a chance? The stars were against him. That was what the sky was trying to tell him. It was indifferent, but then why should it care? Things were going badly for mankind. Most men had to come to terms with the fact that masculinity is merely a column of blood vessels. Wislon thought that, on the whole, he would settle for just that.

Even his mother, her eyes entranced by something in her magazine, was no help.

He kept his own eyes open and stared downwards, but his mind was beginning to wander. He saw himself walking down a deserted road. Suddenly, all kinds of people appeared, all travelling towards him. He smiled at every one of them; young, old, men and women. He even felt comfortable with them. A policeman, who ought to have been eyed suspiciously, was passed with a welcoming smile. Wislon came to a bench and saw that Armitage was seated on it. She had her back to him but he could tell that it was her by the thick fibres of black hair that hung together and swayed slightly in the wind. He took her hand and the two of them walked on without feeling the need to talk. They were too close for that. Wislon could feel that Armitage's hand was warm, dry and supple. This was in contrast to his own hand, which he thought must have been cold, bony and damp. He wondered what it must feel like to hold hands with himself. The two of them moved on, exactly in step. Eventually, they came to a house and the unselfconscious manner in which they approached and entered suggested to Wislon that it was *their* house. Armitage tidied up the sitting room and then made herself comfortable on the sofa. She tucked her legs up and under her backside in the way that she knew Wislon liked. She pretended to be reading a book, all the time stealing furtive glances at him.

'Do you want a drink?'

'Yes, please,' said Wislon, rather too enthusiastically, before understanding that it was his mother who was now asking the question. She stood over him but at a slight distance before moving away down the stairs and into the small kitchen.

Wislon turned his mind back to Armitage. He saw himself outside a door, looking through the keyhole. He could see Armitage on a chair, her legs still twisted and bound underneath her body. He observed the smooth flow of her legs, stretched and emphasised by the sheen of her tights. After a short while, Armitage began to move, taking deep breaths and twitching her body as if awakening from sleep. When she rose out of the chair and stood upright, she wandered over to the window and stood in its frame. Slowly, she took her clothes off. The movements were gradual, polite and restrained. The procedure was an elaborate but practical ritual, accomplished with delicate ease. Wislon's eyes absorbed the tableau as it began to unfold. They blinked and watered, but somehow it didn't matter. He watched Armitage fall on to the sofa, her breasts exposed, her head flung casually backwards, her legs tucked under once more. He watched her rest for several moments, but could resist no longer. He pulled his body stiffly upright, took a number of deep breaths, arranged himself as best he could and quietly opened the door. Armitage did not move or attempt to cover herself. She was neither embarrassed nor compromised. Although the moment was sexual, it was also loving

266

and contained no tension. Wislon walked over and touched the richness of her hair. She seemed to know exactly what to do. After taking him in her arms, she detached herself from his embrace and asked him to tell her things.

'What things?' asked Wislon. He replied without anger or suspicion.

'All things. Everything about you.'

And Wislon talked, not pausing to think what he was saying.

Now he wanted to talk to her and tell her all the things which he could not tell his mother.

When the tea arrived, the feeling that he must leave intensified inside Wislon. It was the only way.

'I thought I'd make another omelette or something later on,' Mrs Needy said.

'Good idea,' said Wislon.

He looked at the article in front of him again. This time it was saying that, on average, men died six years earlier than women and that some men cry in their sleep. Christ, Wislon thought – nowadays men cry *everywhere*.

What have I done? he thought.

This time, there was no going back.

You know you are getting closer. But you also understand that these fantasies are a bad idea and that they will distract you. If you let them get in the way, you won't be able to make it through. And you seem to have gone so far. 'What have I done?' That's good. Almost too good, in fact. What should the next step be? You don't know; that's up to

267

you. Concentrate your mind, perhaps. You can guide, but you can't presume to instruct.

You think of Amy. She's probably still in your bed, but you don't suppose that things are quite as you left them. You can't be too sure. Some people say the dead don't talk. They say that the dead are absolutely silent. But you know that this is not so. In her own way, Amy is talking to you. On quiet nights, when the wind is up, you can stand and hear the dead talking.

You hear Amy, but can you hear your father?

The next time, ask yourself if you can hear him. Ask yourself if you can hear him laughing or weeping or shouting. If you can, ask him whether he loves you. If you can, ask him how he loves you.

What do you do if you take a liking to your father's clothes? Not in the sense that you like the style or the cut or the colour of them. Oh no. Rather, that you just *like* them. The feeling is unencumbered by questions of taste. What do you expect from a fourteen-year-old?

What Wislon did when he discovered a liking for his father's clothes was to wear them as often as possible. To wear them often and in secret. He thought that he might be a lot of things, but an exhibitionist was surely not one of them.

Whenever he was alone in the house, Wislon ploughed through his father's wardrobe. He wore the brown suit and the black suit with thin white stripes which had long since turned a kind of dirty cream. He wore the blue jacket with the hole in the elbow

268

that had been caused by catching it on the bathroom door five years ago. There were three other jackets, all in various shades of brown, and Wislon also paraded in them. Although his mother had developed into a neat ironer of shirts, she hung rather than folded them. He did not have to unpack them. This allowed Wislon to experiment with each of the different shades that his father had accumulated over the years. The shirts swayed gently as Wislon opened the wardrobe door, his father's sartorial history turning slowly before him like so many carcasses in an abattoir.

He had types of white, types of purple, types of beige and types of blue. That was about it. Not ambitious, but enough to allow Wislon almost infinite permutations with the different varieties of suits and jackets he had at his disposal. Of course, he could also mix the two suits up, not only with each other, but also with the anthology of trousers he soon found on the far side of the wardrobe.

After several months of posturing, Wislon began to feel guilty. He felt guilty because he felt that he was taking liberties with his father's clothes. He was showing no *respect* for them. More than this, he began to understand that the real fascination was not in the clothes themselves, but in the way they could make him seem like his father. Wislon began to study the clothes his father wore for certain occasions. He studied what went where, and when. Along with each piece and each arrangement, he observed his father's posture, countenance and demeanour. Soon, he was matching clothes to bearing, and replicating Mr Needy's very presence. Then he managed the

269

stare of the eyes in the black suit with the milky stripes, and then the slight curl of the lips whenever he wore the blue jacket. He noticed the almost rakish sweep of his hair whenever he slipped into anything purple. He copied the jowly, hangdog expression that his father assumed whenever he had to wear a pullover.

Wislon paraded himself in front of the large mirror on the back of the wardrobe door. In the eighteen months after the fancy-dress party, he often transformed himself into a modest version of Mr Needy. Although a part of him was revolted by the sight of his father's baggy garments hanging off his splinter of a body, by far the greater part was now tensed and excited by it. Wislon's blood was aroused and the skin over his stomach quickened, contracted, pulsed and became tender. Soon, it became a case of not being able not to do it.

While he was perfecting his act, Wislon also noticed that the sight and smell of his mother's clothes made him angry and caused unease. He began to understand why his father had grown increasingly cool and distant from her. Who wouldn't? Wislon never told his mother or consciously indicated his feelings towards her. But still, he grew to despise her. He hated the way she cooked and yielded and haunted the house as a thin, airy presence. At times, he associated the thrill of wearing his father's clothes with his feelings of aggression towards Mrs Needy. The two emotions became strangely compatible, willing themselves together as violence and domination.

All the while, Mr Needy was managing his steady twenty-three times a year. Wislon felt violated yet strong, injured but necessary. His father said, 'Don't tell anyone. Not even at school. Not even to best friends. If you do, I'll tell them how worthless you are.' Then he added, 'Even though you aren't – not really.' He need not have worried. Wislon had no intention of telling anyone, especially as he was pleasing to his father. Maybe his father needed him.

While in the sixth form at school, Wislon continually examined his body. Always he concluded that he wasn't enough like his father. He disliked it when people said that they could 'see' his mother in him. It disheartened him and he would sit quietly by himself, waiting for his parents to leave so that he could once again transform himself in front of the wardrobe mirror.

He had plans to put things right, but these needed resources. Therefore, Wislon worked through every school holiday, steadily accumulating money. He transferred his savings into a building society account. He packed shelves, sold fruit, cleaned offices and stood behind counters. Standing behind counters was best because he had access to the till. He often took home an extra five or ten pounds at the end of the week. No one will notice, he reasoned. Besides, it's going to a good cause.

During those years, Wislon effectively isolated himself from his friends at school. Whenever he was troubled by his seclusion, he would go to his room where he would find Mr Needy standing silently amid mercurial shadows and framed by a halo of white light. Pale-faced and solemn, he would draw near. Wislon would run a hand through his hair; Mr Needy ruffled his hair too. Having found consolation, Wislon would then sit down on the edge of his bed and continue to consult the mirror at the far end of his room.

He received his exam results while he was working behind the counter at a small butcher's shop on the Soho Road. He would be going to Leeds, but had already decided to take the year off. The next afternoon, he took a bus to one of the smarter suburbs on the south side of the city. Initially, he had been surprised at the difficulties he had encountered in finding Dr Stubbs. He had been shocked that Dr Stubbs did not work in a hospital. And now he was unprepared for the large modern house that corresponded with the address he had written down. It backed on to a small wood where trees waved and sighed and moved as if in a chorus line. What had he expected? Perhaps a small back street with demolished terracing and too many dogs? Certainly not anything *respectable*.

Wislon rang the bell and Dr Stubbs himself opened the door. He was a tall, thin man with black hair smeared close to his skull and a savage military parting. His skin was mottled and unhealthy. Wislon looked at his fingers which were abnormally long and skeletal. As Dr Stubbs shook his hand, he felt that his own hand was inadequately small. He was led into a large room which contained an old desk. An impressive display of medical books lined the walls.

Sitting down opposite Stubbs, he tried to whisper a quiet, secretive word of greeting, but it just sounded like a parched gasp struggling to escape from the back of his throat. Although his body felt damp, his mouth was completely dry. Wislon felt sweat mingling with the talcum powder he had emptied on to himself that morning. He tasted the remnants of some toothpaste. Other than that, his mouth felt acrid.

Dr Stubbs managed a reassuring smile. Somehow, it didn't suit the rest of his face. He saw the anxious look that had come over Wislon and understood that he must speak to put his mind at rest. He explained that a large percentage of the people who came to see him had a long history of transsexuality.

'I haven't,' said Wislon shrilly, his voice suddenly sparking into life. 'I don't even know if I'm trans-sexual.'

Dr Stubbs nodded and effectively ignored the response. He went on to say that the mean age to adopt male dress was around twenty-three years. 'You are therefore very young,' he concluded, rather obviously.

'I suppose so,' Wislon replied. 'Why? Is it important?'

Stubbs shrugged. 'It need not be a difficulty. In a hospital – yes, probably, unless there were compelling reasons. But here, different rules apply. There is certainly nothing in your medical history that would necessarily deter me.'

Wislon took a sharp breath. He noticed that Dr Stubbs' long fingers were beating a silent but methodical tattoo on the notes he had in front of him. The half-moons of his fingernails were impossibly clean and symmetrical. His face was also bony and blood-less, perhaps incapable of registering emotion. A thin reek of formaldehyde reached Wislon and he wanted to retch.

Dr Stubbs' manner and behaviour were identical on each of Wislon's subsequent visits. The process that he outlined would take longer than Wislon had anticipated. Dr Stubbs was clear that he did not wish to know the precise reasons which had brought Wislon to him, but he was concerned that he should understand the nature of the procedure. The doctor said that hospitals would not usually deal with anyone until they were nineteen. 'You are not quite eighteen. The difficulty is usually one of finding willing surgeons. Even in hospitals. Still, *I* am willing – but that does not mean that I am careless. This is a serious business. You must understand that.'

Wislon nodded. He saw Dr Stubbs' hands, now lying inert and poised on the desk. The fingers were bent and slightly arched. They reminded him of two large spiders.

Throughout their meeting, Wislon was aware that it was important for Dr Stubbs to conserve his self-esteem, yet it was difficult to think of him as a doctor in the usual sense of the word. He decided that it would be easier not to try. Wislon had nodded with these thoughts in mind as much as in response to the question.

Stubbs told him that the youngest male dresser he had dealt with was only twelve, although 'procedures' were out of the question at that age. It was, he said,

274

not only a matter of physical practicality but one of ethical choice. He had doubts about Wislon which he did not intend to conceal. These had increased when he learned that Wislon had restricted himself to his father's clothes and only then in private moments. 'Men's clothing, the male role in general, is not the main issue, then?'

'No. Only my father.'

'I see,' Stubbs said, 'I see.'

When Wislon asked whether he would grow bigger, Stubbs answered that the formula which most surgeons used was ninety-five per cent reliable. He wrote it down.

$$\frac{(\text{HEIGHT FATHER} - 12\text{CMS}) + \text{HEIGHT MOTHER} + 3 \text{ CMS}}{2}$$

Even though he knew that he would not be as tall as his father, this didn't seem at all bad. And he consoled himself by reasoning that he would be moving in the right direction. At least he would be growing away from his mother's shrunken, stooping compliance.

Towards the end of the summer, Wislon told his parents that he would be travelling abroad for a few months, maybe somewhere in the Mediterranean, probably with friends from school. He looked for signs of disappointment in his father, who would only say, 'Make sure you don't get lost.' Then, more thoughtfully, he added, 'And don't get into any trouble.'

He drew some of the money out of his building-society account and rented a small, scruffy flat above a camera shop near Stubbs' house. The flat had a bathroom, a kitchen and a living room which also doubled up as a bedroom. An old folding sofa squatted in the corner, uncertainly covered with a faded print of supposedly exotic flowers. The rest of the money he gave to Stubbs who insisted on providing a receipt.

'Come back next week and we'll make a start. Tuesday. Ten o'clock . . . in the morning,' he added.

Wislon looked at the receipt. It was made out to someone called 'Alice Needy'.

When he saw the name, a surge of panic momentarily overwhelmed him. On his way out, the receipt was crumpled into a small ball before being dropped carefully into a litter bin.

The following Tuesday, he once more made his way to Stubbs' house. For the first time, Wislon noticed the doctor's Adam's apple, which moved lithely up and down his elongated neck like a yoyo. He was not really listening to Stubbs' words. He heard 'androgen' and 'testosterone' and 'masculising effects'. In truth, he just wanted to get it over. He submitted to the first round of injections and promised to complete the course over the next few weeks.

'Not everyone is treated with androgens,' said Stubbs as Wislon was about to leave. 'But in your case, I think it's advisable.'

'To build me up?'

'To enhance your masculinity.'

'Then how long before we can start?'

'You mean operate?'

'Yes.'

'Up to you. But I gather that you want to get through it all as quickly as possible.'

'Yes.'

'I've known people take as long as sixteen years. Some have completed in less than a year. The average – probably about five years.'

'For everything?' Wislon said. 'Mastectomy. Hysterectomy. Phalloplasty?'

'The lot. Of course. Yes.'

'Months. Please.'

'If there are no complications. It's fast and unusual. But feasible.'

A date was suggested and Wislon agreed. He would have just enough money to see him through. He walked back to his flat through the main shopping mall. Already he had not seen his parents for several weeks. His stomach heaved at the thought of the coming months. He thought of his life as being mangled and mussed, but that would soon be at an end. Most important, his father would be pleased. He would soon be more like his father than anyone could be. Wislon stopped outside an expensive clothes shop and absorbed his image in the plate glass. He smiled as he drew his hand back through his hair and glimpsed Mr Needy's solemn stare reflecting back at him. The midday sun was high and the window glistened like a strip of film.

Good news, thought Wislon. All good news.

In the extension that had been built at the back of

the garage, Stubbs was making a last check before completing the final stages of his work on Wislon. The two assistants he had hired had been with him on such occasions for the last three years. They were busy attending to their own responsibilities. One was peering at the pressure gauge attached to a bulbous, scarred canister that contained the anaesthetic. The other was sorting through a collection of metal instruments which were elegantly arranged on what looked like an expensive silver tea tray. Both assistants were men. Stubbs had found that women were not suited to this kind of work. All three of them were dressed in green robes with masks fastened tightly over their mouths and noses. Three pairs of eyes squinted with concentration, the thin gap between mask and headgear framing them in a kind of wide-screened, surgical Vistavision. All were wearing trans-parently thin gloves which compressed the skin underneath and rendered it smooth, as if it had been coated with an opalescent cream. Stubbs' long fingers were wedged tight against the extremities of his own gloves, their new texture and appearance now making them entirely alien.

To the unpractised eye, the array of lights and the battery of steel that littered the room were evidence of legitimate hospital procedure. If there had been a window in the room, it would have looked over a perfectly manicured lawn with woods beyond. Only two days ago, it had been given its weekly trim. Now, alternate strips of light and dark green decorated the grass. A white picket fence led on to a patio area. The strawberries were just about to come into their own, although the large ginger tom-cat from next door had recently taken to interfering with the plants. From the other side of Stubbs' garden came diffuse shrills of delight from four children who were cavorting beneath a sprinkler. The top third of a blue and yellow wigwam could just be glimpsed above the fence. Someone was shouting, 'You told me you'd put it on the compost. Well I can't see it. Where is it?' The October heatwave had taken everybody by surprise and people were busy making what they thought was the most of it.

Inside the extension, the lights and the enclosed nature of the room were already making Stubbs sweat. An air conditioner hummed as it processed the air, but there was something disturbing about a room with no windows. He was thinking about the old man two doors away. His near neighbour had been deaf all of his life. A week ago, at the age of eighty-three, he had been run over by a bus. Someone had said, 'He couldn't have heard it coming.' Stubbs searched for the humour in the situation, but was uncertain exactly where to locate it.

Beneath him, Wislon's body was laid out – inert, pink and vulnerably soft. Stubbs had performed the bilateral hysterectomy and mastectomy during the previous month. Now, he just put his mind at rest about the position of the scar from the hysterectomy incision. It seemed fine and would be unlikely to interfere with the current procedure. He had decided on a transverse rather than a vertical incision. Although the vertical one was less likely to hinder subsequent operations, it was somehow less neat, less

279

cosmetic. Whenever he could, Stubbs went for the more scenic alternative. It was like going on holiday, when he always chose to drive long but pretty. It was the kind of choice which said something about him. Something nice, he hoped. He was also pleased about the scars from the mastectomy. Wislon had had small breasts, which undoubtedly helped. There would still be some scarring, but it would not be of the large, keloidal, inframammary kind. Wislon, he thought, could easily live with the small ridges of elevated purple skin and insignificant bumps around his chest. Before finally concealing them beneath a light blue sheet, Stubbs traced a proud finger along the effects of his previous work.

From the very beginning, from the moment he laid hands on Wislon, it went well enough. Having made three incisions in the left lower abdomen, Stubbs would shortly have to form a tube of skin and rotate it down towards Wislon's pubic region. Although the rest of Wislon's body had been carefully shrouded, the relevant area was open and exposed beneath a hole where a neat rectangle had been cut from the blue sheet. Hospital-issue sheets, with the holes ready-made and appropriately positioned, were naturally out of the question. With the careful incisions and inside its orderly frame, it appeared as a vivid piece of abstract art.

There was not a great deal of blood at this point. One of the doctor's assistants was busy cleaning the wound and mopping up what escape there was. The three cuts also lateralised the blood supply, channelling it neatly as a slow, thick visceral dribble.

Stubbs was good on cutting; careful, precise and even (so he thought) skilful.

He knew what had to happen next, and set about creating a new urethra from the loosened skin. This took longer than anticipated as the folds of skin would not easily be coaxed into a reliable tube. He could not continue until he had satisfactorily completed this part of the procedure. Although resistant and surprisingly plastic, the flaps of skin were also delicate. He did not want to tear them unnecessarily and concentrated hard as he kneaded and twisted the pale, greyish slithers, alternately using fingers and instrument.

The completed duct had the look and texture of a small caterpillar. It seemed pliable yet somehow resilient. Stubbs looked at it with fondness, giving it a final and almost affectionate tug before folding it back between the slender tendrils of skin still lying dormant after the initial incisions. The whole ensemble was then slightly raised and scrolled down to Wislon's pubic region which lay open a few inches below.

In many ways, the most straightforward part of the procedure was over. What was left would be testing and more intricate. Stubbs looked up for a few moments. He considered that everything seemed to be happening as it should. Above the rush of air conditioning, he could just hear the whoops and trills from the children playing in the wigwam. He was surprised. He did not think children still did things like *that* any more. Indistinct childhood memories interrupted his thoughts for a moment.

He glanced at Wislon and wondered whether the person lying there somehow constituted an index of lost childhood and depleted innocence. *That* person and what was happening to *that* body. Then he looked at his hands and understood that it was probably more complex than he had appreciated. He drew an acidic breath and turned back to the torpid figure beneath him.

Although he had effectively created a new urethra for Wislon, Stubbs now had to join it to the existing one. He did this by extending it forward, taking the skin from the labia minor and cross-connecting it to the newly created neo-urethra. First, he made certain that the skin from the labia minor was properly tubed so that the eventual suture would be both neat and effective. Removing the skin was, he thought, rather like trying to cut a thin layer from a jelly or a blancmange. He dared not make the incision too deep, but at the same time, was mindful that the successful splicing of urethra and neo-urethra required a certain amount of slack. His scalpel therefore made a definitive but cool-headed cut. In his own mind, Stubbs always heard the sound of a bicycle tyre being deflated at this point. In reality, of course, there was no sound, but he still prepared himself for the gentle hiss of escaping air as his scalpel made its slice. When it came, he managed a satisfied smile beneath his mask.

Then, a second damp cylinder of skin was fashioned and urethra and neo-urethra successfully joined. Stubbs understood that by incorporating the very end of the clitoris into the neo-urethra, some kind of sensation would be preserved. Although he had no way of actually knowing, he thought this might be important and considered his attitude at this point to be humane and caring. Perhaps in the future he might ask Wislon. But what would he say? Generally, he only felt comfortable once his patients had finished their treatment and disappeared from his life. He dealt with them in a considerate manner. They got what they paid for. But beyond that? No. They were not his concern.

Having created the space and a potential covering for the prosthetic penis and scrotum, Stubbs proceeded to fit them. This part of the operation was probably the most frustrating, although not necessarily the most significant. He took a hollow stem. It was slightly thicker than the drinking straws that were dispensed at fast-food outlets. He had to insert it into the created phallus. It was made from silicon and was known as a Silastic penile prosthesis. The operation was rather like wiring a plug. For a certain period of time, nothing seemed to fit. The proportions and measurements of the constituent parts did not want to match. However, Stubbs reflected, Wislon was easier to deal with than most. After no more than forty minutes of gentle manoeuvring, he had the stem in place.

The clitoris itself had been discreetly buried. What was in its stead should allow enough rigidity for vaginal penetration. It did not resemble a penis in the strict sense of the word, but it would *act* like one. Two years ago, Stubbs had over-compensated and made the diameter of one patient's phallus too wide. He had agreed to reduce it through further surgery. He had found the business of post-operative work distasteful and troubling. If anything, he was now too cautious. Wislon would certainly not have that kind of problem.

The wide tears in Wislon's abdomen and pubic area resembled little more than a number of un-savoury gashes, a segment of ploughed field. The apparently anarchic tension between the various outcrops of skin and the moments of mottled, furry flesh obscured the new ordering of things. The arrangement of tissue was slightly moist from the occasional uprush of blood, but there was no more than should be expected.

Stubbs did one final check of his work, pushing, probing and moving flesh apart. He was not brutal, but he felt that he had to be firm. The stitching was completed with care. When Wislon's hair grew back the scarring and ugly junction of wounds and blemishes would be partially hidden. There was also time for the rawness of the newly built penis to achieve a more pleasing texture. At present, it seemed crude and wounded, like a small herbal sausage.

Stubbs was tired. He left the tidying up to the assistants and went to scrub himself down in a small room which adjoined the main operating space. Soon, they could move Wislon into a bed where he would revolve into consciousness again, some time during the next three or four hours.

He walked through the main door of the exten-sion and into the rear of his garage. Outside, it was now dark. The warmth of the early part of the day had been replaced by the sharp tang of cold air. The moon was up and the clammy smell of compost clung to the air. A silvery cloud passed momentarily in front of the moon's glow. It looked as if the sky had been lacerated. A nice bit of work, Stubbs thought. He turned back and decided to have one last look at Alice. Or the young girl who would now be a young boy. Or whatever it was that now lay before him.

8

Ending Up

Just as the previous nights' suppers had been, so Wislon's breakfast was fastidiously and promptly prepared. He arrived downstairs at exactly six a.m. As his foot left the last of the basement stairs and turned sharply into the dining room, his mother was in the kitchen pouring milk on to a bowl of marshy porridge. He had spent a restless, nightmare-laden night. Despite the cold weather, he had woken up to find his duvet moist with sweat.

Mrs Needy did not eat anything but watched intently as Wislon worked his way through the porridge, a boiled egg, toast and coffee. As quickly as he finished one part of the meal, it was pulled from the table and the next item presented in its place. Immediately, his mother washed and dried the dirty plates before resuming her vigil opposite him. Once again, he noticed the faint bluish tinge on her skin. Although she watched him, her eyes rarely looked directly at Wislon. And despite the cordial neutrality, what they saw in each other was a reminiscence of pain and guilt. Forgiveness was needed from both of them, and yet things had gone too far for its expression to be perceived as anything more than an empty conceit. The notion of reprieve hung unsteadily between them, insistent and tantalising, yet effectively remote and easily displaced.

'More coffee?' asked Mrs Needy at the moment Wislon drained his cup.

'No. Thanks. I ought to be going. Soon. It'll take me an hour or so to get back to Birmingham.' As yet, he still did not know what he was going to do once he had returned. All he understood was that he *must* get back.

'Work?'

'Yes,' he said, 'yes.'

'You ought to come more often. I mean, to visit me.' The words sounded hollow. In any case, they were meaningless.

'Of course. I will.' Wislon disliked the deceit, but felt that in the circumstances it was proper. His mother would understand if she knew the whole story. Then he added, 'I'll get down whenever I can.' This was nearer to though still distant from the truth. For a moment, his hand went towards her across the table. It was only a meagre movement, but Mrs Needy observed it. Wislon saw her eyes widen, expressing something like terror and loathing and the simultaneous will to conceal them. He recognised it as the kind of look which people gave when they were asked to hold a snake or a spider. The thought did not make him feel any better. It reminded him of the time that he leaned across the table in The Lucky Dip and took Amy's hand. The memory sickened him and he was suddenly aware of the contents of his stomach. He brought his hand to an abrupt rest and made an awkward attempt to look at his watch.

'Right. Must be off.'

'Fine,' Mrs Needy said.

Within ten minutes, Wislon had bundled up his belongings, arranged the carrier bags in the back of the Metro and was ready to leave. He brushed his lips against his mother's cheek as she stood in the doorway of her cottage. Momentarily, he gripped her shoulder. In turn, she touched his arm. Whatever their difficulties, they were still trying to act the part for each other.

'Look after yourself,' Mrs Needy said.

'And you,' he replied.

There was something infinitely surreal about the nature of their parting. Its apparent normality was itself a kind of outrage, yet neither dared to venture beyond its ordinariness. He had told some good lies over the past few years but this (he thought) was one of the better ones. Not 'better' in the sense that it was more persuasive than any of the others but because it was much better than the truth. Better for him, at any rate. Probably better for her, too. Best all round, in fact. And that was what *really* mattered, wasn't it?

Wislon turned the Metro's engine over. It caught the second time and he drove away, resisting the temptation to look in the rear-view mirror to see if his mother was still standing in the doorway. Or waving. Or crying. Or something.

At that time in the morning, the small country roads were deserted. It was five or six miles to the main road. Wislon gunned the engine until the dial in front of him registered sixty miles per hour. At that speed, the Metro began to whine and rattle. Both the front windows were oscillating violently and the whole dashboard looked as if it was about to lift free from its moorings. A shit car for a shit person, thought Wislon. Any faster, and the bank of red warning lights would doubtless be blinking urgently at him. But that was half the problem. He doubted whether the Metro *could* go any faster. Even the parameters of danger were being strictly controlled and defined. Still, no point in getting sentimental over a machine, he mused. Buy cheap, run them into the ground, then get something else cheap. No point in getting attached to a car. No point really in getting attached to anything. Run life into the ground. That was the thing.

As he drove through the still countryside, he wondered what it would be like to live more or less alone here day after day. The gentle movements and the feel of isolation. He couldn't think of it in any other way. The murmur of the wind in the grass and the wet, stiff swaying of the trees along the roads. The unnervingly distinct nature of sounds and smells, the manner in which the environment seemed to define and register everything. To live out here on the edge of things in a kind of oblivion, in thrall to its motions and rhythms. To ignore the strange density of life where you could choose the manner in which you were represented. Dissolving everything that was done by human beings. Did people who did this know what they were *doing*?

Wislon shook his head in mock disbelief. What a place the countryside is. You couldn't even shave your wife's pubic hair without the whole community knowing and talking. You probably couldn't even shave your own pubic hair.

Without quite knowing how he did it, Wislon took a different route back to the main road. In the ten minutes it took him to get there, the only two people he saw were driving a milk float and riding a horse. Before long, he was on dual carriageway and passed an Esso station and a Happy Eater. In the space at the front of the eaterie was a large plastic dinosaur, coloured yellow with red spots. Along its back was a children's slide. Its tongue lolled out in a puppyish manner and its eyes were transfixed, expressing something between childlike happiness and adult ecstasy. Then Stratford. Then the Stratford Road.

An hour later, Wislon was taking the large roundabout which would lead into Digbeth. There, he turned left into the Bull Ring and headed up to another roundabout at the junction with the Bristol Road. It was eight o'clock. He turned on the radio. A government minister was busy denying knowledge of the export of naval guns to Iraq. He was a director of the company during the time the sales were supposed to have occurred. Someone else was saying that he would have had to be 'deaf and blind' not to have known what was going on.

There still wasn't much traffic for a Monday morning. Wislon had expected more. Birmingham was having trouble getting itself out of bed.

He raced the Metro directly across the Bristol

Road and negotiated a network of streets before bringing the car out at Five Ways. From there, he passed the Children's Hospital, a disused conference centre and the Birmingham Windsurfing Club. The borders of Winson Green were defined by Cuthbert Road. One end of it was blocked by an assortment of black and white bollards and several concrete stumps. It seemed quiet enough and a mixture of old and modern housing flanked a wide, tree-lined road. Last year it had been identified as the most dangerous street in Britain. Wislon wondered how such statistics had been compiled. Reported crimes per household? Number of arrests per family? A particular weighting for murder or arson or rape? He thought about the insurance premiums, his office, his desk, Fat Mike, the others.

He would soon be back at his flat. The sun was nowhere to be seen but it was definitely getting lighter. It was about eight-twenty and time to make plans.

Wislon was allowed to stay in a small room at the top of Stubbs' house for a week after the operation had been completed. It took longer than expected for him to regain consciousness. However, he had been aware of a dull ache running along the length of his body before he actually opened his eyes. That he eventually did so was due to the fact that he had to be sick. A bowl had been conveniently placed at the side of his bed. It lay on top of a small, white cupboard. Wislon retched but his stomach contained nothing that he could readily bring up. He tried again and managed a thin, irregular trickle of greenish bile. There was a compact bunch of pink carnations next to the bowl. They were tucked methodically into a black matt vase which had a shiny, abstract pattern embossed on its side. This was the last thing he saw before pulling his head back and away from the stench he had created. Still weak, the momentum from his falling head caused him to collapse back on to the triple layer of pillows. Sleep followed. His body stabbed and nipped and there was a constant sensation of nausea as his stomach gathered itself up and then fell away again. After two or three hours of this, he began to be aware of a far worse pain in his groin. It was outside pain rather than inside pain. Soreness, tenderness and distress joined routinely within his mangled body. Wislon decided to keep his eyes closed. It didn't actually make him feel any better, but it was preferable to being *wide* awake and perhaps having to face things more squarely.

Over the next few days, Stubbs saw him two or three times every day. Wislon's crotch remained very sore, but the doctor said that of course it was sore. He made a joke about it and asked Wislon whether he wouldn't be sore if he had been treated in the same way.

'*But I* have,' Wislon squawked. He noticed that his voice was uneven as if on the point of breaking. It was as if his vocal chords had not developed fully or his voice had been injured in some way. Maybe he had larynx damage or a destroyed trachea. Maybe he'd sicked his throat hoarse. Now, to be heard at all, he had to speak through his nose. The noise he made was reedy and abrasive. 'Christ,' he said, 'but I *have*.'

'I suppose so,' replied Stubbs dispassionately.

He then explained how things would now work for Wislon. 'Your new penis can be inflated from a fluid reservoir that is implanted in the soft tissue of your upper right thigh. This is connected to the scrotum by a flexible catheter.'

He paused for a few moments and took in Wislon's expression. In his turn, Wislon nodded agreement and understanding. The ideas were straightforward enough but it seemed strange that the words now applied to him.

'Strange' probably wasn't the right word. Probably a long way from the right word, in fact. He could do a lot better than that. Unrelated. Unusual. Maybe ambiguous. Probably ridiculous. Then, in a flood, grotesque, fantastic and inappropriate, followed by outlandish, crackpot and – his favourite – cock-eyed. But 'strange'. Sod that. And the thing *hurt*.

'Good. Now, pressure on the upper thigh forces fluid *from* the reservoir into the scrotum, and from there into the central tube of the prosthetic penis which is covered by the skin flap. OK?'

'OK'!? Wislon nodded again and glanced down. Stubbs had peeled back the sheet which covered him and rolled up the hem of a white linen nightshirt. He was pointing and gesturing at the various regions he had mentioned. Wislon's pubic area was still wreathed in bandages and neat squares of cotton dressing. He wondered what kind of catastrophe lay underneath.

His mind filled with images of maggots, and he heard moist, chewing sounds. Stubbs had his hand on Wislon's thigh and continued to speak.

'Deflation is achieved by a valve mechanism being activated in the scrotum which releases the fluid back into the reservoir and deflates the penis. This is, in fact, a rather complex and theoretical way of telling you what I think will become fairly natural practice. Think of it like running down stairs.'

'Why?' asked Wislon.

'Because if you think too much about running down stairs, you'll fall over. Best just to do it.'

'Ah. Right.' Wislon did not feel that he would be able to run down or up stairs ever again. He certainly didn't want to activate valve mechanisms in his scrotum. At that moment, he just wanted to die. That and to commit a violent act on Stubbs who was now gently patting his thigh and smiling benignly down at him. The effort had forced his chin comically forward and Wislon wished he had the energy to lean forward and bite it.

It was as if Stubbs sensed his hostility. He took his hand away, restored Wislon's modesty by adjusting his nightshirt and stood up. Finally, he said, 'Never mind. You'll soon get the hang of it,' and walked from the room.

Before he left Stubbs' house, Wislon was warned against the possibility of alcoholism, drug abuse and even suicide. Those who had undergone similar experiences to Wislon were vulnerable to such things due to the high proportion of 'morbidity'. Stubbs also told him not to be anxious about the ability to urinate in public whilst standing.

'Should I be anxious?' Wislon asked.

'You might be. Some are. *Very* anxious.'

Wislon considered. 'Why?'

'Because to urinate in public while standing is a foreign experience,' Stubbs offered gamely.

'Is it difficult?' Wislon persisted.

'Could be. Have a go when you're ready. See what you think.'

'When I'm ready. When will that be?' Wislon's voice was still a ridiculous, gruff falsetto.

'Bandages off end of the week. Not before. Colostomy bag till then, I'm afraid.'

'The bag makes me feel old. Decrepit. You know. Dilapidated.'

'Can't be helped,' said Stubbs flatly. 'And one other thing while we're about it.'

'Oh yes?'

'You don't want a pants filler, do you?'

Wislon looked at him with deep suspicion. 'What's that? Nobody told me about it.'

'Nothing, really. Just a little something we can put in your pants to make you appear more masculine. Some like it.'

'Do they?'

'Especially in their swimming costumes.'

'I bet.'

'And you?'

'No. Thank you. Not as far as I can see. Not at the moment. I've given up swimming, anyway. First, I want to see what it all looks like. Without extras, if you see what I mean.'

'Quite. I do see,' Stubbs reassured him. 'We'll have a look later then, shall we?'

Wislon did not mind Stubbs having a look. His crotch did not even feel like a part of him and the dressings therefore hid an independent object of mutual curiosity. Wislon's body still pulsed with foreboding and pain. He understood what he had willed to happen but had not yet faced its consequences. Besides, it was painful.

When the bandages did come off, it was difficult for Wislon to calculate how he should react. The skin around his lower abdomen and pubic area was puckered and red. There was a faint bristle where hair had started to grow again. The stubble was hard, rigid and unforgiving. Three small scars and one longer cut were still visible. They were ridged and purple. A small amount of pus and blood had leaked from them, although these had now dried into a foul-smelling crust. The penis itself had not changed much from the time of the operation. It could not be mistaken for anything other than a penis, but was somehow apologetic and distressed. It was relatively amorphous and a livid maroon colour.

Wislon stared at it and blinked. He really did not know what to say. Stubbs touched the penis and said, 'Can you feel anything?'

'Yes. Just.'

'That's good.'

'Is it?'

'Yes. Of course. The wounds look reasonable, too.' Stubbs poked and prodded the areas that bordered the four lacerations and made some indistinct grunting noises. 'Yes. They'll clear up a treat.'

Two days later, Wislon was back at his rented flat. The money he had paid to Stubbs only included a week's recuperation after the operation. Although the doctor had been scrupulously fair, he had never implied that Wislon might stay longer. As soon as his allotted time was spent, he was quickly displaced. A regime of drugs and lotions was explained, good wishes granted and then he was on his own. He felt certain that he would never see the doctor again.

Although he had initially felt exhilarated by a vague sense of accomplishment, Wislon soon realised that recovery was not going to be easy. He was sore and his body was still in a state of bewildered shock. He spent the first ten days of his new life in bed, either asleep or dozing fitfully as the sounds of shopping drifted up to him from the street below.

After a few days, he felt well enough to eat again and consumed junk food while watching television. He never cleared away, and the brightly coloured trays and cartons gradually accumulated into a haphazard pile around his bed. Although he re-dressed his wounds every day, he could not yet bring himself to take a bath. Soon, the tiny flat began to smell. The cocktail of sweat, rotten food, urine and stale blood created a corrupt, airless fug. Although he saw what was happening, Wislon was disinclined to do anything about it. He despised his inertia, his smell, his mess and his predicament. He felt ashamed at the uninspired routine of television-watching to which he had succumbed. The garish quiz shows and inconsequentially happy soaps he pored over kept him immobile and unaware of the passage of time. From the church at the end of the road he could hear the remote and meaningless chime of the clock striking the hour. It reminded him that he had nothing to miss. He was in the slow time of panic.

As his body began to heal itself, so Wislon found a new energy. First, he tidied the flat. Even though it was cold, he flung the windows wide open and allowed a cleansing gust of wintry air to work its way around the cramped rooms. He began to take several long baths every day. As fresh routines established themselves, solitude encouraged him to adhere to them rigorously. He would always dress himself in a particular order, brush his hair before cleaning his teeth, and wash the left side of his face first.

Wislon's confidence was not high, but he gradually discovered a sense of purpose. He thought about his father and planned to be at home for Christmas. He telephoned the information, but carefully avoided telling his parents where he actually was. At the barber's, he had his hair cut in a similar manner to his father. With the last of his money, he bought a new wardrobe. Mostly jeans and shirts, but also a few items which aped Mr Needy's dress: a pair of black trousers with thin white stripes running down their legs and a cheap but presentable blue jacket. After a few false starts, he found little difficulty in the urinating-trick. Sitting, squatting, standing, even slightly stooped – Wislon managed them all. However, even if the technique was mastered, he still found its context inside the unadmitted murky exhibitionism of men's lavatories harder to deal with.

He practised shaving. He tried walking around without sensing that his mass, his weight, his flesh were being appraised through carnal speculation. Women were looked *at* but men *looked*.

On Christmas Eve, Wislon felt ready to see his parents. He told them he would be arriving during the day but did not give an exact time. He folded his clothes neatly and pushed them carefully into a new, chunkily athletic hold-all. He was wearing the black trousers and a dark blue shirt. The number thirty-seven took him to Acock's Green where he changed to a bus which went as far as the central depot lodged darkly beneath New Street Station. Another change would take him down the Soho Road towards Handsworth, but he decided that he could walk the last mile or so to Handsworth Wood.

When he set out, the weather was mild. A recent shower had doused the roads and pavements, giving them a scrubbed sheen. The sky was grey-blue and full of small clouds which were energetically skimming across it. Even though he had only been away for about five months, Wislon saw that the landscape of the city had changed during that short time. New shops had opened, warehouses were being built and a few of the larger buildings had been sheathed in steel and smoked glass.

As he reached the end of his own road, Wislon began to feel exhilarated. For the first time since Stubbs had lain hands on him, the real purpose of the past few months was beginning to make itself triumphantly apparent. His father would be gratified. His mother? He didn't care what she thought. Mr Needy, he was sure, would understand and appreciate the intention of his gesture.

On the walk up the street to his home, Wislon was stared at by two builders who were sitting on a wall eating Scotch eggs and drinking cans of lager. A crazy pile of rubble bulged behind them. They wore blue overalls and thick, obscurely smudged shirts. Wislon supposed they were about the same age as him – eighteen or nineteen. Neither of them said anything, but they continued to stare as Wislon walked past. He thought he heard ugly, quavering giggles as he came up to his own front door. He rang the doorbell but there was no reply. Putting his hand into his jacket pocket, Wislon found his keys and opened the door. He supposed that his parents were either at work or had gone shopping.

The small house was exactly as he remembered it. But then why shouldn't it be – he had only been away five months. He did not turn the lights on. It was not yet fully dark and a few sullen, greyish beams struggled through the kitchen window and semi-illuminated the particles of dust slowly manoeuvring and rotating in the suddenly disturbed air. He felt tired and sat down awkwardly in one of the armchairs. Before falling asleep, Wislon tried to arrange himself with care for his parents' arrival. He pushed his hair back and draped one leg over the other in what he assumed was a rakish manner. He took his jacket off, put it on again, unfastened the buttons, did them all up again, and eventually left the middle one plugged through its eye. He moved the armchair so that they would not immediately be able to see him.

Then he turned it full on to the front door before finally pushing it back to its original position. Then he fell asleep.

At about six o'clock he was woken by the sound of the front door opening. It was followed by the characteristic rustle and thud of supermarket carrier bags being rudely handled.

'Enough to feed an army.' Wislon recognised his mother's thin, reedy voice.

'Never mind that . . . let's just get the bloody things inside. It's cold out here,' said Mr Needy. Wislon's eyes flicked open in expectation but he resisted the temptation to show himself.

The door thumped shut and the light was turned on.

'There's somebody in the chair,' said Mrs Needy.

'Who is it?' shouted Wislon's father. Every word was distinctly sounded, as if he was issuing some kind of threat to someone who did not speak the language.

By using his feet in conjunction with its castors, Wislon was able to shuffle the armchair around to face his parents. He tensed the muscles in his cheeks and presented them with the widest smile he could manage.

'Who is it?' repeated his father, even though he was now looking directly at Wislon.

'What do you want?' echoed Mrs Needy.

'It's me,' said Wislon. The smile was rigidly maintained, but it was now becoming self-conscious and strained.

'Who?'

'Me.'

'Bloody hell,' exclaimed Mr Needy.

'What's happened?' Wislon's mother asked, her voice fading into quietness. 'You look so different.'

From that point, things turned bad. While his parents stood aghast in front of him, Wislon explained exactly what had taken place over the past five months. He ignored his mother and directed his words only to his father. As the full extent of Wislon's transformation was made clear, Mrs Needy collapsed on to the sofa. At that moment, she was unable even to cry. Mr Needy's mouth opened and shut several times. The only word Wislon could hear was, 'Why?'

'I thought it would please you,' he tried. The confidence was quickly draining from him. For the first time he noticed the Christmas tree and its beads of coloured lights. He saw that there was a small parcel for him lurking around the base of the tree.

'Why?'

Now it was Wislon's turn to subside into silence. The facts seemed both too complex and too obvious for words. Words were clearly not going to do the trick. He was not prepared for this. He had thought that his father would just *understand*. As it was, his shoulders were beginning to shake as if he was laughing. Normally when he laughed, his whole body shook. Wislon turned away. He could hear carol singers further up the road. *'Awoi in ur main-jer, No creeb for ur bed.'* His mother was still curled up on the sofa, hardly able to move, while his father used one of the chairs for support and continued to tremble violently.

Wislon sat still, watching his parents rapidly going to pieces. It struck him that this was not what parents were supposed to do. Possibly his mother – but not Mr Needy. Watching his father's groggy oscillations, his eyes clenched tight and his forehead manically coiled, Wislon was reminded of an obscure joke. Maybe Mr Needy was waiting for a joke to come to his aid, something that would allow the laugh that was swelling up inside him. But whatever it was he might have been waiting for, it never actually arrived. After several minutes, a deep, breathy pall descended on the room. Instinctively Wislon reached down and picked up the small parcel underneath the tree. He thought it likely that this was the only present he would be getting this Christmas.

Over the next seven days, Wislon kept himself shut away in his room. Somehow, the whole story was unravelled by Mrs Needy. During the week, he heard grief turning into anger and then outrage. This was about the time that his parents began to throw things at each other.

One evening, Wislon went into the bathroom and locked the door behind him. Slowly, in front of the mirror, he took off all his clothes. Standing back, he gazed at the crevices and awkward inclines of his body. His hair was short but a mischievous shank still hung at an emphatically feminine angle. His breasts were pouchy and still slightly inflated. He could see the cuts that Stubbs had made, now like small flicks of red paint. There was something odd and artificial about his nipples, as if they might break off or peel away should anyone tamper with them. His navel and stomach had retained an obvious fleshiness, but they were now set against a pair of crooked bony hips. Here, the skin was stretched and a network of soft blue veins was apparent. Further down things looked worse. The groin was still raw and unprotected by hair. The whole ensemble was a mess of protruding bone, resilient but damaged flesh and the kind of scarring that Wislon now knew would never disappear. The rest of his skin was white, but studded with scores of red blisters and angry fissures of skin which gathered themselves into ugly lumps. At first, Wislon had attributed them to the drugs and androgens and whatever else Stubbs had given to him. But now they appeared to be more permanent. More long-term than a plague. Rather than being a reaction, they had the stubborn, contented look and feel of a *condition*. He looked again at the mirror. To be honest, the whole thing didn't look too good. It looked poisonous and wretched. What's wrong with me, thought Wislon. It's bad, it's *bad*.

Just before New Year, and after the house had been broken up by the shock waves of the violence between Wislon's parents, Mr Needy left home. Wislon looked out of his bedroom window and saw him walking down the road. He recognised the coat his father was wearing. It was not one of his own favourites. He tensed at the memory it initiated. Mr Needy was also carrying a suitcase. It was the last time he saw him.

His father was not dead, but the other thing. Dead to Wislon.

It was 31 December 1988. Storms were battering the country. The skies were irreconcilably black. King Kong had been blown over and gravestones ripped from their resting places. And Wislon wondered whether his mother would ever be able to forgive him.

By the time Wislon turned the Metro into Tailbush Road, he thought he had something like a plan in his head. Really, it was more like a series of objectives, but he would deal with them whenever the opportunities presented themselves. Trust to fate, he mused. Destiny, fortune, Lady Luck. At some point, they always gave you a chance. Just be ready for them.

Tailbush Road was quiet. Those who had been up all night had probably just gone to bed, while the few who had jobs had already left. Nobody else seemed to go out. Animated by his sudden sense of certainty, Wislon parked the Metro in a single, curving manoeuvre and took the stairs to his flat three at a time. Only when he reached the top did he slow down. Out of habit, he stopped and listened for a few seconds. No sounds, not even the furtive shuffle of Raymond Doughty. He fumbled for his keys, opened the door and walked warily into the small hallway. The loose connection and stray leads from the telephone caught his eye and irritated him. Wislon remembered that he had disconnected the answer machine. Now, he pushed the lead back. As he bent down, he became aware of a faintly sweet smell. It had settled, and now hung irresistible and heavy in the airless rooms. As Wislon breathed in, the ambrosial tang also betrayed putrefaction and decay. It seemed to be a manufactured, alien smell and he jerked his head quickly upright.

He did not have to follow the scent to understand its source. Without switching on the lights, Wislon went directly to his bedroom. Amy Facer lay exactly as he had left her. He drew the curtain back slightly and an anaemic light filtered across the room and fell on to her face. The stench was considerable but had not yet become wholly repulsive. Wislon put his face close to Amy's and took a series of deep breaths.

For the next few minutes, Wislon continued to rest his head on Amy's face. Her colouring was paler than it had been two days ago, and there were the beginnings of a scaly, greenish tinge around her eyes and cheeks. The skin was still malleable, but was becoming stiff and unyielding. He remembered that the smudging of Amy's make-up had created an eczema-like texture on her face. Now, he traced the unevenness with his finger and continued to run it down and along her heavy and apparently formless corpse. He brought it to rest between her legs and then used his whole hand to prise them gently apart. Then, he nestled his head again and flung his spare arm around her deflated bosom. His other hand continued to lie inert and delicate on the small mound of bone and hair beneath her blood-stained dress.

He wondered what it would be like to kiss her.

307

Amy's lips had turned a kind of smudged blue. Probably now that she was dead it would be quite like kissing himself. She would not be able to kiss back. In many ways, he would not even be tasting her mouth. Not really. Just *a* mouth. Something like *his* mouth. Kissing was usually like biting up and destroying other people. But not now. Amy was already destroyed. Wislon's kiss could be a proper one, a pure one. There was no need for her to do anything. He leaned slowly forward and managed a dry, passionless touching of lips. On drawing back again, he noticed how the blood had dried to create a brittle cake around her.

The two of them lay like this for almost twenty minutes before Wislon was startled by a weak knocking on the bedroom door. He turned his head to see Zasu Pitts and Tempe Pigott standing apologetically in the doorway. Both had their hands held up to their necks. They were fiddling with cardigans, blouses and necklaces. Anything.

'Sorry to disturb you,' said Zasu Pitts.

'We thought you ought to know,' continued Tempe Pigott.

There was an awkward silence as Wislon stayed where he was. Nor did he even look up.

Eventually, Zasu Pitts said, 'You see, we have to tell you that someone has died.'

'I know,' Wislon drawled with some impatience.

'How?' asked Tempe Pigott. 'It happened while you were away.'

'No. I killed her.'

'Her?'

'She's here. Look. You ought to know. Call the police. Or an ambulance. Someone. It doesn't really matter now. So long as you know.'

'No,' said Zasu Pitts, 'you don't understand.'

'I do.'

'It's Mr Doughty.' It was the first time he had heard them refer to the old man with such respect. 'Something to do with too many sleeping pills or the wrong kind of pills or something. He had a heart attack on Saturday morning.'

'Early.'

Wislon considered the information for a few moments. 'It still doesn't matter,' he said. 'I killed Amy. Look, here she is.' He stood up and disentangled himself from Amy's body before making an emphatic but low-key sweeping gesture with his right arm. Then he wrenched the curtain fully open with a melodramatic flourish and snapped the light on.

'Oh,' said Zasu Pitts.

'I told you there was a smell,' said Tempe Pigott.

'Sshh!'

'Tell them I did it,' Wislon added, 'and tell them it was a bad thing to do.'

He was not quite sure what he ought to do next. He wondered whether he ought to break down and cry. He thought about a long speech that would be full of contrition and would explain to them what murder felt like. (Like sniffing razor blades, he thought.) About telling them that there was always time to wash the blood from your hands. He watched the two old ladies staring at Amy Facer's heavy shape and insisted that they tell the police. Both nodded dumbly in response and moved back into the doorway.

Wislon pushed his jaw out as far as it would go. He didn't feel that it looked particularly impressive but he felt it was the kind of thing that people in his position might do. He walked directly past the two women and chested himself through the open door.

Destiny was doing funny things, but he had a feeling that it would all work out in the end.

Since Wislon had touched Armitage's breast, there had been something of a hiatus in their relationship. In fact, a complete hiatus. Nothing at all. He was not certain whether he should phone her and apologise, just phone her, or just apologise and leave it at that. One thing, at least, was certain: Armitage did not phone Wislon.

He reasoned that most people had a small box at the back of their minds which stored a selection of life's most humiliating episodes. A black box of embarrassment and cringe. The box remained strictly out of bounds and even knowledge of its existence was enough for its owner to maintain a frightened, respectful distance. After all, nobody needed humiliation. Wislon had what he thought was a pretty ordinary box. It included the time at school when he had forgotten the lines to 'Good King Wenceslas' during a solo, the time he saw Grandma Needy with no clothes on, the time he forgot to wear underpants to school, the time he got his foot stuck in a lavatory, and the time his urine sample leaked. Nothing special there. Now it had been supplemented by the time he touched Armitage's breast. Or perhaps it should be the time that Armitage's breast came into contact with his hand. The result was that he could not think about phoning her without his soul withering and shrivelling in shame and self-disgust.

After a couple of silent weeks, he began to think things through a little more carefully. Armitage would not have placed his hand there without a certain amount of desire on her part. Gradually, he pieced the evening together again, the same pieces somehow re-forming for him into a new, different shape. The harder he considered, the more he was convinced that there had been an aura caused by feminine shock waves in the air that night. Wislon had not taken enough notice of them. Maybe he was afraid of them. Of course, it was *his* fault. Armitage must have felt as embarrassed as he had done. Well, almost.

He phoned her. When she answered there was a silence. Then she hung up. Wislon phoned again. There was another silence. Then Armitage said, 'Come round tonight. Eight o'clock. Don't be late.' Then she hung up.

Wislon arrived exactly on time. He was wearing his most daring shirt, a black cotton number with a lilac paisley pattern and sloping shoulders. It was the first time he had been inside Armitage's flat. He knew something was going to happen and he was ready. Poised and cocked. You didn't have to be told about these things – you just knew.

He rang the doorbell. His heart missed several beats as no one answered. Perhaps she had forgotten.

311

Then the door opened and Armitage appeared from behind it. She was wearing a pale blue dressing gown and cables of thick black hair skewed winningly across her face. The dressing gown barely covered her knees. Her face had not been made up.

'I'm not quite ready,' she said.

'Shall I come back?' Wislon replied, half-turning as he did so.

'No. Of course not. Come in. Wait.'

Wislon followed her sheepishly into a small, modern room. He was shown to a tasteful and probably quite expensive wicker sofa.

'Do you want a drink or something?'

'Yes, please.'

'Help yourself. The kitchen's over there.' Before moving away, Armitage flung an arm out towards one of the three doorways which led off the living room. He looked around. There were small piles of magazine clutter on the floor, but everything else was ordered and in its place. The furniture was modish and all recently purchased. Probably IKEA or Habitat. Wislon entered the kitchen and opened the fridge. The only thing of any use in there was a bottle of white wine. He feared for his stomach but felt it was probably part of the price that he would have to pay. He found a corkscrew and, wedging the bulb of the bottle between his scrawny thighs, began the business of trying to get the cork out. His eyes bulged and his wrist ached, but eventually the cork exploded out of the bottle's neck and took Wislon's arm in a crazy, involuntary arc.

He poured two glasses and re-established himself

on the sofa. He turned his mind back to Armitage. Her appearance at the door had suggested that she'd just been in the middle of something when he arrived. Some people had the abiliy to do that. It was a gift and made others feel as if they were merely part of some much grander scheme. Wislon knew that he never gave that impression; he was rarely in the middle of anything. There was also a casual reck-lessness about the way that Armitage presented her body. He wondered what it must be like to have pride and confidence in your appearance.

By the time Armitage reappeared, Wislon's glass was half empty and the juices in his stomach were already beginning to play tricks. She now wore a blue dress which was exactly the same cut and colour as her dressing gown. Her legs were clad in trans-lucent, sheer nylon and her face was daubed in hues of black and a shade of mauve. A matching lipstick did for the mouth. While her head was making a series of important moves, her hair caught the light as it swished round. No shoes. Thick perfume. She collapsed into the chair opposite Wislon and immed-iately brought her legs up underneath the rest of her body.

'Is this for me?' she asked, and gestured at the drink on the glass table.

Wislon nodded. She picked it up, bending her head back to take a mouthful. Then she arranged herself with care, moving as if she was aware of being surrounded by a skilled and familiar camera crew. She was lit in all the right places and exercised complete control over her audience. Wislon had no option but to focus on her face, her lips, her hands, her eyes, her breasts, her legs and her hair. Close-ups, long shots and everything in-between. The lighting and the blue dress gave her a filmic, sexual radiance.

Wislon looked at her but she did not look back. She looked everywhere else, but not at him. This was what he supposed was meant by aura. Eclat. Lustre. *Brilliance*.

'So, what did you want to say?' she eventually asked.

'I . . . I . . .' Wislon began. He stalled to a halt.

She turned to face him without quite committing her eyes. He saw anger in her expression for the first time. 'You're such a baby, Wislon.' It seemed strange to actually hear his name on her lips. Despite the context, it was still thrilling. 'I can't give you any more. You know that.'

'I can't help it.' He knew that he sounded pathetic.

'I know. Well, maybe I know.'

'No. Really.'

'It's quite common.'

'Is it?'

Now she looked at Wislon all right. Her eyes narrowed and her lower lip hung in postured hostility. 'I mean, what's in it for me? I must be crazy.'

Wislon nodded amiably. He could not help noticing that, although Armitage was angry, as she turned her head away once more the beginnings of an unintentional smile curled the sides of her mouth. Was she laughing at him? Was it something to do with power? Wislon swallowed hard. Armitage arranged her legs and dress once again. The sourness of the moment passed, and the two of them talked for a while. Wislon did not quite understand the mechanics of the situation. He hardly understood what they were talking about. She spoke to him as if through rain and from a considerable distance.

Just at the point when Wislon was beginning to wonder whether he had actually lost consciousness, the talking came to an end. Armitage stood up. Intuitively, Wislon did the same. His legs bucked and flexed somewhere beneath him, but he managed to stay more or less upright. He wondered whether this was a defining moment. Maybe *the* defining moment. Armitage and Wislon looked at one another for ten seconds or so. It became twenty. Then thirty. Then forty. Close to, he noticed a number of small imperfections on Armitage's face. There was a faint, pinky blemish on one side of her nose. Her teeth had an indistinct, yellowish patina around them. He was excited by these small signs of neglect, of disrespect, which only seemed to emphasise her beauty by giving it perspective.

When Wislon looked really hard at Armitage – right at her, into her eyes – he saw something rather more disturbing. He saw himself. There he was, in prismatic stereo, coming back at himself. A shag of disordered hair, a pair of pouchy, budding eyes, florid complexion, and a gawky, helpless expression. If it was this bad for him, imagine what it must be like for Armitage. He flinched in horror and momentarily turned his head away.

Once he had recomposed himself, Wislon saw that Armitage was now looking at him in a curious manner. As far as he could remember, no one had ever looked at him in that way before. He suspected what might be on its way and steeled himself.

Their bodies were not actually touching at this point. Wislon could feel the shapes and shadows of her contours, the electric throb of her hair and the steady beam of her skin. Aura, thought Wislon. That's what it's all about. *Aura*.

Wislon's legs started to go again, and he bent and slackened them to ensure that he didn't just topple over. He tried to move himself forward a few vital inches. In turn, Armitage slanted herself nearer and breathed moistly into his ear. Wislon's arm instinctively shot up, its muscles stimulated by an invisible trigger. His hand found itself on the slopes of her body and moved upwards to the damp, aromatic hollows of her armpit. Before he knew what was happening, he had hovered and landed on a breast.

Armitage sighed invitingly. At least, she didn't complain. She withdrew slightly, unbuttoned her dress and slipped out of it. Then she moved her hair as if she was letting it down. Her hair already *was* down, and Wislon marvelled at the eroticism of the conceit. She appeared in front of Wislon as a *mélange* of lace, skin and fleshed nylon. 'I'll take all my clothes off,' she said, 'come on.' Wislon trailed her warily and self-consciously through one of the other doors that led away from the living room and into Armitage's bedroom. When she turned round and appraised him, she saw only fear and ignorance. 'Look at you,' she said softly, 'I'm not sure that you fancy it. In the flesh.' She paused, then leaned closer and began to undress him. Wislon's clothes came away from his body like damp tissue paper. As they did so, Armitage inspected his nakedness. The puffs of skin, the inadequate legs, the blemishes, the slight chemical smell, the dejected scoop of his unmanly shoulders. And worse, of course. Much worse.

Armitage immediately saw how damaged the possibility of love was. She did not seem to mind and took a deep, complex breath.

'I'll be gentle,' she said.

Wislon tried a joke. 'I hope not,' he replied. Quite jauntily, he thought.

'Shut up. Let's get started.'

Wislon wondered why all this should be, how it had come about.

'What about before?' he asked, remembering previous moments of torpor and unreciprocated stickiness.

'That was before. Now is now. I didn't want to then.'

Wislon prepared himself for abandonment. He considered the idea of euphoria and attempted to anticipate it. It was all quite simple really. Men were quite simple when you got down to it. Wislon was being educated. His learning curve was on a sudden and steep spiral. In his mind's eye, Armitage was becoming all that he had ever wanted or needed.

But that was the trouble. It *was* in his mind's eye.

Wislon thought, I can't bear this.

The scene faded and its imagery dissolved. He could not bear the way that she always seemed to be causing pain. He banished her from his mind. He

317

decided that he would never let her in again. It was all too difficult.

When he opened his eyes, Wislon was lying in the foetal position with both hands cupped protectively over his groin.

It wasn't nice, but at least it was the truth.

Wislon drove with confident abandon. The main rush-hour traffic had thinned out and the Soho Road was quite empty. He crunched the gears, accomplished complex overtaking moves and dangerous undertaking ones. As he approached the Hockley Flyover he could see the snarled city strewn untidily before him. He suddenly felt its heat climbing, falling and shuddering into the air. It was the heat of cars and people and tallish buildings. Wislon registered the awful dumbness that covered Birmingham and took in the new mosque that was under construction to the right of the flyover. A plain oblong of concrete with various pastry-cut decorations was already in place. A minaret was waiting on the pavement, extravagantly wrapped in polythene and ready to be hoisted into place. Then, a solid body of black men pointed and laughed before being swallowed by Chas's Snooker Rooms. One of them had a small baby in his arms. Wislon turned away before they could look at him. On the whole, he was feeling good. Really good. He swerved to the left of the flyover, took the road which looped around underneath it and negotiated the small honeycomb of streets that led to the Jewellery Quarter. Although he had arrived later than usual, the space that he used for parking was still available. He brought the Metro to a sudden, clunking halt, ran into the building and climbed the stairs with large, ungainly strides.

The corridor which led to the part of the building he worked in was lined with strip lighting. He turned into the office and saw that everyone had already arrived. Their work surfaces had been designed so that everything was directly in front of them. Any looking around – any not looking at their work surfaces – would be a virtual admission of slacking. Like most mornings, there was a lot of looking around at that moment. Virgil Young was tipped back in his chair so that he could see out of the window directly behind him. He looked uncomfortable, or at least awkward, but it was probably better than what would have confronted him had he been comfortable. His feet were jacked up on the desk surface and his trousers had ridden a couple of inches above the level of his socks. Wislon saw a tanned band of ankle-cum-calf, evenly but not thickly covered in dark hairs.

From the far side of the office, Simon Monks was complaining about the facsimile machine. As usual, the machine had misfired and two sheets had been clumsily run together. Rather than making an exaggerated whining noise, like some large insect, it gave off a wild, irregular ticking. He was surrounded by three filing cabinets, greyish and solemn, with red purchase labels still attached to them.

All the others were actually busy at work. They registered his arrival by discreetly raising their heads.

Other than that, his entrance was ignored. He was about an hour late. There was no reason why they should react more histrionically. After all, they knew nothing. Virgil Young eventually gave him a withering smile and tapped his watch in a meaningful manner before shifting forward and turning his attention back to the concentration of papers on his desk. Fat Mike clumped into view.

'Ah. Wislon. At last. You haven't seen Amy, have you?'

'Yes. This morning.'

'Do you know what time she'll be in?' His voice was only distantly interested.

Wislon answered in a matter-of-fact, even voice. 'She won't. I killed her. A few days ago. She won't be coming in again. Ever. I did it. It was evil and wretched, but there we are. If you'll excuse me, I've just got to check a few things and then I'll be on my way.'

Wislon felt oddly bold and purposeful, strange sensations. He moved quietly to his own desk. As he busied himself in its pattern of drawers, he noticed that an incongruous, confused silence had settled over the rest of the office. Everybody had stopped what they were doing, or not doing. The facsimile machine suddenly gave off a high-pitched twitter. The others were all looking towards him, interrogating his face for some kind of explanation. Wislon wondered what they expected from him. He bobbed his head up for a few moments and said, 'Don't worry. I think the police have already been informed. You won't be seeing me again, either.'

320

He found what he was looking for in the bottom drawer. It was tucked away like a guilty secret, right at the back, inside a rumpled brown envelope. Wislon tore the envelope and took out a small silver bracelet. Its links were chunky and writhed together in a series of curving ovals. The bracelet had space for a name plate which dangled between the clasp and the first of the links. The name engraved on it was 'Alice'. It had been Wislon's Christmas present the year that his father disappeared. Much later, his mother had told him that Mr Needy had bought it from someone he knew who worked in the Hockley Centre. Mr Harrison had one leg and was an engraver who also did some silver plating. Sometimes, he came by small items of jewellery which he sold on to friends. Mr Needy had phoned him to say he wanted it for Christmas Day. 'It's got to be Christmas Day or not at all.' He had driven to the Hockley Centre the same evening. Mr Harrison even found a small box to put it in. The box was covered with a coarse, fuzzy brown material that was meant to look like velvet.

'Do you like it?' asked Mr Needy.

'Of course,' replied Mrs Needy, 'it's lovely.'

Now, the silver was worn and tarnished. Wislon thought that its greeny tinge made is seem vaguely organic.

He picked up his telephone and considered leaving one last message on his answer machine. But there was no need for that kind of thing any longer. It suddenly seemed a useless act. And besides, after today nobody would be listening. He would soon find a different and more enduring kind of reassurance. Now, he knew it all. He smiled to himself. It was a peculiar kind of smile, somewhere between self-satisfaction and relief. An ugly grin, perhaps, but Wislon no longer cared. He put the bracelet into his back pocket, walked smartly back through the office and descended the stairs, vaguely aware of some activity behind him.

His senses were sharpened by the excitement of the moment and the new clarity of purpose he had discovered. He reversed the Metro recklessly out of its parking space and into the road. As the car swung into position, he yanked it into first gear. The back wheels attempted to spin but the engine did not have enough power for such heroics. Instead, the car lurched joltingly forward, wheezing slightly as it picked up speed.

There was a large roundabout at the bottom of the road and Wislon flew round it, taking the route to the centre of the city. He swept past the Town Hall and then on to Symphony Hall. On his right, in front of the Repertory Theatre, there was a sculpture which represented the manufacturing history of Birmingham. It was carved out of something like hard-boiled plastic and showed a small factory belching a crinkled banana of smoke. In front, resolute Brummies surveyed their city with steely, industrious curiosity. As he neared Ronnie Scott's, it started to drizzle. Although it was raining, there were suddenly rays of light, even momentous shafts of yellow sunshine. They fell across Birmingham and for the few seconds that it was touched with gold, Wislon did not recognise it. And yet it was the same city.

Then, almost as quickly, the clouds closed in and the glare gave way to darkness and shadow once more. He heard the whooping innuendo of a police siren. He glanced in his rear-view mirror. The car was too far away to do him any harm. Even so, Wislon could make out the driver, who was fortyish, lean and balding. His passenger was busy on the radio. Most of the other traffic came to a standstill as the police car began its exaggerated weave towards the Metro.

Wislon swung the car left down Gas Street and looked for a gap in the red walls that enclosed the pavement. He felt clear-headed and in control. He was God and Satan. Well, why not? He drove the car with brutal resolution. The area was a slovenly clutter of small businesses, pubs, clubs and empty warehouses. The Dog and Bitch was just over the road.

Quickly, he found what he was looking for. Wislon just had time to turn the Metro at right angles to the opening in the wall. He drove directly at it, crumpling the wings of the car as he insinuated it into the narrow space. Wislon's momentum was temporarily obstructed, but with a ghastly screeching noise and a throaty cough from the engine, the Metro squeezed through and was suddenly catapulted forward. It hit a cast-iron bollard at the side of the canal and the impact turned the car on to its side before it landed with a violent, booming splash in the water. Wislon sealed himself into the car by pushing the locks down into the car doors. They clunked shut with a terminal, metallic 'chock'.

As the car filled with water, Wislon made himself comfortable and folded his arms. He thought, show me a swimmer and I'll show you a drowning man. The Metro was upside down but his seat belt held him awkwardly in place. He had time to think. He had time to think that death could arrive in instalments if you had a mind to deal with it in that way. He caught a glimpse of his face in the mirror just before the brackish water rose above it. He looked at himself with exultation, with relief. He had done it. He had found himself. He was himself at last. Here was death: visualised, planned and co-ordinated. It was Wislon's answer to the unseen powers around him. These were the facts of life as well as the facts of death. What was it that Alice had said? He could remember his father reading the story to him many years ago. 'I shall be punished for it now, I suppose, by being drowned in my own tears. That *will* be a queer thing, to be sure!'

The car continued to fill until its cabin was completely flooded. It settled noiselessly on the canal's greased, muddy bottom. Dying, thought Wislon, as his life started its parodic dash before his eyes. A queer thing. Dying – it's almost as complex, as difficult as life. I didn't expect this.

Then, suddenly, there was water.

Everything was water.